Contents

Characters
(Principal characters in Bold)

Location
Batmalai, Bajaur, FATA, Pakistan
Family
Mehmoud Praang, father; Bibi Rokhana, mother
Sons: Ayub, Sakhi
Daughters: Farikhta, **Shahay Angeza**

***

Location
Denver, Colorado, United States
Family
Nya Shazia Karram, *mother of Ali1*
Ali Karram, father; Ayesha Karram, mother
Son: **Mohammed Yousf**
Daughters: Fariyal, Sabbryya

Some *Pukhto* Words and Phrases

Angrez (pl.*angrezaan*) - English person (persons), (commonly extended to most pasty-faced Westerners); Anglo (s), Euro(s)

Angrezi - the English language (= *Inglisi*, see below)

Arub - Arab

Audas - ritual ablutions before prayer; = *wudu* (Arabic)

Baba - father (used also an honorific, that is, as a token of respect. (cf. *kaka*))

Babaji - grandfather

Bakhana ghwaram - my apology, sorry, excuse me

Badal - redress, revenge (*badal aghastal*) (*e.g.* kill my brother, I kill yours. Here the form redress takes is vengeance); reciprocity (*badal warkawal*) (*e.g.* give gifts to my family, I likewise give to yours) Central to Pukhtun Custom (*Pukhtunwali*).

Badraga - armed escort (provided by local tribes to get through their territory)

Charre - knife, dagger

Cheendak - children's game, (similar to hopscotch)

Daera manana - thanks very much; cf. *manana*

Dakoo - dacoits, criminals

Daktar Sahib - doctor sir (A respectful manner of address for a (male) doctor; ('*sahib*', (pronounced 'seb') an honorific)

Daktara (n.f.) - doctor; (*Daktara Sahiba*, Doctor ma'am)

Dastarkhwan - cloth/blanket/carpet on which food is served (A 'table cloth' if only there were a table beneath it. There isn't in Pukhtun homes.)

Dhost - friend

Dukh'mun - enemy

Enshaallah - As Allah wills (= arab. *Insha'llah*, more fully, *Inshaallah*)

Ezzat (or *Izzat*) - honour, reputation

Gham - grief, sorrow (custom requires commiserative and celebratory visits to friends and relatives. See *khadi* below.)

Gheyrat - physical bravery

Ghin - penis

Hila kawam - you're welcome

Hujra - guest house physically separate from the main house (used for male guests and men's society; useful for preventing contact between non-family men and family's women)

Inglisi - the English language (= *Angrezi*, see above)

Janana - (n.) beloved (cf *jannay khor* - dear sister)

Jaamey - menses (cf. mensez)

Kajoorey - scones (baking powder biscuits) à la Pukhtun

Kaka - (lit.) uncle (Like Baba (see above) an honorific).

Khadi - joy, celebration (cf. *gham* - grief) (Custom demands *gham/khadi* visits to friends and relatives on relevant occasions, e.g., deaths, births, marriage, etc.)

Khairey - badinage, raillery (ranging from the gentle to ferocious, from benign to wicked; between friends, gentle sarcasm, between others, insulting sardony. *Khairey* amongst Pukhtuns doesn't always succeed and may lead to lethal feuds. Widely discouraged.)

Khor - sister

Khwatey - testicles

Kor - home; hearth and home; kitchen

Khuday - God, Allah (also = *Kawday*, *Khoday*)

Khuday pa aman - God be with you

Las niwa - (*lit.* hands held in prayer) a visit offering condolence; (necessary by custom amongst friends and relatives)

Lashkar - tribal militia

Manana - thanks, thank you

Marid - mountain spirit sounding thunder

Mensez - menses (cf. *jaamey*)

Mor - mother

Namous - woman's virtue; family honour

Nang - Pukhtun honour, i.e., honour maintained by satisfying the demands of *rewaj* (see) and *Pukhtunwali*, e.g., reacting with appropriate force to insult; meeting generosity with equal generosity; protecting the virtue of family and tribal women to the extent that if a woman of one's family compromises her virtue, thereby compromising the *namous* of the family, she may be killed; offering *melmastia* (hospitality) to guests; speaking the truth; obeying the decisions of the *jirga*. Where one's *nang* is lost through failure to observe *rewaj* one is *beynanga*. One who consistently observes *rewaj* is *nangyaalay*.

Nya - grandmother (or *Neea*); (affectionately *Nanaji*)

Pairyan - spirits taking the form of men and women

Pa khair raghley - welcome (traditional response: *khair ose* - glad to be here)

Pakol - Pukhtun cap

Partoog-kameez - tunic and trousers. (A national dress consisting of a longish chemise/tunic usually with full sleeves worn over baggy trousers; women wear a *loopata* (veil, scarf); in Urdu these clothes are referred to as *shalwar-kameez-dupatta*.); *kameez* and the English/French 'chemise' are cognates.

Peghore - taunt, mocking reproach; (serious taunts bear on and diminish family honour)

Pet (adj) - hidden

Prraang - leopard

Pukhtanna/Pukhtannay - Pukhtun woman/women

Pukhtun/Pukhtaana - Pukhtun/Pukhtuns

Pukhtunkhwa - the land and nation of the Pukhtun (Pashtun) peoples

Qila - walled compound of rural residents containing home (*kor*) (see), some with guest house/meeting place for men (*hujra*)

Rewaj (or *rivaaj*) - binding customs ('binding' in that breaching custom may result in being forced from the community, in being shunned, in no longer being accepted as Pukhtun)

Saamaan - (sl.) a man's package, his stuff (genitalia)

Sanga yee - hello, hi there

Saritob - (i) manhood=gentlemanliness; (ii) decency, manners, civility; humanity (iii) manhood=male sexual qualities, as in, e.g., Her seductive glance aroused his manhood.

Sar Paisa - bride price, (aka *walwar*)

Shaitan - satan, devil

Sharm - personal modesty

Takfiri - a Muslim believer (a) capable of accusing other believers of apostasy and (b) enough of a zealot to think it's all right to kill such believers on the basis of the accusation alone

Takhalus - nickname, handle, sobriquet

Thror - aunt, (father's or mother's sister)

Tor tap/spin tap – *tor tap*: (lit., black wound), used by US SOF medics in Af-Pak to refer to a wound to the covered part of the body but unfamiliar to Bajauri Pukhtuns who use the phrase *pet zakhem* (hidden wound); ('*tor*' adj. lit. black, by extension, sinful, shameful; as a noun *tor*=illicit sex); *spin tap*: (lit. white wounds) wounds to the uncovered parts of the body. (Conservative Pukhtun custom (which survives) forbids a male physician's dealing with a *tor tap/pet zakhem* on a female body).

Wrandar - sister in law

Wror - brother

Zakhem - wound

Zma num ... dey - my name is ..

Bajaur District
Malakand Division
Khyber Pakhtunkhwa Province

The Leopard's Daughter

A Pukhtun Story

David Raeburn Finn

The Leopard's Daughter
A Pukhtun Story

Published by Lema House, #12, 2655 Andover Road,
Nanoose Bay, British Columbia
Canada V9P 9J5
(www.lemahouse.ca)

ISBN 978-0-9920390-7-3
(Paperback)
ISBN 978-0-9920390-8-0
(Electronic)
ISBN 978-1-7773873-0-3
(Hard Cover)

Cover photo of Snow Leopards in Kashmir courtesy of Pixabay (image # 1994499) and photographer Gerhard Gellinger (gerhard.gellinger@t-online.de)

Lema House

for mercy until the dying man's last breath. Nearby, his friend Baseer worked madly to push a slithering snake pit of intestines into what had been a stomach. Baseer stood when the man gave up his life.

Mehmoud mouthed his question. 'The son of Baseer?'

"Bangar has gone for his truck."

Mehmoud cupped his ear to make out the sounds 'Bangar' and 'truck'. He limped closer to Baseer.

"Ayub and Sakhi will load wounded. Baseer's son will inform the Khan?"

Baseer nodded. "He'll know already. More trucks and help should come quickly from Pashat."

Together he, his sons and Baseer worked silently, tying tourniquets where they could, compressing wounds with rags, some cut from the deads' clothes. Shortly, trucks arrived with unbloodied Pashat boys and men. Ten trucks and eight SUVs drove wounded and bodies for the 40 kilometre drive to Khar's hospital. Too many for scarce ambulances. For many, too little time.

Hours later Mehmoud, matted in drying blood, ascended the gentle slope to his village *qila*. Hearing returned to his left ear. Women and children stood with quiet tears outside *qila* gates. Some stared open-mouthed, others murmured prayers as he passed. Wailing came from within the compounds of the two Batmalai elders killed outright by the suicide bomber. Their wives, now widows, and their families had been told immediately of their fates.

His wife, Bibi Rokhana, had had the household's women fire the *hujra* samovar and put out pails of water and fresh clothing. She helped Mehmoud remove his *kameez*.

"You're wounded. Shall I wash the wound for you? No? Then let me bandage it when you've washed."

"*Manana.*"

"No need for thanks. How many are dead?"

"I didn't count. Many. Perhaps two dozen. Dozens more are wounded. Some of them ..."

Prologue

Batmalai, Bajaur November 6, 2008

The earth erupted, catching Mehmoud in mid-turn, smashing into his nose and ears. A hot blast of wind threw him onto his back. He blinked his eyes open. A painted ball with eyes and black hair flew silently above, bouncing on the ground somewhere behind. He sucked in a breath. Two huge figures ran toward him from his left.

His sons were at his side. They mouthed words he couldn't hear. His hand went to a pain below his left ribs and touched wet and ... something sticking out? Ayub returned the bloody fingers to his eye level. Blood? Ayub's hands revisited the pain. Mehmoud jerked with a sharp tear. His son held up a 4 inch nail dripping red. Sakhi moved a weight across his ankles – an arm, torn off at the shoulder. The two boys helped him to sit up.

Mehmoud looked behind and shuddered. The comic ball was a young man's head, eyes half-lidded, lips open to crimson teeth as if in a mute howl, a red *shaitan*. His eyes followed his sons' to the field below. Bodies and pieces of bodies littered the ground. He stood shakily, leaning on his sons. They descended toward the carnage as quickly as his uncertain legs could manage.

His sons divided to attend separate still moaning bodies. Mehmoud knelt, trembling by a man's head shorn of face, gurgling liquids through two teeth in what remained of a mouth. He prayed

Pak tribals to our side." McPhail's pearly whites gleamed.

Grant stared at him. "That's a bit too mysterious for me, Senator"

"Well, I can't go into details, Captain. Let's just put it this way, the talibs have it in for the tribal leaders on the other side. They may be planning to fix the leaders once and for all, one tribe at a time."

"Sounds a bit scary. How ..." He let it go. The Pentagon and armchair experts were overfond of kinetic lessons. The Senator wasn't finished.

"Right now one of the tribes intent on forming a *lashkar* is finding out how they stand with our enemies. Any doubts they have about who they should support will vanish."

Grant felt his teeth clench. "But if they're forming a *lashkar,* they're almost certainly getting ready to have a go against our enemies. Any attack on them now—"

McPhail shook his head. "It's not *us* attacking them." He paused to look down at his watch. "It's already done."

Grant seethed. Fucking Pentagon idiots and their political bum boys.

"If the Pak tribals as you call them think we have any role, kinetic or passive, in attacking them their *lashkar* will target both us and the *takfiri.*" He hadn't raised his voice, but knew his words were more snarled than spoken.

McPhail's open mouth mirrored that of his two Pentagon companions.

Grant's chin fell. A fucking disaster. "I need to talk with my village headman. Thanks for the visit."

He wheeled and grimaced. Ahead his friend, the *malik,* stood facing him on Mangwel's perimeter, listening white-faced to his cell.

"I understand. More may die. Who would..?"

"*Takfiri.* They sent a boy with a suicide vest."

"Your sons?"

"They're all right. They'll come soon. They've been loading wounded and the dead."

***

November 6, 2008

Kunar Province, Afghanistan

John Grant surrendered a perfunctory smile, trying to forget he didn't give a shit. Yet another Senator, probably prepping for a presidential bid. Outstandingly modest. Just two photographers. Smart. The last group was larger, and narrowly escaped casualties when fire came in late in the visit.

He saluted the two Centcom officers accompanying Senator McPhail. The three visitors grinned at the camera as though it were fresh liquorice. He hid his smile, imagining the liquorice on McPhail's lovely white teeth. Next, the Senator wanted a political money shot, a photo of himself together with him in his Pukhtun *partoog-kameez.*

"I'm told you're doing a remarkable job here in Mungle, Captain Grant."

"Thanks. We've made friends. We help our *Mangwel* friends as we can, Senator."

"Oh, *Mangwel.* Didn't hear the name right first time. Hear you've got trouble with infiltrators coming over the border?"

"Some locals, some from the Pak side, yes sir."

The Centcom brass moved closer as if on cue, and nodded to McPhail.

"I have a military background myself, Captain. You can take it that people have read me in on a few things. We know about the infiltrators. I can't say too much – but events could turn out to bring

Chapter 1

OWL: September 2007, Langley

David Verraeter had never met privately with a Deputy Director before. Why did *two* summon him to meet now? He'd always done what he was hired for, analyzing lists of names using collection algorithms. He couldn't have done anything wrong. Of course he might have made a mistake. But what? ... For the first hour he'd taken the text message as a joke, looking around in the floor of analysts to see who was having a laugh. No one. They ignored him as usual. It came on his safe phone, known only to his Langley superiors.

'Meeting 28/09/07 10:30AM DD Analysis and DD Operations. FYEO. NFD'

Christ! For his eyes only, not for distribution? – What? They thought he'd blab?

He arrived at work next morning bleary-eyed. A well-dressed younger woman stepped from the elevator at 10:25 and came directly to his desk. "Please, follow me." Up two floors she led to a windowless room centred by an oval oak table surrounded by twenty comfortable leather chairs. Two men sat across the table from his chair.

"Coffee, Mr Verraeter?" she asked.

His mouth was dry. But the two across the table weren't drinking. "No, no thanks." She left.

He wasn't *familiar* with Monty L. even if he worked under him. Monty was Deputy Director of Analysis and as DDA led monthly meetings. He'd never met, in fact rarely seen Monty's Operations counterpart, Bill D. They exchanged greetings. Monty led off.

"Any idea why we're meeting, David?"

How could he play it cool? "Not a clue. Is there a problem?"

Bill grunted a smile. "Not one you've created. You okay with David?"

"Okay. Sure."

"Don't want you to think we keep too close an eye on employees." Wups. He squirmed as Bill chuckled. "You were at a party recently, friend's birthday. You used some words that came from the outline you wrote for your PhD thesis a few years back. Monty and I recently reviewed that outline."

Verraeter felt his face drain. What the hell! "I don't remember saying ... At intake I fully disclosed that they'd refused to accept it. I was clear, I didn't complete–"

Bill D. shook his head. "Nothing to worry about. You disclosed everything you should have. No omissions. Relax. Just for the moment, on the PhD side, fact is we think you got a raw deal. We gather a primary stated intention of your thesis was to defend Roosevelt's 9066 order interning Japanese. The University's subsequent placement of Akira Takahashi on your supervisory committee was prejudicial. Did you know she was the grand-daughter of detainees?"

"No, I didn't." *Shit!* He felt his face warm.

"Hmmph. I'll come back to that later. Mind if we go on to a point raised in your outline?"

"All right."

"Good. You spoke of updating 9066 and a contemporary target class potentially more dangerous to the country than WWII Japanese-Americans. Remind me what the target class was?"

He hesitated. He'd prepared his thesis outline in 2004, still in the turbulence of 9/11's wake. The ferment had faded. Was this a sucker play?

"I mentioned Muslims."

"You did. But you were rather more specific. Tell us about that."

Were they serious? This was a high bridge without handrails. What the hell was going on? He chanced a step. "I ... I thought the 9/11 hijackers were expendable riff-raff, not leaders." He took in their faces. Christ, they were interested!

"I wrote that our biggest risk could come from educated Muslims, people who can travel a lot, in and out of countries like smoke through a screen door. Types who'd have money to burn, and foreign friends who have God knows what attitudes toward us."

"And locating them?"

"Initially, they'd be university students in every discipline, maybe interested in the Middle East or in places where we have military and/or economic interests. Maybe they'd join certain clubs, search *jihadi* web sites. The smartest ones wouldn't be that obvious. But they might go to lectures from the wrong people, people that take them in wrong directions. Whatever exposed them, we'd be able pinpoint their families, relatives, friends, foreign and domestic contacts."

Monty smiled. "One of your committee – can't remember who – noted that American university students are off limits for the Agency. Domestic stuff is the FBI's as I'm sure you know. What's your thinking?"

Good. Familiar territory. "The FBI are publicity hounds. They plant provocateurs to set up dopes, stooges and half-wits, makes arrests and claim they averted the massacre of thousands. The press falls all over itself. It's iron clad bullshit. They haven't got the balls or brains to do what needs doing. What needs doing has to be done below the public horizon."

"Well, look who's got some fire in his belly!" Bill chuckled, glancing sidelong at Monty.

Monty nodded. "Right, let's relax." He went to the door. "Becky, would you bring us three cappuccinos." He turned back and smiled.

"Heard you approve." He paced behind Bill as he spoke.

"Going back to your outline David, you wrote about 'virtual internment' replacing physical internment. Explain what you had in mind."

"Physical internment caused post war public relations difficulties with soggy-eyed liberals. Identifying and tracking educated Muslims means following every move, tracking them on line, via their superiors' or doctors' or accountants' reports, emails, phones, electronics. We get to understand them better than we understood the Japs we interned in WWII. No camps, no buildings, no barbed wire, just file folders."

Monty looked to Bill, then back across the table at him.

"So, suppose we constructed a new management group straddling the Offices of Transnational Issues and Collection Strategies and Analysis. The purpose would be to identify and track your target class. Would you be interested in being part of it?"

He couldn't believe what he was hearing. "Me? Yes. Yes, I would."

"Interested in helping to create it?"

He held his breath. "I'd be glad to help."

"You know, so's not to ruffle Congressional feathers or the *hoi polloi,* we'll provide the group with a suitably bland handle, Collections and Resources limps to mind. I believe you had a more descriptive in-house name for it."

"I suggested OWL, the Others Watch List. The foreign counterpart would be FOWL."

"Just between us three, David, Bill and I are looking at you to manage OWL. If you decide you'd like to do that, we're going to look into the PhD thing for you. Bend some academic ears."

He'd never danced on a table or even jumped up on one. Finally someone got it. He'd been right all along.

***

Langley, 2008

Monti's comment unsettled him: 'OWL would be low budget.' He misunderstood. "You mean there's no budget for manpower?"

Monti laughed. "Christ, no need. OWL will have all our worker bees. Names will come from our Customs and Border Patrol personnel, police, military, student bodies, and journalists. The bees don't end there. They include board members of the nation's biggest businesses, their executives, lawyers, physicians, accountants, university professors and administrators."

"Administrators? Deans ... even some higher up the totem pole?"

"Sure. University scholars and administrators will to do anything – *anything* – for CV or reputational enhancement. Sometimes a small grant from one of our fronts will do it – the National Endowment for Democracy is my favourite – sometimes an appointment to a board or a bio ornament. Do you know how many saps we get just by saying 'We'd like you to give a speech to the Council on Foreign Relations. Think about that on your resumé!' We even arrange membership for some.

"Journalists are useful too. They'll give up confidential sources as regularly as hookers drop panties if we promise them 'inside information.' Boy, can we supply that! First we give information – always authoritative, always from an unnamed source – and follow that with a reference to a university expert who, guess what, backs our source up. Never fails. Ditto for the business leaders – a little government business here or there, board appointments, invitations to drink with our stable of insiders."

"So, to go back, 'low budget' just means that we've got pretty much everyone in place we need to feed OWL. Let's hope we can narrow in on the right Muslims."

***

Verraeter met with all the worker bees he could in whirlwind tours of major state and private universities. He'd met interested students, motivated and often enough, pleasantly pliable. He'd been busy.

After laying the groundwork and returning to Langley he'd quickly settled in to a morning routine. He sipped an excellent morning cappuccino and scanned through several pages of weekly University speakers. His eyes stopped short and went back. The name, Major John Grant, rang a bell. A phone call confirmed it.

The Major was trouble – stubborn, rebellious and overly sympathetic to Afghans – America's enemies. Worse, Grant was a draw for impressionable students easily snowed by his Special Ops background. He'd even been quoted as saying he understood – *understood* for Christ's sake – Afghan resistance. As if that weren't enough, early on Grant was made a media darling in the main Washington rag. The paper wouldn't run an article like it now. Langley owned it.

He made a note and called his University of Colorado campus favourite. "Grant may attract students with cultural sympathies for the Afghans or the Pakis. Here's what to look out for ..."

Chapter 2

2007-8: Mohammed

Ayesha Karram swelled looking at him. At six feet two and one hundred and eighty pounds, her son moved like an athlete. Mohammed had her husband's size and ease of movement, but his clear dusky skin, black hair and fine features were those of her father whose photo lay on her bedside table. 2008 was his final year at Anschutz. She'd become a surgeon, guided by her father. She'd started Mohammed even earlier than her father had introduced her to the necessary studies, insinuating him into his uncle's veterinary practice to begin his training.

No better mentor existed than her brother-in-law. Dual qualified, Ali's brother Ahmad did Veterinary Medicine in Peshawar before his MBBS at King Edward in Lahore, and a surgery residency at Hopkins. He shifted his practice late, preferring animals to people. Mohammed took to animals like a finch to sunshine. Even before his eighth birthday he brought home two wandering fawns, a score of broken-winged birds, abandoned chicks, and sundry stray cats and dogs. His fine motor skills were extraordinary. Successful diagnoses led, often enough, to cutting and sewing. Thank God he'd be a surgeon, and not some bow-tied specialist with his nose in books. In his spare time Mohammed swam, ran cross country, and played soccer. On the other hand he'd recently stopped confiding in her. He seemed anxious. It wasn't academic. He was a top student. His sisters

13

adored him. He had everything. Why the constant frown?

She shook her head. It started three years before. His openness clouded. His reserve grew. He deflected or avoided her questions. Was he hiding something? When asked about girl friends, he stonewalled. His sisters were of no help. And why wasn't he more interested in his beautiful Afghan classmate?

***

His mother brought Laila up at breakfast. "She's the brightest of them. Pretty too."

Mohammed caught her drift. Laila Sayyed sat near him in his mother's Primary Care Orthopedic 8001 and Sports Medicine, 8005. Her grades matched his at the top of the medical graduating class. Calling Laila pretty was an understatement. He wasn't blind. "I've asked her for coffee, Mom. We've talked."

"Oh, she's not interested?" His mother's forehead wrinkled.

"Her mind is on Afghanistan. She talks about returning."

He kept the rest to himself, embarrassed. Early on, he tried to stand or sit near her. He wound up feeling like a klutz. She avoided his eyes. His grandmother, *Nya* Shazia, Pashtun like Laila, explained. An immodest Afghan woman was of unchaste character. Easy contact with men, even eye contact, revealed shamelessness. Laila finally accepted his invitation to have coffee, but only after he was introduced. His hopes sparked. She spoke of Asadabad. But later, when he presumed to brush against her in class, she retreated without taking obvious notice. When he asked her to lunch, it was a shy, polite refusal. Her words were apologetic. 'No, sorry.' Shy, eyes not meeting his. But no reason, no explanation, no follow up, no conversation.

On the first Tuesday of December, he stumbled upon her by chance. A shrill male voice filled a sparsely populated cafeteria. Six tables away, a red-faced pug bawled at Laila and her room-mate

Isabel. Laila shrunk into her headscarf. Mohammed hopped quickly toward them. Pug didn't see him coming. As he neared, he picked up the rant.

"I've seen you two dirty dyke ragheads. Go back to fucking Afghanistan, or else."

The man's forefinger punched toward Laila's breastbone. Mohammed intercepted and held the extended wrist. Lean and muscular, he stood over the mouth and fibbed. "She's my girlfriend. Who're you? You're no student!"

"Fuck off. She's your..? Bullshit. You're another lying, fucking raghead."

Mohammed felt his heat rise as he readied his fists. The pug's pimpled face showed scarlet against his white kitchen uniform. Mohammed stepped toward him. Uncertain and outgunned, pimples retreated looking over his shoulder.

Mohammed unclenched his fingers and released his breath. Whew! He was relieved. Pimples likely knew more about fighting than he did. Laila, a dyke? Crazy bastard. He took in a chestful of air. He'd defended her. She thanked him, hand on his arm. Please, leave it there.

Her fragrance and the lightness of her hand stayed with him through the week.

***

His mother arranged her headscarf, a white silk *hijab,* for Saturday mosque. "Perhaps Laila will be there."

Mohammed feigned disinterest. "I'm not sure I appeal to her."

She blank-faced disbelief. "Not what I hear."

He looked up. "What do you mean?"

"Yesterday, I bumped into her. She told me about the cafeteria. I thought she was almost starry-eyed. 'Tall, handsome and the kindest man she's met.' Her words."

"Hmm. Sure she meant me?" His mother frowned. "Okay, okay. Sounds as though I should quick go out and buy a ring." He held off a grin, waiting on further maternal guidance.

"Perhaps she expects you to share her interests."

"What? Politics? Afghanistan?" Her mouth went tight. He regretted his tone.

His mother had been half right. Laila came to coffee more often to chat. She spoke with cautious distance. She said she admired him and was grateful for his friendship. Today, after lectures, she hurried to leave.

"Going somewhere?"

"Hi Mohammed. Yep. A Special Forces officer serving near my home is speaking. Want to come?"

"Sure." He'd go wherever she went. He sat next to her, inhaling her sandalwood and cinnamon. She ignored or was unaware of men's furtive glances. Her gleaming black hair fell freely and shrouded her smile. As the major spoke her eyes shone.

Major John Grant was stationed in a small village in Afghanistan's Kunar province. The headman was his friend, the locals good, brave people. He spoke passionately and well. Laila's eyes led Mohammed's. By the speaker's closing words he too was riveted.

"It's simple really. My platoon helps defend the village against *takfiri* who attack two or three times a month. We're professionals. They're not. The attackers are well armed. We do our best. Now, questions?"

A voice, accented, spoke indecipherably from the back.

"Thanks for your question. I'll repeat it in case not everyone heard. 'How often do we visit the village?' What is its name?' Its name is no secret. The village is Mangwel. We don't visit or drop in. We live there."

Laila's hand rose. "In order to help the village and to live there, did you first have to ask *them* to protect *you*?"

The Major's face broke into a broad grin. "Thank you for that question. Yes, we invited their protection. We earn our place by helping to protect the village. I take it, since you know customs, you're *Pukhtanna?*"

Laila nodded.

"So you understand. We're loyal to each other. We admire and respect Pashtun traditions, even if they're not ours."

She flushed. "I'm an Afghan from Asadabad. *Manana,* thank you for saying this."

"*Hila kawam,* you're welcome."

Mohammed squirmed in his seat, then rose to follow Laila. Grant's eyes flicked to her over the heads of the students bunched around him. Finally, cleared of the crowd, Grant approached, followed by a bosomy blonde appendage wearing a student Sentry press badge reading 'Wendy'.

"Major John Grant, young lady." He placed his right hand over his heart, his left hand to his forehead. "And you are?"

"I am Laila Sayyed, Major Grant. This is my friend –

Mohammed intercepted. "*Zma num Mohammed Karram day.*"

Laila's mouth dropped. "You never ... You speak *Pukhto?*"

"Yes. Gramma, *Nya* Shazia, is Kabuli. Shall we go for coffee? Major?"

"Let's do it."

Mohammed smiled politely at Wendy, who trailed. "You covering the Major's visit for the paper?"

"Sure am. I record everything, to make sure I get it right." He nodded.

Over espressos a grinning Grant pitched them, guns blazing. "Why are you two here, when you really should be in Afghanistan?"

Mohammed reciprocated the Major's grin. "Okay, I'll bite. Why should we 'really be in Afghanistan'?"

"Fair question. Where do I start? First, I get to ask you something. I'm trained to do a lot of things, mostly fighting. What are you two studying?"

The corners of Laila's mouth rose."We're in final year meds."

Grant's eyes softened. He shook his head slowly. "No bullshit, I envy you. I wish I had medical skills." His eyes looked past them momentarily. "Last year, two young women, one from Mangwel another from a nearby village, died in childbirth. The one from Mangwel was married to my friend's son. The myth is that Pashtun men treat women like dogs. Maybe some do. But this boy was crazy about her. He's still a wreck. Some older Afghan men are afraid of all things women. Not all. Another friend in another village was immensely proud of his daughter. She taught in Asadabad. The *takfiri* shot her in the stomach in her sixth month of pregnancy. Her husband's family wouldn't let a male doctor near her. She died horribly. Afghanistan lacks doctors, especially ones who speak the country's languages."

Mohammed studied Laila. Her brown eyes gleamed. She wagged her head gently. She included him, her champion. Her eyes were on the Major's. Her words were for him too.

"I'll return as soon as I can, Major. My mother is American, my father is Pashtun. I'm a Cadet First Lieutenant in the ROTC. I've spoken with my superiors about serving in the Maui Clinic in Asadabad."

Mohammed sat back in his chair. "I'd no idea, Laila. You've never said ... Major, I still have an internship and residency to do."

Grant grasped the opening. "If that's all that's stopping you I'll have someone from Walter Reed call. They offer intern programs. You'd train first, but gain credit toward your internship in Afghanistan. You'd help where you're needed without delaying qualification."

The words slipped from his mouth before he realized what he was saying. "Please, have them call me."

"Mohammed?" Laila's hand was on his. She met his eyes. "Your parents, you should speak with them."

She rarely touched him. Her hand was warm, soft, electric. What did she say? "Y..yes." A stammer.

He stewed later. Laila was right. Damn. He had to speak with them. But Afghanistan? He didn't know whether he was up to dealing with the kitchen thug. Beyond childhood jiu jitsu classes and a single attacking move his father showed him, he knew nothing about self-protection. But Afghanistan was the land *Nya* loved. Grant said doctors were needed. It wasn't as though he'd find peace living at home and seeing Laila or anyone else.

*****

Wendy waited until Grant and the two students departed to order a cappuccino before dialling.

Verraeter picked up."Hi Wendy. How's the weather in Denver?"

"Hi sir. It's clear and bright, thanks. You were right about the Major's speech. It brought out new faces. I'm sending information on two. Both are final year meds. Laila Sayyed, Asadabad resident. Pashtun. She's ROTC, a junior officer. Grant's idea that Afghanistan needed more *Pashto* speaking docs sold her. Laila's classmate, Mohammed Karram, speaks the lingo. He asked Grant to have Walter Reed call him. These are the types we want to identify aren't they?"

"Perfect. Pashtuns in Af-Pak are the worst. You recorded the conversation? Good. Into the dropbox. Work on family connections. Excellent. Text me. By the way, I'm out Denver way next week. If you'd like me to drop by again to, umm, go over details on these two. Maybe a drink?"

"I'd like that. I remember last time."

He picked up her giggle on the other end and smirked to himself, remembering their first drink together in his hotel room the day after her nineteenth birthday. Dinner with a bottle of wine followed, and breakfast.

He added two new names to the OWL list. The names, circulated to seventeen agencies, came from DV:Mgr, Collections and Resources. Insiders referred to it as OWL.

***

His mother's eyes swam. His father's voice was quiet, flat. "What could possibly make you want to do something so dangerous? How could you make this decision before discussing it with us? Please tell me, going to Afghanistan has nothing to do with 9/11?"

His father's neck veins bulged. His own throat was dry. He'd never seen his parents like this. "No. I know Afghanistan's role in 9/11 is BS. I understand it's dangerous. But I could help. People are being assassinated, teachers, doctors, university students. I'll see more surgery, more illness, more everything. Laila's returning. She's described conditions. *Nya* gave me *Pashto* and some *Dari*. I need to go where I can feel useful. Trust me. I'll be careful."

His father wagged his chin. "It's Laila's country, not yours. She knows what to look out for. You won't. You'll be in harm's way."

"So will Laila. She's a friend. After my training, I can catch up with her." He swallowed water, and regretted his hint of certainty. Over a final coffee, when he spoke openly about joining her in Afghanistan, Laila was strangely cautious.

"Mohammed, we don't know each other that well. You mustn't count on ... You know I admire you. But ... I've a lot to learn about myself. When you come I'll know better ..."

He nodded, troubled. He had no idea why she was confused. Was there someone else? Did her parents rule the roost?

Passing the kitchen door before dinner he overheard his mother crying softly as she shared her worries with his sisters. All right, there was risk. But the Major hadn't shrunk from it. He'd talk to him again.

Privately he felt unburdened. From high school on each time he'd shown interest in a girl, his mother sought to direct him toward his future – marriage, family responsibilities, setting up a practice. In defence, he'd asked for and gained his sisters' silence in whatever furtive social arrangements he pursued. He thanked God they remained silent about a delicate misunderstanding in his first year at Anschutz.

Peggy and he knocked around for a month after a meet and greet. Their mutual attraction wasn't booze-driven. Neither of them drank. She'd stood out, literally sparkled, in a revealing blouse studded with sequins. She proved lively, full of fun and laughter unfuelled by drugs or alcohol. They had coffee for a couple of weeks, went to the movies. She went to church at weekends. He attended mosque. Things warmed up in the privacy of his home, when both had time.

His parents were teaching, his sisters in school. For the first time, she hadn't clamped down on his hand as it slipped under her skirt. Her heavy breathing spurred him on. He reached the top of her knickers and slid down to find her moisture. Lips locked with hers, holding his breath, he began lowering her panties. Suddenly her hand restrained his.

Her cheeks flamed. She stared at him open eyed. "I want to ... but ... will you come with me ... to church?"

His growing enthusiasm drooped. "What? Now?"

Her eyes immediately welled, droplets starting down scarlet cheeks. "Dad said ... he said I have to ... to marry a Christian ..."

He stood, shaking his head. She'd seemed more attractive moments earlier. "Peggy, I didn't understand. You had a plan."

Her eyes spilled. She blubbered. "But I want *us* to have a plan. You knew I was born again ..."

His teeth set hard. "Right. You did say that. I thought I'd been clear too. I'm a believer too, a Muslim. Your plan, marriage, prayers, conversion. We should have talked more. My fault. It's all right. I'll drive you home."

Fariyal and Sabriyyah arrived early from high school to find Peggy in mid-wail. He wasn't comforting her. His sisters looked daggers at him, all the while reassuring Peggy, whose whimpers descended rapidly to sobs. He shook. It could not have been worse. Damn. Double Damn. He stood in the kitchen, burning, trying unsuccessfully to drown the conflagration with cold water. When his sisters murmurs and Peggy's sobs muted, he drove her home in silence.

On his return his sisters rounded on him, apparently on principle. He explained, sparing details.

Fariyal frowned. "But you accused her ... you said she had a plan. That was cruel."

He wagged his chin. "Sorry. But sometimes the truth is cruel."

***

Nya Shazia lit up. She smiled and shrugged. "Mothers need weaning as much as offspring. Distance sets in – always too quickly for mothers. I don't see eye to eye with Ayesha. Parents don't know what children must do. What you want is right. Many Afghan teachers are attacked. Most are women. Doctors are scarce everywhere. You'll be rewarded in unexpected ways. Pashtuns need more like you. I'd love to go with you. I envy your gifts. Listen to Pashtuns you meet, especially those who don't want Americans there."

He was grateful. *Nya* had the biggest part raising him and his sisters. A rock.

Chapter 3

May 2010: Kunar, Recon

Mohammed woke with a silent prayer. He thanked Allah: no more night raids for their platoon. He and checked and rechecked weapons and med pack. He prayed for innocents caught in the dirty war.

Today was more recon and interdiction. The platoon had taken up his mantra, even if sceptical repetition would make it true: stopping hostiles meant fewer night raids and fewer dead Afghans. This morning he was edgy. The previous three days scouting proved barren. Just after sunrise, they set out with a young Frank Kudlow on point.

They moved silently through the mountain's blue and chir pines. High up sunlit fascicles began their melt, pelting shaded needles below still tipped with overnight frost. His ears perked up to the morning's rhythm. Finches and thrushes sat in treetops' first light, drinking melt water while chorusing the rising sun. *Nya* named them the forests' parishioners. Their songs hushed to peeps as the platoon's laden giants and their shadows passed below.

The forested path avoided pebble-strewn hillsides, where a crunch of heels or errant dislodged stones might alert an enemy. The ground's pine straw damped the tramp of their boots. Mohammed inhaled the familiar scent of Colorado's pines.

Two miles east north east of the Pak Army Ghakhi checkpoint,

Frank led the twelve man Operation Detachment Alpha across the Durand line. A further two miles into Bajaur, the platoon split up. Mohammed would lead his spotter-group of four farther east into Pakistan. Captain Chris Montoya's interdiction ODA-eight, armed with two M249gs, would set up a mile west.

Twenty minutes later, Mohammed signalled a brief halt. The pines were behind them. The mountain's slopes, barren of trees but boulder-strewn, were an area of increased risk. "Tony, take point."

Montoya had entrusted Frank to him for the first time. At barely twenty Frank was sharp, but green. Unlike Tony Mitchell, he'd not yet been under fire. Frank still wrote a daily journal for his parents and girl friend in Virginia. He spotted for Barry Hanko, their sniper. Barry was a Chicago native with a keen eye and steady trigger pull. The four walked on, alert and silent.

A mile farther on he motioned halt. He studied the hillside. A clear view of the trail's westbound traffic coming from Bajaur toward Kunar and Asadabad. They could ignore a blind spot, a bank above a sharp bend briefly blocking a view of eastbound passersby below. Mohammed relieved Tony on point, leading along a faint path above the crude but better defined mountain trail. Now, his hand signalled a move uphill, above both path and trail.

He took stock. Their camo was solid, blending well into the boulder-covered slopes of golden scree. He punched his Multiband Intra Team Radio to confirm a surveillance drone pass. The MBITR confirmed the mountainside above was clear. He shook his head. Drones were fallible. "Double check. Thirty yard intervals."

Their check found nothing. He set them up on a twenty-foot-wide pebbled shelf. His four men flattened across the ledge fronting a low ridge to their rear. At seven thousand feet, each breath pushed puffs of steam into crisp, clean morning air. A veil of light cloud hovered over the rise about two hundred feet in elevation behind. Bare, wind-swept patches were covered by frost. A few low banks of eddied snow lay in shaded patches behind the larger boulders.

Mohammed murmured to Frank at his left. "What's up with the frown? Worried?"

"Nah. Just thinking about Sandy."

"So why aren't you smiling? She seeing somebody else?"

"Nah. I've haven't seen her in a year. It's her birthday next week. She'll be eighteen. I wish I were there."

"In two months and a bit you'll be home. I bet she jumps on top of you and won't let you up for couple of weeks."

"Wow. I'd sure like that."

"Well, don't ask me afterwards for any medical advice on damaged parts."

"You're just making fun." Frank coloured and laughed.

The frost still painting the ground began to recede under noon's high sun. He squinted through glasses southeast down slope for any movement coming from the Bajaur side. Hanko lay beside him muttering complaints.

"Three days of nothing but smugglers and families. No bad guys. Think they've got other trails? Maybe over the top, on the slopes behind?"

"Patience, Barry. Whatever trails they have, we'll find them."

"Mind if I slide back to take a piss, boss?"

"Better there than in my ear."

"Maybe, maybe not." Barry bellied back, preparing to rise to his knees.

Mohammed refocussed on the trail. An unfamiliar thud, a gasp, warm liquid on the back of his neck. He rolled instinctively, scrambling toward cover at the delayed crack of a sniper's Dragunov. His fingers? Blood from his nape. A round brought up dust where his head had been. He made cover – a boulder. Shuddering, stunned, he stared at Barry's body. Sprawled, eyes and mouth wide, motionless except for the blood washing through his headgear and onto frosted golden pebbles below his face. Movement!

"Frank! What are you doing! Get down! Down!" Frank knelt over

Barry's body, trembling, sobbing. "Barry. Get up. Barry. No. You – !"
A slug exploded Frank's neck into open arteries spraying blood. His
legs thrashed. His body spasmed, gurgled and lay limp.

Mohammed flattened behind the boulder, snorting for breath,
shaking. Tony was on his belly wedged under the low back ridge.
Their shouts crossed. "Hold position!" "Hold! Hold!"

Stop shaking. Think. Med Pak. On ground. How? Useless. Barry
and Frank DRTs: Dead Right There. Tony's safe. For now. He took
a deep breath and stared at his opened med pack. When? Disorga-
nized. Items out of place. He clenched his teeth, shook his head to
stop his eyes spinning. One hand repacked mechanically. He held
his MBITR radio in the other. Montoya. Damned voice, shaking.
"Chris – Frank, Barry. DRTs. Snipers. Under fire."

In the background Tony screamed curses. "My mirror ... They're
fucking moving! They're going for firing position!" Tony's voice,
stressed, unsure.

His radio hand trembled. "Chris, have to move. Two hostiles,
maybe more above us ... descending."

Montoya's tone was clear, steady. "Leave the bodies. Move downhill. West to the main trail. Toward us. We're coming for you."

His offset mirror rose cautiously. A bullet smashed off the
boulder. Shards of granite clattered off his helmet. Damn them!
His breath came fast. His eyes steadied. Sons of bitches. Rounds
screamed and cracked into the boulder. The mirror. Two likely firing
positions. Hillock a hundred and fifty yards east south east. Rise due
east two hundred feet up and three hundred yards out. The sniper's
barrel showed on the hillock.

One. Confirmed. He cast a belt around the barrel of Barry's
scoped MK12 Mod 0 and retrieved it. He raised the brim of his
Kevlar ACH helmet on the M12's barrel above his boulder. Shoot
at this, you bastards. A shot from the rise knocked the ACH off.
His M4 thrashed the hillock. He dropped instantly. Granite chips
exploded off his sheltering boulder. Good, fire not coordinated.

Four paced shots kicked up dust, gravel and granite above and beside him. He fed another clip into his weapon, readied and motioned to Tony to belly across. Kneeling low, he rose suddenly and fired a burst, ducked, waited, then rose to sweep both hillock and rise with staccato covering fire. He knelt and fixed another clip. Tony. At his side.

In the mirror a slight movement amidst the hilltop scree. The high Dragunov. He sprayed cover as Tony sprinted hell for leather through a choke point below. Thumbs up. The snipers' attention was divided.

Tony set up and waved. He took off, zig zagging to cover while Tony swept and reswept both positions with rapid bursts. Screened by intervening boulders and small ridges, they scrambled down toward the trail and Montoya. Intermittent rounds hit behind ... Behind? Chasing?

He paused with Tony below a chest high ridge. So far so good. Two hundred yards below, the trail. Once there, they'd move south-west, toward the remaining eight members of the platoon. His neck hair was rigid.

"Tony, the bullets keep hitting behind."

"Better than hitting us."

"Maybe. Sharp eyes ahead. I'll take our six." Fifty strides on he stopped short and tapped Tony to drop. He pointed back uphill between boulders. A huge Pukhtun crouched below cover, looking uphill. They'd run right past him!

"Uh oh." He ducked and looked at Tony. Two bearded Dragunovs stopped five yards below the Pukhtun's boulder as if sniffing danger. He raised his mirror. The big man levelled his AK47. Mohammed held his breath. *Watch out!* A sniper spotted him. The Pukhtun's burst dropped them both in mid-turn.

Mohammed and Tony rose into the open. The Pukhtun looked down toward them. They waved a salute before resuming their descent. Mohammed approached the blind trail bend carefully, sighted the trail below and hit the dirt. What?

A *Pukhtanna*, striding long, smiling under the sun. Loosed from her scarf, black hair gleamed and tossed in the breeze. Two mules plodded behind her, followed by two lads carrying AK47s. Her head turned back toward them ... A boy's shout carried.

"*Mor!* Behind you!"

She turned to stare at him, palms up, uncomprehending.

Mohammed slid forward to the bank's edge. Behind her from boulders at the cliff's base, two men were onto her. One seized her arms from behind. A second faced her, hands groping. More armed men stood behind the boulders. His M4 cracked. One down. Tony dropped a second. Fierce return fire whistled over their heads.

He spat the dirt from between his teeth and looked for the woman. She'd freed one arm to draw a knife. Damn. No shot. Both attackers had drawn knives. God help her. Unexpectedly, the boys' AK47s opened up, spraying ricochets off boulders into screaming flesh. His barrel swung back to the armed men below, now in a cross fire. Someone ran behind to his right.

"The big Pukhtun!" Tony shouted.

The corner of his eye caught the *pakol*-topped beard setting up, fifty paces right. Triangulating ... a pro. The giant's rounds flushed two rifles toward the mules. A flurry of the boy's auto fire dropped them. Tony's and the Pukhtun's fire knocked down men below. Mohammed's eyes raced back to the woman. One attacker was on the ground, throat open. *Alhamdullilah.* Look at her! Crouched, circling, she feinted in a lightning flash toward the second man's neck. He raised his arm to defend. Her slash blurred beneath it. The brachial artery! *Mother of God. Who is she?* A third attacker had come, black garbed, slender, knife drawn. She faced him, ready. A boy's scream turned her head. Shit! No! The attacker sprang instantly, his blade grazing her inner thigh as she spun away. She flinched, looked down only momentarily, wobbled and fell to her knees. Ruby liquid flooded into her *partoog* legging.

The slender man readied his knife, grinning, voice rising. "Now you die, whore daughter of *shaitan*."

Mohammed shouldered his M4, sighted, squeezed the trigger. His round struck the attacker's chest, knocking him off his feet.

"Tony, hold and cover!" *The woman. Femoral. Allah, help me!*

He left his M4, scrambled down the cliff's incline and ran headlong, releasing his pack as he knelt. Combat gauze to thigh ... No time. *Her knife.* No. *"Dhost! Dhost!"* Friend! Friend! His forearm blocked her wrist. Fainted. Praise Allah.

Eyes fluttering. Breathing steady. Neck pulse racing, thready. Bending low, ear over her mouth, his hands moved in a blur. Thumb on femoral artery. High Israeli tourniquet. Ringer's Lactate. Hang ... Where? A child's sandalled feet raised dust beside her. Small brown hands moved into his field of vision. He put the bag in them without looking up. Boy. "Please."

Disinfectant. Gloves. Can't see. Raise *kameez*. Widen *partoog* slash. Expose wound. Three inches long. Deep. Arterial, vertical. Praise Allah, inch and a half. Extend surrounding flesh. Spread. Isolate artery. Sop up blood with tamponade. Pry artery up. Gently. Gently. Need vein. There. Tie off. Section two and a half inches. Slit open. Seat over slash. Suture. Thirty stitches. Not too tight. Release tourniquet. Good pulse. Check seepage, again. Check. Good. Close. Heparin, Cefotan into line.

His knees and legs were numb. He fell backwards, eyes closed, head spinning, silently grateful. *Praise Allah. Let her live...*

His eyes opened momentarily to the sound of footsteps. Three Pukhtuns stood over him; two boys and a man who seemed a Goliath viewed from Mohammed's position. The towering *pakol* they'd seen behind. Of course. He was with her. All three faces wore concern. Goliath's weapon barrel pointed down. The younger boy, teary and anxious, continued to hold the intravenous bag. Where was Tony? Why didn't they speak? Were they suspicious? ... Oh ... my manners. *Nya* gave me the words.

"May Allah forgive me that I didn't ask your permission to assist your woman. The assassin's knife opened her artery. The wound would have taken her unless I acted. I ask your permission to continue."

The giant looked at Mohammed briefly before nodding. "You may help my *khor*."

"Your sister?"

"*Aw.*"

"*Manana*, thank you."

He nodded toward the younger boy. Put a new bag of O-Neg into the intravenous line. He'd start with the boy's name. "*Sta num tse dey?*"

"I am of the house of Mehmoud Prraang. I am Zarhawar." He looked down at the patient. "She's *mor*."

"You shouted to warn her?"

"Yes. She didn't understand."

"Gathered that. She is ..?"

"The daughter of Mehmoud. She is Shahay."

"Your uncle?"

"The son of Mehmoud is Ayub."

"And your brother?"

"No. The son of Ayub is my cousin. He is Faridun."

Ayub's brow creased. "*Daktar sahib*, please. She'll live?"

"Yes, *enshaallah*. She's too brave to die. I've never seen anyone use a knife as she did."

Ayub brightened. "It's true. Thank you for helping her. When she was young I carved her a wood play knife. She thanked me by blooding my brother and me with it. She moved like a mongoose and mastered it quickly. Her hilted kukri *charre* comes from Dir. It slaughters lambs and chickens and seems good for *dakoo* too." His grin widened.

"So the ambushers were dacoits, bandits?"

"*Aw.*"

Zarhawar touched Ayub's sleeve and pointed. His mother's eyelids fluttered.

Moments later Shahay's eyes opened to find Ayub and Zarhawar at her side. Mohammed stood away, assisting Faridun who'd started water for tea. Would Tony and *Daktar Sahib* share?

"Thank you. We'd love to. First, a cup for the mother of Zarhawar." Faridun nodded.

Mohammed placed the tea near her hand while Ayub murmured to her. He heard only the words '*Amriki daktar.*' Her eyes flicked toward him and shied immediately. Her voice was weak.

"*Daera manana, Daktar Sahib.* You've helped me. May I know your name?"

"My name is Mohammed Yousf." He smiled, fixing his eyes on her tea.

She and Ayub drew a collective breath. Her words slipped out. "But these are Muslim names. You are a believer?"

"I am. Please, have tea. Faridun prepared it. It's not American tea."

He looked to Ayub. "May I speak to your *khor*?"

"You may, *Sahib.*" Ayub stayed.

Her eyes steadied. Training manuals gave the words *tor tap* to describe a wound to the covered part of the body. He tried them out. Her brow wrinkled.

"You speak of my wound? I don't understand *tor tap.*"

"You don't? I was told it meant *pet zakham*, a hidden wound. His gaze lowered. "No matter. The *zakham* opened your artery. I bound your leg to stop the blood, then used a small piece of vein from your leg to close the wound."

He avoided mention of cutting her clothing. *Nya* forewarned him. Family honour, *namous*, is founded on women's purity. Women were never to be made vulnerable to men's predations. In Nya's youth death might be preferred to a physician's exposing a female patient's flesh.

For the moment Ayub was distracted both by Tony's return and his tea.

Mohammed fought his gaze. She stood better than five feet seven. In stride and combat she was lithe, athletic. Distracted by Zarhawar's sudden movement his glance aside caught the flash of blue-green eyes set wide in an extraordinary face, full nosed, wide mouthed with a pure café crème skin. His gaze locked momentarily. She drew a quick breath.

He choked his apology. "I ... *Bakhana ghwaram.*" Nya's warning rang in his ears. 'Staring is overtly sexual, an attempt to penetrate the veil.' How could he be so stupid! He saw his embarrassment in her eyes.

"Thank you for your help, *Sahib*. May I speak alone with my brother? We must soon continue our journey."

He turned away, grateful for her dispensation. Montoya's eight arrived to distract him from his gaffe. Mohammed began the debrief.

"... After they hit Barry and Frank ... the bullets seemed to chase us. We looked back and saw the big Pukhtun, Ayub. We'd passed him without noticing. The snipers stopped and sniffed him out. He took them out as they raised their weapons. His sister, Shahay, she's the wounded. Frank and Barry... I couldn't help..." His voice shook and broke.

Montoya gripped his shoulder. He steadied, head lowered. Tony came to his side.

"Go look after the patient. I'll catch Captain up on the rest."

***

Montoya nodded. "See to her, Sergeant. I'll be with you in a few minutes. Carry on Tony."

"Mohammed thought the snipers were herding us. Didn't know why. Couldn't see much 'til we saw over the bank's edge. The woman led donkeys and kids. One kid shouted a warning she didn't make out. Two men ran out from behind her. Eight more were in the boulders below. She and the kids surprised them. The eight had good firepower, but poor position. Ayub came and set up for crossfire. The kids opened up with AKs. We had them from three sides. She killed two of them with her knife."

"Say again."

"Two, in face-to-face knife fights."

"Luck?"

"No chance."

Montoya muttered. 'Jesus! None of us could—" His eyes went to Mohammed who rejoined them. "How is she?"

"She'll need watching. In field operations ... it'll be a small miracle if her wound stays free of infection. The stitches have to hold. She's lost a lot of blood. Ayub tells me their compound, the *qila*, is miles away. In Batmalai."

Montoya listened, nodded and moved away. Mohammed rejoined the now sparring Pukhtun siblings.

***

Mohammed had sparred with his sisters, but never witnessed a sibling row like this one. His father had described post-op pain for femoral artery surgery – a red hot poker burning through the thigh. Shahay gritted her teeth and looked to Ayub.

"Brother, help me stand. We need to set out for home."

"Sister, you're mad. Please, ride a mule. Your wound brought you close to death. You're weak from lost blood. Your face shows your pain."

"No. Help me. My head will clear as I walk."

Mohammed suppressed a grin. Ayub's voice rose. "You're too weak to continue on foot to Batmalai!" *Nya* called it the impotent imperative.

Shahay was smiling too, lowering her head to mask it. She

continued to ignore his presumptive authority. "The tea has refreshed me. Help me rise, brother. I'm not a child."

Mohammed shaded his eyes. He sympathized with Ayub's sigh, a giant worn down by a wilful sister. His stone against her steel. So far steel had it. Ayub glanced to him with suddenly eloquent eyebrows.

***

Montoya returned after contacting base and approached Ayub. Mohammed translated.

"*Salaam*, son of Mehmoud. *Daera manana*. We're grateful for your assistance and happy Mohammed was able to help your sister. How is she now?"

The giant smiled and sighed again. "She'd go on as if her wound were a scratch. I worry she's in more pain than she shows and not as strong as she thinks."

"What if Mohammed accompanies you? He could ensure your sister heals... Sergeant?"

"If Ayub permits, I'd be happy to accompany him to Batmalai. I'll need to restock from Vargas's med pack."

Ayub's face betrayed relief. "My father would welcome *Daktar Sahib* as a guest."

Mohammed dropped his eyes to his boots. Montoya saw potential intelligence. He suppressed his own guilty pleasure. He'd be a guest in a Pukhtun *kor* and oversee her recovery. His attention was drawn back to the siblings.

Clearly impatient with Ayub, Shahay enlisted Zarhawar to regain her feet. As she leaned into him she sucked in a breath, her face chalk. Ayub's grimace reproved her while his eyes sought Mohammed's with a silent plea.

Mohammed nodded. He joined Zarhawar to lead an older mule to her side and spoke quietly with bowed head. "Please, sister of Ayub, I've seen your courage and know it tells you to walk. No one can doubt your bravery and endurance. May I give you something that will lessen your pain?"

"*Manana, Daktar Sahib.*"

His eyes fixed on the task of filling the syringe. "Your wound might have taken your life. Allah's mercy allowed me to close it." He injected the painkiller. Her continued silence suggested he take the risk.

"I pray my words won't offend you. Until you've healed, what seems your wound alone is also mine. If your stitches burst with walking, or if the wound becomes badly infected, my help would be wasted. I beg you, on behalf of *our* wound, please mount the mule and walk another time."

Shahay's reaction caught him flat footed. Her jaw fell. Her face, drained with pain, now coloured. Was it ... the analgesic hadn't yet taken?

***

For the moment Shahay's pain vanished. His *words*! She looked away, her hand covering her mouth. She felt a quiver within her chest. He dared to address her like this! On her exchange with Ayub! Yet *his* words ... '*Our* wound'? ... '*Our* wound?' Did he test her? He meant kindness. But the words!

She turned back, her insides tumbling. Recognizing the unease on his face, she retrieved her voice. "Thank you *Daktar, Sahib*. I'll ... I'll honour our wound as you ask." She turned to conceal the smile tracing her lips. She'd met his dare.

Her concessive nod beckoned Ayub. He lifted her carefully to sit sidesaddle onto the mule. She sucked in her breath, and objected no more.

Zarhawar looked at her, then quickly grinned at Mohammed who winked back.

***

35

Henry Vargas, a second 18D in Montoya's ODA platoon, picked through the second dead sniper's poke. Food, a rag-bandage, *chapati* ... What? His fingers felt it. Paper, folded into a two-inch square. He unfolded it.

"Christ!" His hand shook. He broke into a downhill trot. Montoya stood with two others. Vargas's wide eyes drew the captain aside.

"Find something?" Without words Vargas handed the find to Montoya. Montoya's face went white. "Mother of Jesus! Where was this?"

Vargas's voice wavered. "In the pouch of one of the Dragunovs... Boss, what's it doing in a hostile's possession?"

Montoya turned away and paced head down, hand on his chin. He gathered the men.

"Listen up. For your ears only.Vargas found something on one of the snipers – an intake photo of one of us. It's from *our* files." He hissed the words as he continued, "It's from someone with top secret clearance..."

Murmurs burst into curses. He passed the photo around. His raised hand settled their voices. "Someone from our side is targetting Sergeant Karram. The ambush was for him. Ears up at base for any mention of his name. Say nothing about this, and don't talk about it between yourselves. Report anything you hear to me, and only to me."

Chapter 4

1992: Nya Shazia: Husay's Story

Mohammed stared at his plate. When his parents went out for dinner, they never returned for bedtime. Why not? They always said they helped sick people and saw friends. Why did they have to do it all the time?

The doorbell rang. He bounded from the table. *Gramma!*

"Were you glum again, dear boy? Do you have a kiss for *Nya*? That's better. You miss them. When you finish your dinner we'll have a story. I'll put your sisters to bed while you eat."

He wolfed the chicken, cleared his plate, and found *Nya*. "What's the name of the story? Is it a new one?"

"Yes. You smile. Good. It's the story a man and woman who lived in a country far away. It's good your sisters are in bed. It's not a story for them just yet."

"Why not?"

"It has scary and sad parts. They're little. When they're older like you, I'll tell it to them."

"It's about Pukhtuns, isn't it?"

"Yes. How did you know? It comes from the people of a village near the town of Pashat, from the mountain Pukhtuns, people of honour. You remember their word for honour?"

"I remember. It's *nang*."

"Right. But I've told you many stories. Do you remember what *jinni* changes shape to make mischief?"

"The *pairyan* of the river beds and forests where they hide."

"And who's most devilish?"

"Hah! the *shaitan*!"

"Have I forgotten any?"

"Yes, the *marid*. He's the powerful one who makes thunder in the mountains."

"You remember well, Mohammed. So, I'll tell the story. Already you speak *Pukhto* so well, I don't remember whether you know all the words. Ask if you don't understand. Before I start, I warn you, this is a story for a boy soon to be a man, a story of courage, love and death."

"Death?" He sat closer.

"In ancient times, a beautiful girl named Husay grew to love a village boy named Rekhteen. Her heart near burst with happiness when he was promised to her. But before they could marry, his bravery called him away to war. She waited. Weeks became months, and months years. Still, she pined for his return, and rejected many suitors greedy for her beauty. She heard nothing. At last, a visitor related the story of her village's young warriors. A cruel king from afar captured and enslaved them.

"Husay resolved to journey with her brother to the distant kingdom to seek Rekhteen. For weeks they travelled, through snow covered mountain passes, raging rivers and sun burnt deserts. They endured cold and sickness made worse by hunger and thirst. At last, so thin they cast no shadows even in the brightest sun and all but unrecognizable, they arrived in the land of the cruel king and approached his soldiers. Before they could say they came in peace, an arrow shot from the bow of the king's archer struck her brother's leg, crippling him. Throwing her cloak over him as his shield, she calmed the soldiers and asked to see their ruler. And he came.

"What is it you want, woman?"

"Your majesty, I have come to your kingdom to beg freedom for a prisoner named Rekhteen, to whom I was promised."

The cruel king looked down on her crippled brother. A crooked smile came to his face. "If one from your family can jump across a pit of burning coals, I will free Rekhteen."

His eyes opened wide, when Husay stepped forward.

"I'll jump" she said to the king.

Nya stopped to look down at him. "But you my grandson, you know the secret of Husay's name."

His eyes narrowed. "It's a kind of deer. Doesn't it mean gaz ... gazle?"

"We say 'gazelle.' Yes. Good. Back to the story!"

"The truth is, Husay's limbs were strong. From childhood, she could jump great distances. Now, here in a distant land, her heart lifted. She didn't weigh how the journey, her hunger and thirst had weakened her.

"When the coals were prepared and burning blood red, she knotted her *kameez* above her knees, and steadied herself against her shaking legs. Summoning her courage and all her strength, she ran like a desperate antelope and leapt across the long expanse of glowing coals toward safety. Her feet found solid ground beyond the fiery embers. Stunned by her triumph, she momentarily closed her eyes in joy. Alas, she hadn't noticed her *kameez* unravel behind her, trailing into the blood red coals. The *kameez* caught, and burst into flame. Women watching screamed a warning, ran to her, pushed her to the ground, and threw charred sand upon her to extinguish the flames. So fierce were the flames, so great was the amount of burnt sand thrown upon her that she was blackened from head to toe.

"The king, true to his word, had Rekhteen brought forward.

'Do you know this woman who jumped the coals for your freedom?' the king asked.

"Rekhteen peered onto the face blackened by soot and blinded by sand, a body torn by fiery agony, unable to speak, shaking with pain, hollow with starvation.

"Perhaps, but no. I'm grateful, but I don't recognize her."

The evil king's lip curled, and he nodded. "Then go without her. You are freed."

Rekhteen turned to leave, but hesitated. Did he not owe the woman a debt?

The king saw his hesitation and grew furious. "Depart now or be my slave again and watch her die!"

Rekhteen had little choice but to continue on his way.

"For months Husay lay between life and death, her burns infected and her pain beyond suffering. Her strength and love for Rekhteen saved her. Sadly, her brother didn't survive. His leg blackened, and he died.

"Meanwhile, Rekhteen returned to his village. He searched everywhere for Husay, but didn't find her. In his long absence great misfortune had come upon the village. A terrible plague left homes empty. No one from Husay's family remained. Memory of her vanished, just as she had. In despair he married one of the few remaining village girls. Sadly, she died soon after giving birth to a daughter.

"Rekhteen named his child Husay, in memory of the woman he'd once loved and forever lost. In the sixth month of her life his daughter Husay became gravely ill."

"As it happened, a strange woman had come to live in the abandoned home that earlier belonged to Husay's father. The stranger called herself Sparghai."

Mohammed looked up at *Nya* with brightened eyes. "'*Sparghai?*' It means embers."

Nya nodded. "Sparghai's weary face was lined by pain and thin from hunger. One cheek and ear bore strange rough scars. Her hair on one side had begun to show grey. When she heard of Rekhteen's dying child, she came to care for her. With Sparghai's help, Husay slowly regained her health.

"Marriage and death had emptied the village of girls. Rekhteen needed a mother for his daughter. Sparghai proved kind to Husay. By and by they married, and the happiness of their home flowered. They grew old together. Rekhteen never tired of telling how he gained freedom from an evil king through an unknown woman's gallantry and courage. Sparghai never tired of listening to his story. As much as he smiled to recall his good fortune, she smiled to show her happiness.

"Illness overtook Sparghai late in her life, and in her final days Rekhteen's daughter Husay came to care for her. As her last breaths left Sparghai whispered her secret to Husay, asking only that it be kept from Rekhteen.

"But after Sparghai's death, Husay couldn't withhold the secret. So Rekhteen learned the woman he came to love and now mourned, his wife marked by fire, was none other than his beloved Husay who returned him to freedom.

"Each day that remained to him, he wept as he told, to any who would listen, of a woman whose courage saved him from captivity, and whose honour returned her to him."

Mohammed's young eyes narrowed. "He was brave to go and fight, grandma. But she ... she was braver, wasn't she?"

"I think so too child."

Chapter 5

April 2010: Shahay

Bibi Rokhana watched her daughter from the porch. Shahay, glossy coal hair stirring in the breeze, knelt weeding the vegetable patch. She'd looked up too late to shout after her son who'd scampered off through the gates. Shahay wore her exasperation on her face. She mopped her forehead with her sleeve as her lips mumbled an empty reproof.

Bibi left the porch and went to kneel alongside. "Zarhawar is young. Where Faridun goes, he'll go too."

Her daughter wagged her chin. "He's disobedient. He didn't listen again."

Bibi chortled. "What! You, Mistress of Disobedience, say this of my grandson? How many times did you abandon your sister to follow your brothers through our *qila* gates?"

Shahay smiled. "But they were my brothers. Farikhta liked *cheendak*. I preferred doing what my brothers did."

Bibi nodded. "Yes. You began when you were four! You left the *cheendak* hopscotch with Farikhta and scurried after Ayub and Sakhi with their slingshots."

"Yes, I remember."

"You should. They jumped like ibexes across the torrent-boulders up the stream bed to hunt chukar in the fields above. Somehow, you

followed them. How you leapt across those boulders with your little
legs I'll never – you might have killed yourself."

***

Shahay waved off a fly. "Their voices were far ahead. When the gaps
between the largest boulders were too great, I jumped down and ran
between them. They seemed like giants to me."

"Ayub told me you startled them."

"Yes. They whispered in the long grass. I crawled toward them.
They stared into bushes. A chukar sounded there. Sakhi put a stone
in his sling. I think grass tickled my nose..."

"You sneezed."

"I didn't know the chukar would fly away."

"You wouldn't leave until they showed you how to use the
slingshot."

"No. Why would I? They wanted to bring me back right away.
But I followed them because of the slingshot."

Her mother's chin wagged. "They let you have your way. That
helped make you stubborn."

Shahay uprooted some crabgrass... "You mean my marriage to
Angar Malak?"

"Your haste to marry a *jihadi* was wrong. But you were stubborn
even before that. You insisted on sparring with your brothers with
their knife fights. And as for crawling into a cage with a wild animal..."

Shahay felt her cheeks warm. "Both Lema and I were young.
Neither of us knew better. Angar Malak is dead. I don't think of him.
Yes, I married too young... I knew little of men. As for the knife, at
first sparring with my brothers was a game, one I wanted to win.
Now, I know better what it does."

Her mother met her eyes. "Yes. May you never need to use it as
men do."

She left Shahay to garden, returning to the kitchen with carrots.

***

Bibi had made only one visit to her daughter during the brief marriage. Shahay still wouldn't disclose all that happened when, eight years earlier, she'd married and following custom, moved to her husband's family home. It wasn't until seven months after the marriage that Angar's mother summoned her. It was the morning following Angar's and his father's departure for Afghanistan to fight the *angrezaan*. Shahay was pregnant. Her face was a mass of bruises, her eye blackened, the sclera blood red. Bibi invited Angar's mother to sit with them for tea. She'd chosen her words carefully as her daughter sat quietly, head bowed in the presence of two older women.

"Have you met my sons, mother of Angar? They are giants with a quick, cruel hands. They are lethal with knives and excellent marksmen. It would be a pity to lose a son as brave as Angar, would it not? For now, I'll say nothing to them. My mind may change when I next visit."

Angar's mother's face turned white. She stomped off. Bibi instructed Shahay to sharpen her knife openly while Angar was away.

A week after Angar's return, his family, with Shahay's exception, travelled by truck to a wedding in Khar. Shahay, near due, was left behind to give birth to her son. On its return, the truck rolled into a gorge, killing everyone. Bibi and Mehmoud welcomed Shahay's homecoming.

Bibi's concern remained. Time had permitted Shahay's spirit to return, even if that spirit included her wilfulness. Now she insisted on joining Ayub on the forthcoming *khadi* visit to Farikhta and her husband on their first child's birth. The celebratory visit would be the longest journey Shahay and the boys had taken. Travel by foot to Asadabad and back over the mountainous Hindu Raj wasn't without risks.

Chapter 6

April 2008: Medic

Mohammed had been naïve. His parents were in shock. He hadn't sought their permission because that invited prolonged dispute. On the other hand, he'd not been forthcoming. His mother avoided his eyes. His father's silence remained resolute.

To protect himself he needed training. After years of vet surgery followed by years of medical training, it was time. He'd be amongst Nya's people. Laila would be there.

"I'll join as a medic."

His mother paled and left the dinner table. His father rose in silence, staring fixedly onto the garden. His sisters' faces went white. Fariyal and Sabryya went to their rooms.

He went for a run to burn off tension. His Dad intercepted him when he loped back.

"We should sit and talk."

"Good. Let me shower first."

Their faces remained glum. His mother's lips trembled. "A regular soldier?"

"An NCO, so pretty much a regular soldier, yes. I'll return for a residency after training and deployment."

"How long will those take?"

"A couple of years. I'll have a better idea what I want afterwards.

The medical combat training includes a couple of months of hospital trauma rotation and usually, eight months of advanced training. I might be able to shorten some of that."

His father's head wagged. "You'll be a common soldier? Getting shot at and shooting people?"

"I'm not planning to shoot people or be shot at. But it'll probably happen. I want to meet some Afghans, to see how they live. I've never even been abroad. Gramma's told me so much..."

"She hasn't been back for forty years" his father snorted.

"True. But I won't meet Pukhtun patients in a stateside hospital."

His mother's face coloured. "You could be an officer working in a military hospital here. Instead, you'll be what they call a grunt..."

"It's a non-commissioned officer's rank. They call it an 18D, the same rank as all twelve men in a platoon except the Captain. Most will be like me, specialists. So I'd be one of a dozen grunts... You've given me everything, a great education, no debt. I need more. I have skills, but chances are other guys will have different ones. If I can help out, I will. It'll be okay. Laila will be in Asadabad. By then she'll have made captain."

Their pretence of easy optimism next day left him with more guilt than relief.

***

Jaime Gomez, a retired SOF instructor turned recruiter, listened to him, evidently gobsmacked.

"Okay, let's start with a simple question. I assume you're not playing me. Why does a doctor want to be a soldier?"

It was the question Mohammed expected. "Fair enough. My parents groomed me as a surgeon. Lots of veterinary surgery from early on. I won't bore you with details. I began to wonder why I should do what they expected – graduate, get a big time residency, marry a nice girl, settle down in a good practice. At Anschutz I listened to a speech by a visiting soldier, John Grant.

Gomez straightened. "Major John Grant? He's a legend."

"I didn't know that. What he said impressed me. I was with Laila Sayyed, another med student. She hails from Asadabad. Near where Major Grant served. He said they needed docs in the field. Teachers needed protection. I've got *Pukhto*, Arabic and some Dari. Languages might help. I need to set my own course. This is it."

Gomez's chin acknowledged the story. "Okay, that's better. Understand, we don't get university medical grads willing to be SOF grunts. Plain and simple, I'll submit your name and the forms once I have your details. A few warnings. They'll typically want to place you in officer's ranks. You'll need to resist that to get into the field. With Arabic and *Pukhto* you can challenge language courses, and you'll skip a lot of the basic medical training. I'll talk to friends at Bragg. Second. Physically and mentally it may be a stretch for you. One more thing ... you'll mix with some tough dudes, some who have strong opinions."

"About – ?"

"Yeah, not only about your name and religion. You're a civvy meds grad aiming to be in the field with them. Experienced soldiers will wonder kinda like 'Can-we-trust-this-guy-with-our-lives?' Without prior military training you'll enter as an 18X. The X is a question mark."

"But if I'm in, I get the same training everyone else gets?"

"Yup, at least the same as every other 18D. I get the impression you think you'll measure up. I hope you do. You've got something I haven't seen before. I'll say that in my notes to Fort Benning."

***

Mohammed understood the inevitability. First it was at Benning. Fifty of them completed a four-mile ruck march. He'd looked sharply toward a small group huddled to his left, laughing and glancing at him. Abdul? Was that what they'd said? Perhaps he'd misheard. He'd picked up the forty-five pound ruck and turned to walk back.

He knew being a physician wouldn't cut any ice. But he'd grown up and gone through Denver's schools without problems. At Benning and now Bragg he'd heard Abdul, diaper head, sand nigger and variations on the tired, ... no wonder he runs so fast – Arabs invented the running shoe.

Today he sat back with his head against the plane's headrest and closed his eyes. Three days of leave after the Special Ops Prep Course and, better still, a friend made in his first real scrap. He'd have to make something up about his bruised face for his family. When he popped in on Jaime Gomez, they'd have a laugh.

***

Shoulders hunched, Mohammed walked toward barracks from the mess. Larry flanked by his two friends followed. What was it? Were they frustrated he'd ignored them? They somehow survived pre-training at Benning. It wasn't their fitness. They came in fifteen minutes after his fifty-four minute ruck march. Washout range. Hadn't the brass picked up on them? Now in the Bragg intake group, they'd brought their taunts. At first he'd been annoyed, but curious. Did they mean anything? Unopposed, they'd become more frequent. And blindingly coarse.

"Hey nigger, we heard you Muslims fuck your sisters and mothers, then whore them out for money." Laughter. Guffaws. "Guess you can't say nothing when it's true."

He stopped and set his jaw. He could use his Dad's technique. It was all he had. He'd still probably get his ass kicked. The thugs' laughter quieted. He turned, walked back, right hand extended as if in peace. Larry's snarl wavered momentarily. Good. He looked puzzled. His left feinted toward Larry's groin while his right thumb gripped deep under Larry's chin and fingers stabbed claw-like, deep into both eye sockets. Larry screamed, stumbled back, and fell to the ground holding his face. Stunned at his success, Mohammed unwisely stood still. Big arms seized his from behind in a full nelson. Fists pelted wildly into his unguarded stomach and face.

Running sounds behind. A gasp of warm air on his neck. His arms suddenly freed. What? Fists stopped. Now the pummeller fronting him backed off, eyes wide, hands dropped, staring. Behind? A scream. A wet thud. The crack of a bone snapping.

Mohammed turned, wiping blood from his chin. The big one lay on the ground, howling, holding an unnaturally bent leg, shaking. A smiling face on a sturdy body slipped by him.

"Please, allow me..."

Sturdy grasped a flying fist from the standing attacker, opened its fingers and bent the wrist inwards, dropping its owner to his back. A short kick whipped into the dropped ulnar bone, snapping it like a twig. The assailant scrambled away screaming, holding his shattered forearm.

Larry continued to writhe on the ground, tried to get up only to fall back.

His cavalry looked down at Larry. "Looks like he's out of action. What'd you do to him?"

"Dug into his optic-thalamic nerve. His heart's running a bit slow."

"Nice. What's that called?"

"It's an eye-heart reflex, the Aschner phenomenon."

His defender's smile widened. "Don't know that one. You'll have to show me. Heard you were medical. You o.k?"

"Little sore. Thanks. I've seen you around. I'm –"

His companion waved him off. "I know who you are. Mohammed, right? Heard about you. Seen you here and there. I'm Tony Mitchell. No thanks needed. Didn't look like you were making much headway. Three against one is tough sledding." His hand was out.

"Well, thanks for stepping in. Stupid of me. Anger made me too ambitious."

"I'd say so. Worth it?"

"It was time. Months of nigger, mother and sister whores. Started at Benning."

"Hmmph. Charming. You aren't exactly pink and blonde, but *nigger*?"

"Yeah. Heard that once before, as a kid."

Tony's smile left. "Who'd come after a kid like that?"

"Long story."

"I've nowhere to go."

"Hmmph. We were up at the cottage in Nederland. "

"Where's that?"

"In the mountains, west of my hometown, Denver. Friends and I, running around, stumbled on a doe nursing fawns. Next thing I saw was a guy kneeling behind a bush drawing his bow back. I couldn't believe it. I shout. The doe is startled, starts a run, takes the arrow in her haunch and drops. Shock I guess. The bow starts moving toward her drawing his knife. I ran to stand in his way."

"Jesus. How old were you?"

"Maybe twelve. Don't remember exactly."

"What were you thinking?"

"She had fawns. I thought I'd take the arrow out and patch her up."

Tony's chin wagged. "At that age? What the hell made you think you could take an arrow out and patch her?"

"I'd done it before. My parents had me helping out at my uncle's vet practice. They're surgeons. They set me up. I helped on weekends, and pretty quickly did more. I guess that was the plan. Anyway, I'd already helped take out arrows from a couple of great Danes, a cat, a fawn, and a calf. I knew the drill. If it doesn't kill outright, it can be pretty straightforward. Sometimes not."

"So he's coming at you with a knife..?"

"He was shouting, *move away nigger*. That confused me. I turned my head to see if he meant somebody else."

"Hah! Like who, me???"

***

Mohammed's adolescent fists were clenched, his knees shaking. The hunter growled. "The doe's mine. Move you little prick, or I'll put an arrow through you."

If he moved, the doe was dead. No way. The bow notched another arrow. Who? His tall neighbour stepped out from behind the hunter ... Bert!

"You should calm down, fellah. Deer's out of season. You aren't from these parts. Tell you what – leave my neighbour's kid alone and take off while you can."

The bowman spun the arrow toward Bert's chest. "I've got the arrow, buddy. Fuck off. Leave, or so help me, I'll let this one go."

A woman's voice came from his right. "My Ruger shotty is locked and loaded, fellah. It's just a 12 gauge pointed at your fat ass. Course, I might miss. But I might not. Best do like Bert says. Drop the bow. Leave and don't come back."

"Okay. Okay. Christ Almighty."

The string relaxed. Bow and arrow fell on the ground. Bert smashed the bow against a tree. His wife, Fern, grinned.

***

Tony shook his head. "And the deer?"

"Fern took her pickup and got Dad with his medical bag. A foot or so of arrow was in her hip. The point sat a half inch or so below her hide. So, it was shallow. We'd covered the doe's head to calm her. Bert put light pressure on her neck. I injected lidocaine, then slit her skin above the arrow point. We pushed the point through the slit, broke the fletched end off and pulled the business end out. Simple enough."

"Fletched equals feathers?"

"Right."

"No blood?"

"Plenty. I wiped some onto my face to yuck my sisters out. But no gushers. Missed the artery. I stitched her up, entry and exit wounds."

"Surgery in a veterinary clinic? How long?"

"Right through medical school, so until about four months ago."

"You finished med school? That's a hell of a lot of surgery. Didn't get turfed for killing anybody?"

"Yep, finished. Med school didn't let us kill patients. Pity, it was the only place we could have practiced without killing paying customers." Tony grinned.

Mohammed's curiosity spilled out. "How about you? You sure learned to take care of yourself. Where?"

"New Jersey. Some big guys took to whacking me around in school. One day four of them were tuning up a small Italian kid. It pissed me off. I stood up with him. They thumped the hell out of us. Mom was poor. My new Italian friend's dad paid for karate lessons for his son and me. I took to it. Turned out his dad was connected, like the Mob. My last trainer was Israeli. He made sure I knew how to break bones. My friend's dad offered me a job with his, hmm, organization. I joined up instead."

Mohammed breathed easier when the enquiry wound up. Larry and his friends proved reluctant witnesses, shy on details. He and Tony admitted simply to defending themselves as well as they could. Eyebrows were raised over the broken bones. Larry and friends washed out.

***

Verraeter paused as he scrolled through the growing file.

OWL: Karram, M.J.:05'14'2008 Accepted: SOF training, Ft Brg,

18D. Enquiry. Disciplinary enquiry. Whines of racist insults. Injuries to fellow trainees. Anger issues? Temperament? Co-opted candidate Tony Mitchell (separate file) into fighting alongside him.

***

Laila's email congratulated Mohammed on finishing his 'courses,' digging with 'What's taking you so long?' and 'What courses?' Fair questions eighteen months after their last coffee. He replied simply 'Mil 100, 101,2 etc.' He promised to contact her in the field. How he'd do it wasn't clear. A lot of water under the bridge. He didn't offer to explain why, for two months preceding deployment, he hadn't written.

He'd shortened his training, as Gomez foresaw. Bragg's medical trainers allowed course challenges: Basic Sciences, Pharmacology, Trauma, Clinical skills, Cardiac Care. He'd also skipped languages with the exception of the Basic Combat component. He thrived in hand to hand fighting, tutored by Tony. Before deployment, he accepted and needed a two month stint at a Phoenix Level One Emergency Department.

***

Mohammed had Nadia Sikorski's name and a short bio. A former nurse, she'd attended medical school after divorcing, did brilliantly and quickly rose post-residency to Emerg Head in Phoenix. He walked in to the humming ward, toward a lanky woman wearing scrubs and a saucy grin. He'd meant to ask where he might find Dr Sikorski. Her name was on her scrubs.

"You have to be Mohammed. Sorry, I haven't gone over your file in detail. 'Just graduated but 'some surgical training.' What's that about? Oh, wait. Sorry. Have to take this." The buzz turned her eyes away to the text message.

"Tell me later. Knife wound incoming. You'll start now. Everyone else is tied up." She continued as they trotted toward an open exam room. "Explain to me how a fresh-faced MD winds up as a SF medic. Was it – ?"

He was relieved sirens interrupted. Senior docs he'd met made the same assumption. 'No one selected you for a residency?' Translation – 'As a moron at the bottom of your class you couldn't find a residency even in outer Mongolia.' He didn't hold it against them. His reply was to the point. 'I didn't apply for a residency. Afghanistan was always first.'

Friday night was an ER zoo. Two nurses already prepped and hooked the patient up. He masked and gloved.

Nadia looked directly at him. "Right. Tell me about our patient, Dr Karram."

He locked onto the patient's eyes. "What's your name, fellah?"

"Gary. That sonofabitch cut my neck."

He spoke through the patient to Nadia. "Okay Gary. Zone 2 laceration. No larynx involvement. I'm going to move you around a bit while I take a look. Meanwhile" – he took in the nurse's name tag –"Sally is going to continue to press Combat gauze lightly down on the wound."

"Right. Alert, strong pulse, 100 bpm, good bilateral breath. Elevated BP 140 over 100. Penetration Zone 2, platysma is scored. No evidence of hematoma." He motioned Sally to pull back the Combat gauze and placed his left thumb on a small pulsing stream of port coloured blood mid-wound and listened to the neck sounds with his stethoscope. "Stridor – likely a tracheal nick. Blood's arterial. Probably another nick right carotid. The platysma isn't transected, absent hemoptysis, absent hematemesis."

"Treatment?"

"Trendelenburg–"

"Why?"

"To prevent air embolism." He motioned to Sally who adjusted patient's bed. "Careful intubation for the tracheal leak. Shall I?"

Nadia nodded. "Go on, keep explaining." Mohammed narrated as he worked.

"Combat gauze under light pressure on the bleed. Doppler ultrasonograph CTA the neck for confirmation and call a surgeon, Cardiovascular or neuro. They'll likely just suture this. If it's more extensive than it seems, he might use an ePTFE patch on the carotid. I'll use a cuffed 11mm ID to intubate."

Nadia's eyes widened. "All right, remind me. What's an ePTFE patch?"

He first explained to Gary what he was doing and intubated before answering Nadia. "Okay, I know you're testing. The patch is basically Goretex. Dad used saphenous vein grafts elsewhere, but for neck work he likes the synthetic."

"Your Dad's a surgeon? Cardiovascular?"

"Yes, Mom's an Orthopod."

"How old are you?"

"I'm twenty-three. Why?"

"Just getting to know you. You graduated when you were *twenty-two*? Your resumé – what's 'some surgical training'?"

"Almost twenty-two. Surgery? The short story, I worked in my uncle's veterinary clinic for thirteen years. Dad and Mom would come by, showed me stitch techniques, first superficial hide or skin-lacs, then deeper tissue and vascular repair. In med school, in spare time, I visited their surgeries."

***

Nadia listened and nodded, bemused. Next day, she had lunch with the heads of cardiovascular and neurosurgical services.

"A young doctor's arrived from, of all places, Fort Bragg for two months Emerg tune-up before he's shipped out. I've a hunch you two might be interested in him. I don't know what a surgical prodigy looks like but... Ken, do you know of an Ali Karram from the University of Colorado..?"

"Yep. He's head of cardio surgery there. His wife's at Anschutz too... Ayesha, I think. Orthopaedic."

"Mohammed Karram is their son. He's had unusual training."

Nadia sent him with emerg patients bound for cardio and neuro-surgical surgeries. Curious surgeons invited him at first to observe and pose questions. That progressed to enquiring about his parents' techniques in comparable cases. The neurosurgical head remained skeptical. Were the young man's surgical skills up to his knowledge of procedure?

"So young man, scrub in and close this neck. I'll finish inside while you scrub."

Mohammed scrubbed, gloved and masked. He closed deftly, precisely, at lightning speed. The neuro head looked on, confounded. From then on he was asked to scrub in on vascular cases. Theatre viewing galleries filled with curious nurses, envious residents and nervous surgeons.

Nadia passed along the whispers, not without envy. 'Surgeons are giving him final year resident treatment.' So far as Nadia could see, he didn't seem to notice.

***

Mohammed tried her cell. No answer. He'd followed the neurosurgeon's suggestion ... 'You'll see blast Traumatic Brain Injuries in Afghanistan. Do some TBI research.' But the neuro head was off to Hawaii. Nadia said she'd help in the interim if he found something. She'd given him her home phone and address. He'd spotted something he wanted to discuss.

She opened her apartment door to his knock.

"I'm so sorry. What an idiot I am. You're in your pyjamas. What time is it? I'm ... I tried your cell. I found some research – I wanted to tell ... I'm so embarrassed." He turned to go. "It can wait."

Her smile relaxed him. "No. Come on in. You must have rung while I was in the shower. Tell me, what you've found. I'm having wine. A glass? ... Do you drink?"

"You sure? Wine? Never had any. I'll try a bit."

He sat, sipped the odd tasting liquid and recounted what he'd found. "... but the processes are similar. So, the same injection used for Alzheimer's may suppress post-TBI neuroinflammation..."

Nadia nodded and simultaneously stifled a yawn. "It might well if I understand the process. You've found something interesting."

Nadia's hand covered another yawn. He stood ... "I'm ashamed. You're tired. I've stayed too long. I'll get going." He half-turned to leave.

Her hand on his shoulder stopped him. Her eyes lowered. She spoke haltingly.

"Please ... I'm hopeless at ... I don't want to embarrass either of us... Would you... I've never asked anyone. Would you like to stay?"

He tried to catch her eyes. "Stay?"

Her colour was up, and her eyes were full. "I'm sorry. Damn. I've made both of us uncomfortable. The wine... since my divorce..."

He felt his cheeks warm. "Please, I'm not uncomfortable. But ... It's not just that I've never ... never been asked. I'd love... look, you may not want – I've dated, fooled around but ... bad experiences. I don't want to disappoint you. I've never..."

Her eyes seemed ready to pop out of her head. She placed her empty stem on the table, put her finger on his lips, then her arms around his neck and kissed him. He opened his eyes when she backed off, her arms still around his neck.

"I understand and I'm astonished. I assumed these days that every good looking young man has had girls galore. You're unusual. Please, don't worry about disappointing me." Her lips opened to a wide grin. "I promise, I won't let that happen." Her hand covered a chuckle that came from deep in her chest. "No time to waste."

He smiled, took her hand and followed, stepping over her pyjama bottoms somehow now on the floor.

***

Mohammed read the email notification. Two months already? Tomorrow back to Bragg. This evening she'd cooked penne draped in lightly sautéed pieces of tender chicken breast with mushrooms, sun dried tomatoes, onion, in a brandied cream sauce sprinkled with fresh thyme. They drank a white wine she called Meursault. He shook his head.

She noticed. "Don't you like the wine? Is it something else? Are you worried about going back?"

He looked up to meet her gaze. "I'd never drunk wine before the first glass you gave me. I'm enjoying this. And dinner was delicious. I'm not *worried* about going back. It's... I'll miss... well, our pleasure. I don't want to leave someone I've worshipped."

Nadia's grin spread ear to ear. "Worshipped? I love it. Is that what you've been about all this time? Little did I know." She undid the top button of her polka dot blouse. "Speaking as a goddess wholly deserving of your devotion, I hope you'll stay for breakfast prayers. We goddesses are always gratified to be here for our worshippers."

Chapter 7

March 2010: Karzai

Six miles below the land looked like the Mojave with attitude, bleached desert with wind-blown sand plains and tawny, rock-strewn hills and mountainsides barren of life. Life had to be poor, hard and scant. He'd have been happy to be stationed anywhere in this country, even the bleakest outposts. Nya's land. He couldn't wait. As for the base, it was even better. They'd lucked out. It lay on a mountain top.

They'd touched down at Kandahar to overnight. He inhaled his first deep breath of Afghanistan's air. Tomorrow morning the Chinook would take them up to their post, three miles above Asadabad into the mountains. Laila was in Asadabad. He wondered how she'd changed. She would have, wouldn't she? He prayed she didn't have a boyfriend.

***

Bouncing out of the Hook he breathed deep. It was Nederland's air, pine and conifer. At 8000 feet, Camp Karzai was loftier than Denver. He lowered his eyes, keeping his smile to himself. Barren sands, hills and poor villages were one thing. But for much of the rest, Afghanistan was as *Nya* Shazia described in her parting letter.

My country is a land of coursing rivers, valleys bedded with carefully tended fields of red poppies, terraces of wheat, corn, apricots and olives. Villagers are always curious about visitors. I pray you respect those you meet. The children are brown, dusty, inquisitive. Their smiles are friendly. Walled homes have small gardens and orchards of almond, walnut, pistachio, apricot, apple and cherry trees. Beyond them are high mountains with conifer forests rising to crowns of snow. You'll feel at home.

He was grateful. She'd filled his young and empty, if capacious head with stories of the heroes and heroines of the land of her birth, stories told in her native *Pukhto*, with occasional interspersed moments of Dari. The twinkle in her eye signalled cheerful and abundant sprinklings of fictional mendacity and historical hyperbole. He remembered asking about Pukhtun heroes. She recalled their stories in her letter.

"Remember our heroes and heroines. Thieves and murderers made many wars against us. But Pukhtuns are warriors. Our great hero was Khushal Khan Khatak. He united the Pukhtun tribes against their Mogul enemies. He defeated the murderous Moguls making them forever fear Pukhtun bravery. Then he wrote beautiful poetry about Pukhtun courage and his love of Pukhtun women."

He recalled his boyish question. 'Your cheeks are pink when you speak of Khushal Khatak. Did you know him?'

"Oh no. He lived long, long ago. But I would have liked to." She'd giggled. Why did she giggle? And her cheeks?

"Who else was a hero?" Her letter reminded him.

"Remember Nazo Tokhi. When her father fell against the invading Persians, what did she do? Did she weep and wail, and hide from the terrible enemy who killed him? Recall what you said as a child? 'I bet she hid if she was afraid.' And I said what is true: She picked up a sword, charged into battle on her white horse, leading her people against the Safavid Persians. She and the Pukhtuns won. Remember above all Malalai of Maiwand, a simple village girl. Thieving British redcoats made war on Pukhtuns and wounded many. Malalai cared for the

wounded but when the Pukhtun flag bearer fell dead, she ran to raise it high and stood against bullets and swords, dying with the pennant in her hands. When they saw her courage the Pukhtun men gained strength and won the battle against the angrezaan."

For him as a child, Pukhtun men were warriors, princes and kings. Their women were their equal in bravery, in pride and in endurance.

***

Camp Karzai sat above the Ghakhi Pass on the border of Kunar Province and Bajaur. His Captain Chris Montoya, on his third Afghanistan deployment, briefed Mohammed on background.

"Karzai was to be super-secret, unknown, invisible. The CIA, the 'Other Government Agency' (OGA) and JSOC were close mouthed. We're – that's 'we' as in SOCOM – joint operators. We get to tidy up after the ninjas do the really important work. The CIA guys and their operatives, known for infallible intelligence and a devotion to self-licking ice cream, are after 'high value targets.'

"Things didn't begin well. The countryside here is quiet. Somehow villagers were tipped Karzai was abuilding, possibly by bulldozers thundering and creaking day and night above the sleepy gullies and valleys below. On the other hand, it might have been constant dynamite blasts and crashing rock. Or, massive nighttime floodlights, maybe even giant Sikorsky Skycranes flying in with loads of construction equipment – those may have alerted them. Who knows? Naturally, the villagers told no one ... except insurgents who attacked several times during construction."

***

Mohammed welcomed the humour. "So other than insurgents, local villages on both sides of the border and everyone in Asadabad, we're completely unknown?"

"That's about it Sergeant. Mind you, Pak intelligence and military knew as well."

"Excellent, super secret it is then. Count me in. I won't say a word."

As much as he admired the Captain Mohammed was wary of Montoya's take on some Karzai colleagues. Montoya said CIA Special Activities Division operatives bore a consistent reputation. No one trusted them. At the business end of SAD was the Special Operations Group, a mixed swagger of private contractors, Delta Force and Seals. Their handle was Task Force Grey. According to Montoya, they were a law unto themselves.

He'd wait to see.

***

The *malakan*, headmen of local villages remained quiet during a first meet and greet. Mohammed watched and listened as the headmen's words were translated by an Afghan interpreter. They asked to pause for afternoon prayers. Silent until then, he now spoke up.

"*Mehruba'nee, ze tasu sara moonz kolay shum?*"

The elders' eyebrows rose as one. Surprised by a request to pray with them, they asked the obvious. "You're a believer? Yes. Of course you may pray with us. How do you speak *Pukhto?*"

"My *Nya* is Kabuli. She taught me *Pukhto* and some Dari. Her husband was Lebanese. At home we spoke English, Arabic, *Pukhto* and a little Dari."

***

Nya predicted Mohammed's birthplace and Arab father would be incidental. For villagers, he would be Pukhtun. Mud brick village mosques welcomed his prayers. Brown and dusty children followed him in chattering troops as he knocked on doors to introduce himself. The whitebeards, the *spingeray*, saw his eyes drop respectfully when village women, young or old, passed by.

While he quickly gained credibility, the villagers remained guarded about his platoon mates. Slowly, respect for him extended to Montoya, then his mates.

***

Karzai's commander, a bird colonel, held Montoya back after a daily briefing.

"So how is Karram working out? I gather he speaks fluent *Pukhto*. He must be useful."

"He is. He prays in the mosque with them. They seem to be taking to him." As he left, Montoya saw the colonel hasten to his desk computer. Why the interest in Karram? Notes?

***

Mohammed puzzled over a new Afghan interpreter assigned to the platoon. The Colonel touted the Afghan as 'one of our best.' Advertising? Mohammed arrived unexpectedly to stand beside Montoya listening while the new interpreter conversed with the *malik* of Marah Warah village.

The interpreter's words were unmistakeable. "If the village won't pay, I'll make your words those of the *takfiri*. Then we'll see what the good captain here will do with you and your family."

Mohammed caught the village leader's alarm. He slowly pulled his sidearm. Running his fingers down the barrel, he fronted the ANA translator and addressed him sharply in *Pukhto*. Montoya backed off, mute, watching.

"You're Tajik. Perhaps you harbour ancient anger toward Pukhtuns. But you're now in a Pukhtun home. You'll apologize to the *malik,* who greeted us courteously ... Good. Now remove your boots and drop your weapons. Yes. You'll leave on foot. If we see you again, we'll arrest you. Your name will be known to your ANA commander and to mine. You won't be hired again."

The *malik* shook Mohammed's hand. "We don't want *Amriki* here. But you're honest. You won't be our enemy." He gave Montoya the gist.

Word spread to other villages.

***

Montoya reported the incident to command next day. "Sergeant Karram caught the translator red-handed trying to blackmail the *malik* and ordered him off."

The Colonel's face went beet red. "That's Karram's story. Who gave Karram the right to fire the guy? I appointed that translator."

Montoya stammered. "We ... I didn't know that. But if he hadn't, I would have, Colonel."

The red in his face deepened to purple. "Get out, you stupid son of a bitch."

Through the tent flap Montoya saw the Colonel go to his computer.

***

Mohammed noticed it first. Outside his platoon conversations regularly stopped as he passed. Muttered slurs floated from the midst of muted conversations. 'Dune coon', 'haji', 'racoon', 'kebab'. It was crude logic. His acceptance by Afghans meant he was Afghan. Since Afghans didn't want Americans around, he was suspect, possibly a traitor.

Meanwhile, his platoon mates griped about countless cups of villagers' tea. He dealt easily with their grumbles. "Their code demands generosity. They have nothing else to offer. They're embarrassed that they can only offer tea."

Where he pointed to starvation, Montoya managed to designate some supplies as surplus. The surplus enabled the platoon to distribute chocolate, rice, tinned tomatoes, biscuits, meat, even flour, to locals. That, along with help without the use of bribes or insistence on *quid pro quo*, bore fruit. *Malakan* and villagers began to warn of IEDs, building enemy forces, potential ambushes. Previously wary villagers began to show hospitality.

Montoya tapped him. "How're we doing?"

"Okay. The locals think we might be civilized. But I have to ask about something else. The rumour is we're getting new orders. What's up?"

Montoya's face went stony. "Simple. Mullah Omar took off for Quetta in 2001. We got our regime change. The *Taliban* were spent. The Five Sided Puzzle Palace decided to milk the victory. They said we hadn't punished the bad guys enough. Add some inter-service rivalry. The air force crowed they broke the Taliban's back. Fort Fumble needed to show regular grunts could kill bad guys too. The navy wanted to show off killer seal pods. How? Beat the bushes. Pay locals to name former Taliban, even if the former Taliban who remained in Afghanistan supported the new government we installed. A brilliant strategy wouldn't you say? In a land of tribal feuds and mass poverty, how could paying for leads go wrong?"

Mohammed closed his eyes. "Shit. It all fits. The *malakan* are asking why we stay."

"They don't get it. *We* don't know why we're here. Poor bastards in villages did us no harm. What'll happen when we round up former Taliban and their friends based on bullshit leads?"

"For real? Simple. We'll lose them all."

Montoya scowled. "Right. But remember, tribal rebellions mean we need to stay. As they go hostile, we'll kill them. When Afghans kill Afghans, it's a feud. When we kill them, we're an invader. Any

Afghan, Pashtun or not, will fight us. The more hostility, the more need for our military. Success means bodies. For us, improving body count means anyone who winds up dead is a hostile."

Mohammed winced. "Innocents?"

Montoya shook his head. "Innocents? Where's your cynicism? Why are soldiers here? Bridges, schools are window dressing, stateside advertising. Soldiers kill people. Promotions come from bodies. Trust me. Whether our guys wanted them dead or they're collaterals, they'll be hostiles. Innocents? There can't be any."

Chapter 8

April 2010: Night

Helicopters increasingly took off on night forays into Kunar, the Korengal and Laghman. Safi tribesman, jealous of successful Korengali timber smugglers, identified smugglers as hostiles. Americans killed them. The Korengalis learned the Safi lesson. They informed on Safi leaders. Americans killed them. The whole valley allied against Americans.

Mohammed accepted Montoya's prediction reluctantly. Arrested and dead villagers were hostiles by definition. Hostiles' mobile phones were scanned for contacts. Contacts were deemed to be hostile. A contact name that appeared on too many phones identified a High Value Target. HVTs abounded. Platoons of suspects became legions. Afghanistan became more dangerous each day. The arrests and deaths of countless hostiles proved it.

***

Karzai's Bird Colonel cracked his knuckles. Time to test Montoya's favourite *haji*. He summoned two senior operatives. "Take Montoya's platoon for backup. Watch the *haji*. Any sign he consorts with the locals I want to know about. Keep an eye on him. Let your men know."

***

Mohammed heard it from Montoya. Command needed the platoon on a night raid near Yaka China in Manogai district. Mohammed's Pukhto singled it out.

He asked who led the raid. Montoya duly asked the Colonel, who ignored the question. Montoya came back shaking his head from a briefing.

"I asked John Wayne. He pawned me off to Bruce Lee, who referred me to Indiana Jones. No one identified command. The raid's pretext is that somebody fired a rocket at FOB Blessing."

Mohammed had grown used to the raw edge of Karzai tongues. As a group Task Force Grey ninjas swaggered toughness. Unimpressed, Tony referred to them as 'prancers.' If the prancers were under orders to achieve results Mohammed would need to be careful. With Afghan interpreters available, why was *his Pukhto* needed?

***

Aloft, nearing the ground Mohammed sucked in clean air and held it. The Hook shuddered into touchdown's choking dust storm. Thumping rotors winding down blew the din of shouted commands into shreds. Flying grit burnt into his nostrils, ears and clothes. Once beyond the grimy cloud, he released his breath at the village. Villagers offered no resistance, no gunfire. *Alhamdulillah.* Blinding bright lights stunned sleepy-eyed men, women and children as they tumbled from huts into a chaos of crashing doors, voices bawling in incomprehensible *Pukhto* and expletive-laced English. People were afraid and fragile. His eyes darted toward a wailing woman kneeling in fear, sheltering her bawling two year old.

"I'm Mohammed. Comfort your son. We won't harm you. Join the other women. Please, tell them what I've said." He turned to village elders. "We mean no harm. Please be patient. We're searching for men who make trouble for your village. We'll try to be quick. Tell your men. Thank you."

The herded villagers nearby began to calm, the din of their voices receding. Shouted commands of the soldiers seemed to let up except ...

Across dirt lanes, an American bellowed curses from behind a clutch of floodlights focussed on a single dwelling. Great. When they don't understand, shout louder. He trotted toward the racket.

Montoya's hand stopped and cautioned him. "The headman, the *malik*, is resisting Rambo – refuses to come out. Apparently he's proud and his door's thick metal."

The lights silhouetted Rambo. Big, heavily armed. Alerted to Mohammed's approach Rambo stalked toward him hissing seniority. "You're the one who speaks the local lingo. Tell the fucking *malik* if he doesn't come out I'll lob a grenade through his window."

Mohammed turned and walked, barrel down toward the flood-lit door. Rambo screamed from behind.

"Wait! What do you think you're doing? Come back here! That's an order! Don't go near that door!"

He ignored the shouts, conversed through the door and returned. He spoke through his teeth, ready. "He's the village headman protecting his wife and three teenage daughters. We're armed intruders at night. He asked us to come back in daylight for tea."

"Fuck tea. Fuck tomorrow. He comes out or it's grenades."

"He *invited* us to come tomorrow."

The operative sneered. "I might've known we'd get one camel-fucker siding with another! I'll decide how we get him out. You have five seconds to translate or he'll come out my way." He fingered a M68 frag, eyes fixed on an open window.

Mohammed sucked in his breath. "No way!"

"Fuck off, Abdul." Rambo pulled the pin and took his arm back to throw.

Mohammed drove his elbow hard upwards into the bellower's

nose, splattering blood up into his eyes. The grenade dropped; he quickly picked it up and threw it into an empty lot. It exploded harmlessly.

In mid-turn toward Rambo, a rifle butt smashed into the back of his helmet knocking him face down. On the ground trying to rise, hard knuckles slammed into his cheek. The fists stopped. Above him someone gagged. He looked up.

Tony Mitchell's arm sank into the attacker's carotid sinus while the toe of his right boot met the solar plexus of an oncoming second operative, crumpling him. Mohammed regained his feet in time to see a bloody Rambo coming hard. His left foot met the charger's groin, dropping Rambo midstride. Tony slid by to receive another attacker. He deflected a low kick and straight right before crunching the heel of his right palm upwards under the spook's chin. Tony smiled silent menace at two other would-be toughs. They thought better of it, and instead stooped to help their comrades to their feet.

Tony offered solace. "Sorry you super killer ninjas are bleeding and bruised. We'd heard heaps about how tough you were. How could we know it was bullshit? Hope you haven't injured any of your vaginas. Need any kleenex?"

***

Mohammed watched the Colonel's face flame as Montoya described the dustup.

"We were unclear on the chain of command. The result was a tactical disagreement in the field."

"What kind of horseshit is that, Captain? Our guys asked you along as fucking backup! *Our* guys were in command! And what the fuck do we get? Karram sides with one of the locals instead of following my guy's orders. You sure about Karram's loyalties, because I'm not?"

Montoya went purple. Fists clenched, he stepped toward the CO.

"Go ahead you little fucking burrito! Take the court marshal."

Mohammed pulled Montoya away.

Through the tent window they saw the Colonel, whiskey in hand, sit at his encrypted computer.

***

Three days on, Montoya came to Mohammed, grim-faced.

"They raided the village last night. The SAD ops blew the head-man's steel door and snatched him. The poor bastard didn't make it back. They said he 'fell' from the helicopter. 'An accident.' It's worse. They brought back two young men, nephews of the *malik*. The colonel says they're under interrogation."

The delegation from Manogai arrived four days later. They asked for Mohammed to interpret. "They're asking for the two nephews of the *malik* taken by our soldiers. Can they see them?"

"They're not here" the Colonel said. "They were interrogated and released three days ago."

The old men looked back impassively. Mohammed recognized the look. Bragg's instructors portrayed Pukhtuns as flat, emotionless, unfeeling. The villagers' eyes betrayed nothing. They hadn't believed a word.

Next day, twenty villagers massed below Karzai with shovels and picks. They were surrounded by a guard of seventy men with AK47s. The base went on full alert.

Mohammed walked to them, unarmed. "I know why you've come."

A white beard turned to him. "We've found their bodies. Please, look at the young men your commander said were interrogated and released. He lied. Tell your commander his men may no longer to come to Manogai's villages. We're his enemies."

Mohammed recoiled. The corpses were missing ears and fingers.

A week later he accompanied Montoya to Command's briefing.

"A force of our operatives with an ANA group raided another Korengali village. Return fire was heavy. Our guys called in a C130 Gunship, then bombing runs. The bombing runs came late, two hours after the firing stopped. Fourteen are dead. Three women, three girls, eight boys. Locals say the dead were gathering wood on the hillside above the village. The wife, two daughters and two sons of a *malik* were amongst those killed outright. Precision Paveways and gatling guns sometimes go astray."

Montoya stood, shaking. "Let me understand, Colonel." His lips quivered. "We're getting villagers onside by showing them we can slaughter more of them than the talibs?"

"You make an assumption, Captain." The colonel snarled. "Who says we're in the business of getting villagers onside?"

***

Mohammed outlined it to Montoya. "All right. So, we're suspect. Banned from helping ninjas. I wonder, rumour has it Camp Monti up the road is tasked with obstructing hostiles coming through the Ghakhi checkpoint. But they're still coming on back trails to threaten villages and recruit young locals. Could our platoon help locate the militants' alternate routes?"

Montoya's face slowly broke into a grin. "Good idea. Let's try to get asshole on board."

***

The Colonel paced, frowning, as Montoya broached the subject of retasking. Reconnaissance. Scouting for infiltrators. The frown gradually disappeared. Montoya noted a momentary smile flit across the SOB's face.

"Frankly, your platoon is useless to us on this side, Captain. You want to finish the deployment doing something. Recon would split the platoon, four and eight say? Four scout, eight lay back for fire-power? Top guys in the scouting foursome? You had that in mind. All right. It's yours. Infiltration scouting and interception across the line."

***

Once alone, the Colonel broke into a full-on grin. He poured himself a triple Evan Williams Black and summoned an Afghan lieutenant.

"I seem to recall your cousin across the line has kept some bad company. Here's something he might be able to sell to his contacts. One of our platoons is crossing the line to do recon ... Yes. You've got it. They'll divide. There'll be four in the scouting group, high over the trail. Here's the guy to look for." He passed over a slip of paper.

***

Mohammed's sense of relief wasn't without unease. "Chris, he's been a thorn in our side since we arrived. Now agrees double quick to the retask? Didn't you get *any* resistance?"

"None. Look on the bright side. Across the line we can run our own operations."

"I hope you're right." He hesitated and turned back before leaving. "Listen, I have a school friend in Asadabad. Any chance I could use a proper phone?"

Montoya's quizzical stare became a smile. "I won't ask. Okay."

"Laila. It's Mohammed. How are you? Good. You sound happy. Yes. I'm here, in Afghanistan. You're right, time's not my own. I don't know when I can visit. Sorry, can't tell you where. Near enough. If I have time, shall I come to see you? ... You're hesitating. You have a new roommate? Malalai. You're together? You mean –? Your girl-friend. Oh, I didn't understand."

He sucked in his breath, hesitated too long, and steadied himself. "Okay, I'm ... I'm surprised. But I'm happy for you. Be careful – local customs. Maybe, when I have time, we might all meet."

He'd lied. His shoulders slumped. He'd been foolish, a blind insensitive muttonhead. How could a suet-brained cafeteria bully recognize something about Laila he'd missed? He sat alone, chin in his palms.

***

Verraeter scanned eleven recent file additions before coming to the JSOC Kunar commander's.

OWL: Karram, M.Y.:04'12'2010 Threatened and chased off translator appointed by CO. Eliminating potential witness to MK's conversations with possible local taliban/sympathizers???

OWL: Karram,M.Y.:04'23'2010 Sided with hostiles in field standoff. Disobeyed command. Instigated fighting between commands. Growing camp-wide sense MK not to be trusted. Immediate superior Capt C. Montoya fails to perceive danger.

Chapter 9

May 2010: Batmalai

Mohammed pinched his shoulder blades. After five hours of mountain trail under a sixty-pound pack with additional gear and weapons, his quads and hamstrings burned. Ayub led toward a *qila* on the village perimeter.

He'd seen Batmalai on drone surveillance snaps. A few mudbrick-walled homes lying on a gentle slope forty miles north west of Khar, Bajaur's administrative centre, and two miles due west from busy Pashat. Three corner turrets marked the enclosing walls, fronted by large solid plate-steel entrance gates. As the sun's crown sank, the gates creaked open unsignalled. The emerging brown face and white teeth of another Pukhtun giant gleamed welcome.

"*Stari me shey!*"

Ayub embraced his brother. "*Salamat osey!*" The two chatted briefly in muffled tones. Ayub gathered Shahay from the mule's back and carried her into the *kor*, the main house. Her face paled.

Her brother's eyes followed Shahay with concern. He turned, smiling, to introduce himself. "*Assalamu alaykom, Daktar Sahib. Zma num Sakhi dey.* Ayub tells me of your meeting. You are like a *wror*, a brother. *Pa khayr raghle* to our father's home."

"*Alaykom assalam. Khayr ose.* You're kind to greet me like a brother. You should know that your own brother helped save both my life and my friend's. *Manana* for your welcome."

A firm handsome face, leathered, clear eyed, with grey-streaked beard approached. Sakhi introduced *Baba,* his father, who took Mohammed's hand warmly. At six three Mehmoud was an inch shorter than his sons, erect with broad shoulders, slim waist and lean muscled arms. The brothers spoke of him as *plaar,* father. Mehmoud released Mohammed's hand only after what seemed several minutes.

"Welcome to my home, *Daktar Sahib.* I'm pleased you're our guest."

"I'm honoured to visit, *kaka.* I've visited with Kunari villagers, but never been a guest." Mehmoud introduced his sons' wives and his own. "She is Bibi Rokhana."

The women buzzed and brought a *kut* for Shahay. Mohammed smiled to himself: they were neither leaving nor veiling. No *purdah*? But Nya had said..? Another mystery – someone was missing. Where was Zarhawar's father? Shahay couldn't be single. Pukhtuns didn't divorce. Wives lived with the husband's family. What was going on?

"May I ask, *baba. Nya* Shazia told me to expect *purdah* when visiting. Yet in your home the women seem excited, happy to see your son and daughter and a guest. They don't veil or remove themselves. This is comfortable for me, since it's as it is at home. You don't practice *purdah*?"

He saw the knot forming in Mehmoud's forehead. Impatience? A sensitive area?

Mehmoud turned to him. "Your *Nya* isn't wrong. In older times *purdah* was widely practiced. We did it in my father's home. Many still do *purdah.* It doesn't come from Islam. You come as a son after defending my family. We don't veil for sons and brothers. Your respect for *namous* is clear. If you're comfortable, I'm pleased."

The *kor* bustled. Chattering women took themselves off toward the kitchen carting Shahay on her *kut* with them protesting all the while she should help. Clucks instructed her to rest instead.

Sakhi brought a basin of warm water for hand washing. Bibi

gave her sons huge steaming platters to bring to the *dastarkhwan* dinner carpet. Roasted chicken, *cherg*, and *polau* with onions, tomatoes, and carrots, filled his nostrils with the aromas of ginger, cloves and cinnamon. *Dodai*, breads, *wriji*, rice, and kabobs of roasted peppered lamb still on wetted sticks. The brothers ate like bears!

Mohammed's chuckle escaped and was noticed. Conversation hushed. "It's like being at my own home, but for one thing..." A nervous silence descended on the *kor*.

"Here, you pay close attention to my words. At my home no one listens."

"Heed our *melmast*, our guest" Mehmoud parried. "We must disregard him for the duration of dinner."

Mehmoud now prevailed on Ayub to recount the day's events.

"Our boys fought like lions. They used the incline of the roadside for cover and fired steadily into the dacoits, the *dakoo*." Ayub's eyebrows arched. "Then, two enemy giants, easily twelve feet tall with bloody knives in their teeth, charged the boys clearly meaning to cut them to pieces. Our sons stood like granite, unmoved and calm. With the giants' knives almost at their throats, they cut the monsters down. I've never seen such courage facing certain death." Zarhawar and Faridun beamed.

Ayub's face went deadpan. "As for me, earlier I heard two men speaking *inglisi* galloping down a path near me. They were so intent on where their feet would fall, they didn't see me. Fire from above chased them. I crouched behind a boulder when two more men sporting scoped rifles ran a short distance past my old rifle. I'd leaned it against a boulder while I answered nature's call. Of course, it has an uncertain trigger. It toppled, and as if I myself aimed it, killed them both. I had trained it well.

"More gunfire arose below. Strolling downhill. I came upon *Daktar Sahib* and his friend firing toward the *dakoo*. Their first shot felled a passing pigeon, the second a chuff. I worried lest I be mistaken for an eagle. It seemed certain their ammunition would

soon run out. Naturally, I took pity on those unlikely to hit a teth-
ered sheep with a grenade, and shot the rest of the *dakoo* myself with
the exception of two. The daughter of Mehmoud slaughtered them
like chickens with her *charre*. Alas, when the boys cried out her eyes
left her last attacker. His knife caught her leg. *Daktar Sahib* raised
his rifle to shoot him. Certainly, he would have missed. Luckily, he
stumbled, and by a miracle, his bullet ricocheted off a boulder and
killed the criminal."

Mohammed rolled on his back, wiping tears from his cheeks.
Ayub nodded, poker-faced. "You see. He confirms what I say without
correction."

The women's hands hid their guffaws. Sakhi chuckled while the
boys looked into their laps, chortling like piglets at play.

Mehmoud's commodious grin settled the hubub "Ayub recounts
the battle with unmatched modesty. It could only be his renowned
humility which prevents his taking credit too for the surgery saving
our daughter's life." Mehmoud's gaze went toward Shahay. "Her eyes
show that her wound and surgery have exhausted her. For her life
we're grateful to our guest, *Daktar Sahib,* for our entertainment, our
older son."

Throughout dinner, Mohammed blindly fought her presence,
forcing his attention to the onion *polau*, savouring juicy peppered
lamb, focusing on cups of green tea, *kava*. With each mention of
her, his eyes flitted to her, then away. Now fatigued to the point of
blackness, she flinched as fentanyl began to shed its mask. Her face
was flushed under her family's attention.

Momentarily, his ears were deaf to the table's chatter. She'd
turned away when he spoke of sharing her wound. Was she flustered?
Her home was fragrant, nourishing, and lively. His mind wandered
to Husay, a heroine, injured, marked and restored.

Mehmoud rose from the *dastarkhwan*. Mohammed stirred from
his reverie and regained focus. Shahay's eyelids drooped, opened, and
fell again.

"With your permission, *baba,* may I reexamine your daughter's stitches before she retires?"

Mehmoud nodded.

More than stitches. Meds were wearing off. She needed pain free rest. From his kit he took a syringe. Should he humour her about the injection. Hold on. Needles? Dad had warned...

He turned to Ayub. "Your sister will need her sleep. I'll inject a pain reliever. Will she laugh if I tell her I'm going to use a needle this big?" He gestured.

Ayub fought for a straight face. "Best not mention the needle in the manner you suggest. You may frighten my poor sister to death, and *baba* will surely draw his knife. In our slang your words and gestures say, 'I'll have sex with you and my *ghin* is two feet long.' Still, my brother will enjoy your question."

Ayub hurried off to whisper to Sakhi. More guffaws.

"Thanks for sharing" Mohammed muttered.

Bibi, Ayub's spouse and Mehmoud attended Shahay with him. She rested wearily on the *kut.* The wound had to remain clean, the stitches closed. He draped, minimizing the visible wound while checking for seepage and inflammation.

"May I touch your forehead, daughter of Mehmoud?"

"*Aw, Daktar Sahib.*"

"Do you feel pain? Any throbbing, hot or stabbing feeling?"

"It's all right, *Sahib.*" All right! All right? Liar. Post-surgical pain for this surgery is shattering. "This medicine will allow you sleep without pain."

He injected the fentanyl. Her lids became heavy under his gaze.

"Good night, daughter of Mehmoud" he said quietly.

Shahay and Bibi nonetheless caught his words.

"Good night, *Daktar Sahib*" Shahay breathed.

He turned to Mehmoud and Bibi. "I haven't eaten food so delicious since I left home. I'm grateful for your hospitality. Like your daughter, I must say good night. *Daera manana.*"

In darkness, he followed Ayub under a quilt of mountain stars. The compound's guest house, the *hujra*, opened at one end to the courtyard. A curtained entrance separated the meeting benches from a modest room with two beds and a smaller room with a covered clay chamber pot, the *koza*.

The rough interior west wall of the mud brick *hujra* retained the sun's warmth. A small round table flanked a *bistara*, a made-up bed with pillows and blankets. A tabletop candle flickered off the bedroom's wheat coloured walls. A second candle warmed the grey-bleached open rafters, bedside screen and gaily cushioned benches of the men's meeting room.

"Thank Baba, son of Mehmoud. His *hujra* gives a warm welcome. It must have seen many guests."

He blew out the candles, and exhaled exhausted tension from his belly. Within minutes his eyelids grew heavy.

***

In darkness he writhed, panicked. *Barry! Your skull – it's open. Don't move. My hands ... it's wet, heavy, pulsating. Allah, help me to put it back. Why don't my arms and hands work? No, no. Frank, not you! Your throat is split. Your blood's splashing on my feet. Your eyes ... Don't look at me! Please don't make that noise. I can't move. Don't die. I'll help.*

"No!" His shout woke him. Allah, let no one hear.

He shuddered and shrank until fatigue overtook him again.

In intruding light, he woke to the familiar call. Where..? The *hujra*. Mehmoud. What time? The sun was high. But the *azan*? The call to prayer wasn't to morning's prayer, *sahar*. It was already noon. He'd never slept so late!

A jug of water for ritual pre-prayer ablutions, *audas,* sat unbidden at the *hujra* table. He washed thoroughly. For the first time in weeks, he prayed alone. Even if night terrors had shaken him, he felt comfort as the guest of believers. He positioned the prayer rug, faced west and knelt.

"*O Khuday, in Your mercy guide me. Lead me to help Shahay's recovery. Help me to understand the deaths of men I failed. In Your mercy guide me to those I may help, to those whose wounds and sicknesses I may heal. Allah, Most Merciful, in Your mercy lead me to a place of peace. Ameen.*"

***

He stepped from the *hujra* into a walled courtyard of espaliered apple, plum, apricot and fig trees. The blossoms, now tiring, dropped to carpet the earth in still pastels. A small garden with carrots, onions, beans and squash lay on one side of the house. Grape vines grew against a perimeter wall bathed in bright sunlight. A missing stone in the wall showed fields adjacent to the compound where corn had begun its rise. Two boys in the field abutting the corn tended a sizeable flock of sheep. Within the walls Ayub's and Sahkhi's wives were tending the garden.

"*Salaam,*" he greeted.

"*Maspakheen mo pa khayr, Daktar Sahib.*" They giggled. The greeting, 'Good afternoon doctor' was amiably sororal, even a tad cheeky.

Passing behind them, below the porch, he scooped up fallen blossoms unnoticed, then approached them stealthily as they kneeled. His shadow foretold the silent floral petals loosed over the saucy tyro sisters. More giggles.

He greeted Ayub and sat beside him. Bibi smiled and brought unleavened fried bread, *paratta*, and *chai* with lightly boiled eggs. Mehmoud and Sakhi arrived. Bibi, and the brothers' wives, Niazmina and Gulalai, prepared more *paratta*, eggs and *chai*.

"How did our wounded warrior sleep?"

Laughter greeted his question.

Mehmoud smiled. "The wounded warrior slept well. Like you,

she slept through morning prayers. Unlike you, she also sleeps through *maspakheen.*"

Beneath Mehmoud's bright tone, Mohammed sensed purpose. Was Mohammed's family well? Did he have siblings? Were his parents and grandparents still living? Did they go to mosque? Did many believers live in his village? How were they received and treated? Were there any troubles? Were his people, like most Pukhtun, Sunni?

"Both of my parents and three of my grandparents are alive. Yes, we are Sunni. Our mosque is Masjid Abu-Bakr. My two younger sisters, Fariyal and Sabriyya are in school. Both want to be teachers. About fifteen thousand Muslims live in Denver. But Denver is more Peshawar than Batmalai. It has six hundred thousand people. Muslims are accepted. Most are Christians. There are Jews, Sikhs, Hindus and Buddhists too."

"Are there troubles amongst peoples?"

"Some. When I was twelve, a Jewish schoolfriend and I liked the same girl. We argued. He called me a towel head. I called him a stupid Jew. When we fought, I gave him a black eye and bloody nose. Peter told his parents that someone called him a stupid Jew. His father reported it to a local newspaper as anti-semitism. He was embarrassed to learn that Peter's slur started the fight. Our fathers made us apologize. We remained friends. Sadly, another boy wound up with the girl."

Mehmoud nodded. "This is Pukhtun blood. You meet insult with courage. The loss of the girl was unfortunate. Tell me. You aren't married. Aren't there suitable women from whom your parents could select?"

Mohammed grinned. "Few American parents make matches. Some men my age marry. But I've more training to do. And I haven't found the right woman. Besides, I was off to war."

He weighed Mehmoud's silence and fleeting scowl. *Nya* said, silence shelters impatience. Mehmoud straightened.

"Pukhtuns rarely divorce. We understand this unpleasantness is frequent in your country. Perhaps it would be better if American parents chose for their children."

Mehmoud's furrowed brow didn't release with his retort. Now what?

Chapter 10

Bones

Mohammed waited, watching while Mehmoud pawed his beard.

"I would speak of another matter."

"Please."

"Amongst Pukhtuns we say: Enemies make us smile, friends make us weep."

Ayub deciphered. "Enemies flatter while friends speak the truth."

"I see. *Nya* has another saying: When people are anxious to tell the truth, prepare for bad news."

They grinned and nodded. Mohammed's hands relaxed on his knees. "Please, speak your mind."

"I don't ask about America, but about you. Pukhtuns know *badal*, revenge. After America's towers fell, it came for *badal*. I don't believe *Sahib* came for this reason. If not that, why?"

Ayub and Sakhi studied his face.

He hesitated momentarily. "You're right. Not for *badal*. My sisters will be teachers. I read of teachers intimidated, beaten and killed, of schoolgirls attacked by bombers and burned by acid. My grandmother, *Nya* Shazia, is a Kabuli Pukhtun. When I was young she filled me with stories about *Pukhtunkhwa*. Later, I listened to a soldier speak. He said, as a doctor I could help. *Nya* agreed."

Mehmoud's smile revisited. "Your answer shows honour."

"Do many Salarzai agree teachers deserve protection?"

"Almost without exception. Opinions about girls' education are more divided. As for my family, we accept the *hadith* according to Al-Majilisi Bihar al Anwar. The Prophet's words, peace upon him, are *the pursuit of knowledge is the duty of every Muslim, man and woman.* My children read and write. My daughter in Asadabad teaches, and has been threatened. She is Farikhta."

"May Allah protect her. Might I visit her in Asadabad to see about her safety, after I return to Kunar?"

"First, make yourself known to her husband. I'd be grateful."

"May I too raise questions?"

"I'll try to answer."

"Some of my questions are my own. Some I raise because my Captain expects me to."

"Yes, thanks for saying this. It's as I expected. May I first return to your question about veiling and *purdah*. You said the women's presence made you comfortable. *Purdah* is much observed amongst Pukhtun Khans, others too. I trust my household's women to observe modesty. *Purdah* is *rewaj*, a custom. I find no authority for it. Not all Salarzai agree."

Mehmoud looked into the distance. "While I was a child my father fought wars. My mother raised me. How she'd learned to read, I don't know. She read aloud the poetry of Khushal Khan Khatak, of Rahman Baba. She read the Qur'an's verses. After father returned he insisted on tradition – on *purdah*. She rarely ate with us after that. From then, she withered. When I was sixteen, she went with women for water. They said she'd fallen amongst boulders and died. Father insisted it was an accident. I wonder still. The lives and hopes of my daughters and of my wife will not go unnoticed as my mother's were."

Mehmoud paused. He put his hand on Mohammed's shoulder and met his eyes. "My son told how you met, how you helped our daughter. *Purdah* is not necessary. Yours were acts of family. My family is dear to me."

Ayub rose. "More tea?" He brought and poured more, sitting beside Mohammed opposite his father. "What else surprises you?"

Ayub posed the question. Mohammed knew his answer should be addressed to Mehmoud. "*Nya* said a daughter who married into another family lived with them. Yet the daughter of Mehmoud lives here with her son."

Mehmoud's eyebrows arched. His reply bore the brevity of impatience. "She lived with her husband's family in his village. He was *mujahid*. When she was with child and near her time, his family left her alone while they attended a wedding in Khar. As they drove back home, their truck rolled over a cliff. All died. It was Allah's will."

"No one survived?"

"No one. She was alone. A neighbouring midwife helped her give birth to her *zoi*, Zarhawar. When we informed her of the accident, she asked to return to our home. We welcomed her."

"Of course." His hands trembled. He clamped them together. "She suffered great misfortune."

"Only if her husband was worthy," Mehmoud snorted. "I'll say no more. Now, my bones feel old. Shall we walk? Let's look to our fields to see how the youngsters tend our sheep."

They exited the gate and rounded the compound to find Zarhawar and Faridun throwing small stones at each other from the back corners of the sheep pen. Mehmoud's glare halted their war.

Mehmoud wasn't satisfied. "Are you curious about other matters?"

"Yes. For one, your daughter fought with courage and skill. Ayub spoke of test combat with her brothers."

Mehmoud swatted at and missed a wasp. "Few men, and no women amongst us possess her skill with a knife."

"Few of our soldiers possess it!" Mohammed laughed.

"That's a compliment." Mehmoud said. "She emulated her brothers and bested them. They taught her well."

"Do others honour her skills?"

Mehmoud sniffed. "Some Pukhtun honour women only for

purity. Yet many believing women have been warriors." He shrugged. "At the Battle of Uhud, Um Sulaym and Nusaybah bint Ka'ab fought alongside men with their swords for the Prophet, peace upon him. His wife Ayesha went into battle as the commander in the Battle of the Camel. Malalai of the Afghans died fighting the British at Maiwand. Naazo Ana and her daughters took up the sword against Persians. If courageous women don't deserve honour, neither do men.

Mehmoud's attention went to the returning wasp. His hand knocked it to the ground and beneath his sandal. "My daughter shares her brothers' courage. If a woman's honour came solely from purity, it would come neither from men nor custom. Pure women exist in every land. A daughter who shows physical courage, *ghayrat*, to defend her purity is twice honoured."

"Grandmother told me stories of Malalai, but also of Naazo Tokhi. Is she Naazo Ana?"

"The same."

"You've been patient."

"Not at all."

"Thank you *baba*. May I ask about war?"

Mehmoud nodded. "Yes, but I warn you. You won't like my answers."

"Please, speak your mind. We worry we're seen as invaders."

Mehmoud exhaled. "You've said why you're a soldier in our lands. America's reasons are more complex. You say America worries how it is seen. How different is it then from a whore who worries about how her lipstick colours her lips? She and America would better worry about what they are.

"America *is* an invader. Worse, it assumes it knows better than ancient inhabitants of the land it invades. Imagine believers invading America, offering to improve women's lives. Would Americans accept this? It boasts it stays in our lands to protect women's interests. Is it a pretext? Arrogance? A lie? Is it that we are Muslim, and Muslims don't protect and esteem women? We read of America's treatment of dark skins. Does it invade our lands to save brown women from brown men? Do you know Pukhtun proverbs?"

"Not really."

"America builds a school here and a road there and boasts of helping. They're like the man who finds a horseshoe and deems it progress, because now all he needs is a horse and three more horseshoes."

"It's true we know little of what is needed."

Mehmoud's lips curled. "But 'little' may be 'almost nothing.' Some of our proverbs are less delicate. We say "If you wish to swallow a bone, first take careful measure of your asshole."

Mohammed's grin matched those of Mehmoud's sons. "I worked in an animal clinic. Some dogs hadn't measured."

Mehmoud's gaze remained stony. "Then you know the dangers of bones. Afghanistan is America's bone. For revenge, it bombed and claimed to have killed a mere few thousand innocent civilians. It lied. It killed hundreds of thousands and counted only a few scattered bodies. Whole villages vanished, leaving only vapour. Everywhere Pukhtuns walk, even now, we smell death, the decaying flesh of unknowns. Thousands starved because cluster bombs denied them their fields, their produce and animals. Thousands of injured came to Pakistan to die in agony. Widows and children starved to death after bombs slaughtered their men.

"America arrested, imprisoned tortured and murdered men and boys who protested. When it paid criminals for names, they identified innocent men for money. Once the innocent were imprisoned, the criminals stole their livelihoods. It tortured and killed innocents and *takfiri* alike and denied that they'd done this. It armed ancient enemies of the Pukhtuns for Afghanistan's army and promoted their revenge. Northerners continue to act against all Pukhtuns, hostile to America or not.

"Your country might have left after forcing the Taliban to flee. It didn't. Instead it swallowed the bone and cannot get rid of it. It took revenge and began a war it could never have won. Winning would come only by eliminating all of Afghanistan's and Pakistan's peoples. How blind are America's leaders not to see this?"

Mohammed bit his tongue. He was the first American Mehmoud had met. Politeness ensured *baba* would eventually get to the hostiles. For now, Mehmoud's understanding of Mohammed's nation took precedence over formalities.

"Before I come to what America calls *Taliban*, I'll relate a Persian visitor's tale. He supported a leader, Mosaddegh, whom America replaced with a Shah. The Shah's Secret Police seized and interrogated him. He remained silent despite beatings and thought threats to his family to be hollow. They gagged him and tied him to a chair. They brought in his wife and young daughters, stripped and used them, then burnt them to death. He lost his mind. His guards bragged they were trained to torture *by Americans and Israelis*.

"I see you lower your head, *Sahib*. Regrettably, our guest's story did not finish there. He survived and moved to Iraq. There his second family's grandchildren died of disease because America sanctioned medicines. His adult children died beneath tank treads when America urged them to revolt against the ruler. He wandered to us after his wife died."

Mohammed raised his eyes to meet Mehmoud's and shook his head silently.

"I believed him truthful. Your captain asks about those America calls *taliban*. In Pakistan *taliban* are students. In Afghanistan Taliban was the name for Omar's government. Our enemies and yours are *takfiri*, Muslims who slaughter Muslims. The *takfiri* say, be with us or die. These are also America's words. Are the *takfiri* better or worse for us than Americans? Ah, your face pales. But I haven't spoken to offend you."

Mohammed nodded. "I know you haven't, *baba*. I heard in the mosque of the Iraq sanctions. I knew nothing of the children, nor of the Shah's secret police and torture"

Mehmoud's face was stone."It's a mystery. You are *daktar*, educated. The Persian describes America teaching torture and causing hundreds of thousands of children's deaths. Did the wanderer lie? You're honourable, *Sahib*. But your leaders are criminals without honour. Do you doubt his story?"

"I'm sorry to say, I don't."

Mehmoud nodded. "We're not America's friends. You're an exception. Pukhtuns want America gone from our lands. Now, you're curious about the *takfiri*. They're the most dishonest of the *ummah*."

"How so?"

"They seek their way by force and claim Islam's blessing. Do you know the story of Tufayl of the Bani Daws? No? He heard the Prophet's message, then professed Islam. He converted almost no one of his tribe. Angry they ignored the Truth, he asked the Prophet to curse them. Instead, the Messenger prayed for their guidance and advised the traveller to call them to Islam, and deal gently with them."

"Gently? Of course. I'd never heard this."

Mehmoud shrugged. "Can we imagine the Prophet today using suicide bombers against believers, and shooting schoolchildren? The widow Khadija, his beloved first wife, proposed to him. She was a leading figure in Mecca, wealthy, beautiful, literate, pursued by many suitors. She took in orphans and widows alongside her own children. Khadija didn't esteem a selfish, self-centred, cruel man. She would scarcely have swooned over a miserable, hateful man. Clearly, she admired his richness of character. His charisma became apparent to all when he was chosen to bring the Word of God."

Mohammed adjusted his seating. "Where do the *takfiri* fit in?"

"Nowhere" Mehmoud sniffed. "No *takfiri* can be, as the Messenger was, a model, a *salaf*. Some quote Wahhabis. But the Qur'an gives no authority to Wahhabis. Who, except a Wahhabi, suggests a Wahhabi is the best *salaf*? Even if the Wahhabi is devoted, devotion doesn't establishes truth. The Qur'an doesn't proclaim scholars as teachers of its meaning. No authentic *hadith* informs us that killing Shias is permitted, as the most insulting *takfiri* mullahs teach. No *ayah*, no word uttered by the man chosen by Khadija, authorized Islam's greatest tragedy, the slaughter of Hussein and his followers. The *takfiri* claim religious authority. They have none."

Mehmoud made to rise. "Your captain asked for our views. The Tarkanri Salarzai oppose the *takfiri*. They began by assassinating three leaders from our village. When our *jirga* met to organize a *lashkar* to fight them, a suicide bomber blew himself up together with twenty-six of our finest men."

Mohammed nodded. "A soldier named Grant told me of it. Two years ago?

"Yes. A month earlier the same happened to the Alizai of the Orakzai at the Ghiljo Bazaar. They lost dozens of elders, their leaders. Many more were injured. We're not alone. All Bajaur's Pukhtun tribes share our view of the *takfiri*. The *takfiri* aim for an emirate with their version of *sharia*, not a *jirga* based on custom and secular law.

Mehmoud's eyes jerked suddenly toward Ayub who stood, cocking his ear and signalling for quiet. He rose and cupped his ear. A car's horn blared. Now nearer. The dogs drew close, barking fear.

The brothers grabbed their rifles and ran headlong toward the *qila* entrance. Beyond the gate, the horn blaring amidst shouts and screams blasted calamity. Faridun and Sakhi clambered up flanking towers with their weapons. Zarhawar stood behind the right side, Ayub, AK 47 levelled, behind the left. At Sakhi's command, Zarhawar opened the right panel.

Chapter 11

Blood

Shrieks shot from cab's window. A woman stumbled from its door. Below her bulging belly blood coursed into her leggings. Mohammed bolted for the *hujra*, shouldered his medical kit and turned, only to have Mehmoud momentarily block his path.

"Take care, *Sahib*. Her man, Bangar, is America's *dukh'mun*, an enemy."

Mohammed heard only sounds. *An enemy.* He raced toward the gravid woman now bracing herself against the truck's cab. She took two steps then fell to her knees grasping her swollen middle. The legs of her white *partoog* were soaked scarlet.

Her man roared. "Wife of Mehmoud, help us!"

Bibi knelt next to the shrieking woman. The brothers' wives scurried to help. Shahay limped behind. Bangar collapsed, wailing, praying.

Bibi wagged her downcast head. "Too much blood. The afterbirth comes first. She'll die."

Mohammed tapped her shoulder. She moved aside. "Please, wife of Mehmoud, a *kut* with a clean sheet." Bibi gestured to the brothers' wives.

He knelt beside the panicked woman and interrupted Bangar's invocations. "Please let me help."

"Who are ..?" Bangar nodded bewildered assent.

No time to explain. He turned to Bibi. "Roll her to her right side." Allah, stop her shrieks. "Please hold her." Spinal, 20 mg marcaine. "Now on to the *kut*. On her back. Hold her shoulders, arms too." Intravenous Ringer's lactate. His eyes met Bangar's.

"Please, pull her *kameez* above her waist!" Bangar blinked, mouth wide.

"Her *kameez*" he pointed. "Up..!" Ignore vaginal blood. Please God, make the marcaine work! Belly. Betadine. Scalpel. Vertical below umbilicus. No reaction. Good. Marcaine working. She's moving!

"No! She musn't see!" Too late. She twisted, raised her head to see and sighted her open belly. Her scream died as she fainted.

Steady. Steady. Two passes. Uterine wall. Through. Combat Gauze on torn placental nexus. Small. Boy. Thirty-six weeks? Praise Allah. The placenta was below, behind baby.

"Wife of Mehmoud, please splash this Betadine on your hands. Yes, rub them together. Now lift the baby from the womb." Clean blood, vernix. "Yes. Please continue with baby." Placenta. Bright green meconium. Clean up. Tie off cord. Detach placenta. Good. Bleeding slower. Mop pelvic blood. Suture uterus, musculature, abdominal layers. Mefoxin into line.

Bibi swiftly and expertly cleaned blood from the baby's nose and mouth. He smiled and nodded to her at the baby's wail.

"Wife of Ayub, please move your hand over mother's belly. Like this. Yes, circle around the incisions." Bibi put baby on mother's breast. Gulalai, Ayub's wife, moved opposite to mop mother's forehead and murmur reassurances. Nursing and massage helped shrink the wounded uterus.

On his knees at the patient's head, Mohammed breathed easier. In a few moments her eyes fluttered, then opened as she regained groggy consciousness, brightening at the weight and warmth of her suckling newborn. The baby nursed noisily to his mother's hoarse moans. Gulalai held the bag of Ringer's Lactate. Mohammed straightened his back and spoke quietly.

"Congratulations, *Ombarak sha*. A fine healthy boy! This medicine" he pointed to her intravenous "helps replace lost blood. It makes you strong again."

Bibi Rokhana made introductions. "*Daktar Sahib* is our guest. He is Mohammed. This is wife of Bangar, son of Baseer. She is Gul Sanga."

Eyes averted, Mohammed gestured acknowledgement.

"*Daktar Sahib* helped our daughter when she was wounded. *Ombarak sha,* wife of Bangar. Allah's blessings for your family and your *zoi*." Gul Sanga's eyes darted from Bibi to Gulalai, and back uncertainly to Mohammed.

"To stop your bleeding, I removed baby and closed your wound. The injection lessened your pain. Your legs won't work for a short time. They'll be weak a little longer. As numbness wears off, you'll feel more pain. If bleeding begins again, I'll come. The Khar Agency Hospital is a long drive."

He provided Tylenol 3s for pain with instructions to drink plentiful fluids. The women lifted cot with mother and baby into the shade. Gul Sanga whispered as he rose and turned toward the *hujra*.

"*Daera manana, Daktar Sahib.*"

***

Shahay gasped as his blade opened the stained belly. How quickly his hands moved. His manner remained calm and gentle amidst blood, shrieks and panic. *Mor* said mother and baby would die. He saved them, then reassured Bangar and his wife.

Why were her knees trembling, her feet leaden? She leaned heavily on her good leg. He was covered in surgery's blood. He glanced toward her for an instant and smiled. Her gaze held his, until she felt her eyes well. She looked down.

Her hand went to her cheek. She recoiled. It was hot. He will know. He must not see. He approached.

"Are you all right, daughter of Mehmoud?"

"Yes. Thank you, *Sahib*. Thank you for our friend."

***

Mohammed's attention drew away to the truck's door slamming. What was Bangar doing? He'd pulled an ancient *topak*, a Lee Enfield, from his truck and tapped the carpet by his wife's head. Greeting the newborn? Mehmoud and his sons joined the call to prayers, *azan*. Bangar held the baby aloft. After prayers they fired into the air in celebration.

Somehow two pails of fresh water and a large basin were on his small *hujra* table. How had they managed? He stripped, washed blood from his skin with one pail and rinsed his clothing in the second. In fresh garments he performed *audas* and prayed, grateful he'd helped. Still kneeling, he straightened and yawned, refreshed. A shadow crossed the sunlit floor of the *hujra* as he came to his feet. Who? Oh, oh!

Bangar's face wore a stoney scowl. His fingers clenched into fists.

"You're *Amriki*. I fight crusaders. You are *dukhmun*, an enemy. Why do you help my family?"

He met Bangar's eyes. "I'm Mohammed Yousf. Yes, I'm *Amriki*, but a believer, not a crusader. We've done each other no harm. Please, I don't wish to be an enemy. Your wife needed help. Allah has blessed you with a fine *zoi*. Your wife will be well, *Enshaallah. Ombarak sha. Badd Amriki Daktar pa bada wraz pakaregi.*"

Silently he thanked *Nya*. 'A bad American doctor helps on a bad day' was the second of two set speeches he'd rehearsed, this one useful if treating a hostile. With the first, he'd begged Ayub's *post facto* permission to treat Shahay.

"May we have tea to honour your son's birth?"

95

Mehmoud, nearby, overheard Mohammed's invitation. "Son of Baseer, please join us for tea as *Sahib* asks. Allow us to honour you and your new son." Bangar's scowl released. His fists released.

Mohammed nodded thanks to *baba*. Difficult to lean on a grudge over tea. Women bustled in the courtyard. Sakhi's wife, Niazmina, filled and fired the *hujra* samovar then repaired to Bangar's wife. Bibi had taken clear charge. She and Gulalai covered mother and baby with a blanket, propping them up on the *kut*. Faridun brought sweet green tea, *kava* and Zarhawar, *barfee*, a milk dessert for their nursing guest.

"Come Bangar, sit with my sons and *Daktar Sahib*" Mehmoud said. "Our families' friendship is old. Praise Allah, you came with your wife's and child's lives in danger and our guest helped." Bangar nodded without raising his eyes. His shoulders softened.

"May your *zoi* be blessed with the qualities of his father and grandfather" Mehmoud proposed.

Ayub joined. "We haven't seen your father in the village for some time. Has he recovered from his illness?

"No, he hasn't. We pray for it, *Enshaallah*."

Ayub's glance signalled Mohammed to listen. "Tell us, son of Baseer. How does his illness affect him?"

Bangar threw up his hands. "He's weak and sleeps much of the day. His skin is pale. *Mor* gives him much *chai*. It doesn't help. His belly spills out, yet he's lost weight. Five years ago he carried large burdens through the hills for hours."

Mohammed chanced it. "With your father's permission, I can examine him. A medicine might cure him quickly. Tomorrow may the wife of Mehmoud and I visit to ensure your wife and baby are well?"

Bangar hemmed and hawed before consenting to the newborn visit. As to the offer to examine his father: "Thank you. We'll consider it."

***

Mohammed turned to Ayub. "He didn't warm to my examining his father. Did I offend him?"

Ayub shook his head. "No. Your help in his son's birth means he's already obliged to you. If you treat his father too, their debt is increased. He isn't rich. They'd likely accept your offer if you found a way they might repay you."

"I'm not looking for payment. There *is* no obligation. Hmm. Soon I'll return to base. We'll go through Salarzai lands. I should have an escort, a *badraga*?"

"You know our custom. Why am I not surprised. Yes. A *badraga* to your camp would take a northerly route to Salarzai borders. Your camp lies near where Mamund lands meet ours."

"So your village knows of our camp?"

Ayub chortled. "FATA's Pukhtuns say it's a fly, and your enemies are like the frog watching."

He shook his head. "I'm hoping it doesn't become the frog's meal. May I ask Baseer to have Bangar join the *badraga*?"

"Yes. Baseer must permit Bangar to come. If he's no longer your enemy, he may be useful. His contacts are hostile to *Amriki*. You should seek Baseer's consent as soon as possible. Otherwise, Bangar may alert others to your presence. If they know of you, they'll know you must return."

Chapter 12

Baseer

Mehmoud led on the gently descending dirt lane. Mohammed's sandals followed *baba* on the shallow twin ruts. Better to avoid the grassy median dappled with cart donkeys' droppings.

Behind *qila* walls lining their route dogs barked interrogatives, hopeful welcomes and fierce warnings. At the outskirts as the lane turned eastwards, the view opened toward Pashat. They turned to a compound off to their right.

The grey-bleached wood gates of Baseer's *qila,* cracked with age, opened to greet Mehmoud's party. Bangar led to a *hujra* somewhat smaller than Mehmoud's. Rickety benches were decked with red, yellow and green tea-stained cushions. The aged roof had long given up on any claim to level. Sagging rafters resting on wanton wind-cracked purlins imparted the impression of rolling hills and shallow gullies.

Mohammed stood behind Mehmoud who clasped his sallow friend's hand. Baseer, grey bearded like Mehmoud though younger, shifted wearily from foot to foot. The two friends exchanged unhurried pleasantries before introducing him.

"Father of Bangar, please meet our guest, *Daktar Sahib.* He is Mohammed."

Baseer took Mohammed's hand warmly. "As Mehmoud's guest,

and *Daktar* who helped my family, you're twice welcome."

"Then by Allah's grace, I'm twice blessed." He acknowledged Baseer's wife – Bibi whispered her name – Gul Lakhta. She stood behind her husband, eyes downcast, a momentary trace of a smile responded to his gesture before she and Bibi disappeared. Baseer beckoned his visitors to sit.

Mohammed addressed the immediate concern of the *tapos*, the visit of enquiry that Bibi led. "The wife of Bangar bore great pain in the birth. Is her pain lessening?"

"Yes. *Manana* for asking." Bangar's face betrayed nothing.

"And the *zoi* of Bangar is nursing well?"

"Like a hungry lamb, yes."

"I'm pleased to help, if I'm needed."

"*Manana, Sahib.*" Baseer smiled carefully.

Mohammed drank tea, listened to village gossip, commiserated at news of attacks on anti-militant *malikan* in neighbouring villages, heard of government corruption and of suspicious acts of government agencies. In due course, Mehmoud acted on Mohammed's request.

"Son of Baseer, my son and I will soon look for rifles. Yours is newer than ours. May we come with you to fire a few shots?"

Baseer nodded permission to Bangar. "Of course we may fire my weapon, *kaka.*"

Mohammed began. "Father of Bangar, your hospitality welcomes me. May I ask, would you permit me to speak to you about your health? Your son said you're unwell. Might I return tomorrow?"

Baseer weighed his request in silence. His eyes rose to meet Mohammed's. "We spoke of this when he returned with his new *zoi*. You're right; I'm ill. How will I repay you for help you've already given?"

"I'm grateful for your frankness, *kaka*. May I be equally frank?"

"Please."

"I helped simply because the wife of Bangar was in distress. I ask no payment. I wanted to assist, and could do so. You owe me nothing. There is a way in which you might help me."

Baseer's eyes widened. "How might I do that?"

"Your son said he's my enemy. I'm an American and a believer. I don't wish for enemies in your village. May we speak of this matter?"

Baseer studied Mohammed's face only briefly. "On this matter I can offer guidance. Our conversation will remain private. I must ask, what do you want from this?"

"Our soldiers and Kunari Afghans are attacked by infiltrators. Perhaps the same *takfiri* who sent a suicide bomber to slaughter your *malakan* here in 2008. I hope your son won't be amongst the infiltrators. I must also return to base. If word reaches enemies, my escort and I may be at risk. I don't doubt the bravery of Baseer's son. Might he consider being a member of my *badraga*?"

Baseer was silent save for weary breathing. Momentarily his voice returned. "We'll speak further, *Sahib*. I'd prefer he neither be your enemy nor act with them. But be clear ... America has no place in *Pukhtunkhwa*. If it hasn't learned this already, both it and Pukhtuns will suffer more."

He entered the gates with Bibi to see Shahay up. Bibi muttered concern.

"The Leopard's Daughter is still limping."

Mohammed looked up. "I haven't heard this name for your daughter. How did she come by it?"

"Ah. Then you must learn how *baba* became the Leopard. Daughter, please tell *Sahib* how you and your father came to your nicknames. Let me gather the others."

Bibi told the women of Mohammed's curiosity. The chance to hear the story once more brought her sisters-in-law with with the youngsters.

Chapter 13

Lema

"The story of my *takhalus*, my nickname, began when I was a child. *Baba* brought a kitten back from his hunt in the Chitral. I thought: 'He shows it to me, not to my brothers and sister. It's *my* gift.' I skipped after *baba* through the vegetable garden, under apricot and apple trees to the back of the enclosure surrounding our home. Naturally it was my role, not my siblings, to help him prepare the pen against corner walls. My eyes wouldn't leave the animal. It was a spotted *peeshu*. I'd never seen a kitten so large, nor one with spots. *Baba* corrected me. 'You're mistaken' he said. 'It isn't a *peeshu*. It's a baby *prraang*, a leopard cub.'

'Yes. A *prraang*' I said. I pretended I knew. But how could I really know? I'd never seen one. Its eyes were different from a cat's. I would ask Farikhta. She'd know.

"When *baba* left, I remained behind, peering at my pet. *Baba* warned me: 'Don't leave the pen door open.' But I thought, I could go in and close the door. After all, it was mine. Father brought it for me. I could play with it.

"I crawled in, closing the door behind. The *prraang* looked soft. I wanted to stroke it. I looked into its eyes and smiled, so it would see I was a friend. I crept closer and closer on hands and knees, silently and slowly, so as not to frighten it. It seemed to me that it smiled back. Its mouth was wide and its little teeth showed. A low rattle came from its belly. I thought it must be chuckling, speaking to me. So I spoke back. 'I'm Shahay. You're my pet.'

"I was so close I could touch it. Slowly, carefully, I reached. Its eyes fixed on me and grew even bigger. I didn't know then that it saw a crawler-animal, showing teeth from an open, noisy mouth, an unknown animal with large, greedy eyes. In the voice her mother taught, the baby *prraang* made a different sound – a desperate squeal.

"Spotted fur flashed at my forearm tearing it with its razor claws, puncturing my finger with its needle teeth. The *prraang* retreated to its corner glaring at me, snarling a high pitched whine.

"I trembled, mouth open. Blood soaked my sleeve from ripped skin. My finger dripped a red pool from the punctures. I held the wounds. My eyes were full. I wiped them on my sleeves so my brothers and sister wouldn't see. No sobs came from my mouth. I scolded the *prraang*. 'I meant only to touch you. Why did you hurt me?' I left silently, securing the gate. I thought '*Baba* will see blood, not tears.'

"*Baba* cleaned and bound the wounds. He was wise. He didn't mew sympathy. Sympathy makes children soft and cowardly. He washed the blood streaked across my face where my bloody sleeve wiped the tears. He explained.

'You say you crawled in to play. Why do you think the *prraang* hurt you?'

'Is it a cruel *prraang*?'

'Did it speak to you before it attacked?'

'It made a noise. Was that its voice?'

'Yes, a voice saying 'Beware! I don't know if you're friend or foe. I'm a warrior. Come no closer or I'll strike.'

'Warriors are strong and brave.'

'Always. The warrior strikes hard and endures with courage.'

"After that I stood back. She was savage, wild. I envied *baba* who went into the pen. The *prraang* didn't attack him. One thing was different. I saw it.

'Why do you wear the spotted skin?'

'It's her mother's skin' *baba* said.

"That must have been it. The cub didn't fight *baba* because her mother's skin covered him. He named the cub Lema. Lema rubbed against him. He was her friend but she hated me.

"I stood watching. I held my tears. But *baba* saw my lip trembling. I turned to walk away when he called. 'Come little one. I need your help with Lema. She needs milk and doesn't know how to lap it from a bowl. Crawl in to show how a mother drinks ewes' milk from the bowl. You'll wear mother's skin. Show no fear.'

"I gulped. He was father. I couldn't disobey. My arm's red scars were still sore. My brothers and sisters came to watch. Ayub taunted. 'You're afraid aren't you?' I was angry with him. 'No, I'm not. Watch me.'

"Father helped tie the skin around my arms, over my back, and across the back of my legs. My arm wouldn't bend against its stiffness. Beneath it, I was hot. It stank of old blood. I blinked, held my breath and crawled slowly, cloaked in the skin. Lema cocked her head and looked at me closely, but didn't speak. I peeked, then went to the bowl and began lapping noisily. She came to my side and sat looking from milk to noisy tongue, to milk, to tongue. Lema's nose touched the tip of my milky tongue, sniffing. Her rough tongue wiped across the end of noisy-tongue's nose, tickling it. I wanted to giggle but didn't. Now she pressed into my side, lapping milk as I did. We drank together, licking our lips. As I crept out I looked back. She stared after me.

"Each day after teaching her to drink milk, she brushed against me as I entered, greeting me, purring soft rattles. I imitated her sounds. Soon, as I went to leave, Lema would leap on her mother's back – my back – and put her teeth into the neck's skin, roughhousing. I rolled over into a ball and she bounded, bounced and rolled with me, chewing at the leopard skin cloak, pawing gently.

"As Lema grew and her excitement was too great, she bared her teeth and unsheathed her claws. I hissed and growled in return, answering her quickness and threats with my own. She was my playmate. There was still something I didn't understand.

'Why did you bring Lema for me *baba*?'

"Our hunts succeeded only after seeing the leopard" he said. "The *prraang* is rare now, the stealthiest of creatures. Each year it appeared as if by magic. It became our talisman.'

'What's that?'

'It's a magic charm.'

'You brought no ibex from your hunt. I like the *korma* mother makes from it.'

Baba nodded. 'It's true. Our hunt didn't bring the ibex. Do you know why?'

'No, what happened? Didn't you find one?'

'No. We found one. We stalked a huge ibex, shy and wary, for three days. At last we sighted him, late in the third day on a rocky ledge above a fast-flowing river. I raised my rifle and had him in my sights. Something stopped me, a movement on the boulder above him.'

'What was moving? What was it?'

'A beautiful *prraang* crouched above my ibex readying her pounce. Our friend Baseer, urged me to shoot. I couldn't.'

'Why, *baba*?'

'We owed the *prraang* a debt. For years, though her kind reigned over her kingdom and its animals, she allowed us game for our families. If Allah let her come to take the same prey we meant to kill, it was for a reason. She and her family needed the food more than we did.'

'They were hungry.'

'Yes. So next morning, for the first time, we started to leave the hunt without game. We weren't surprised as we walked out to come across the fresh corpse of a female leopard, dead from starvation.

Nearby a cub mewed, relenting only to menace us with fierce growls when we approached."

"The baby didn't want to leave his mother."

"Yes, child. I could think of no better way to keep Lema with her mother than to skin the corpse and wrap Lema in the skin to bring them home."

"When *baba* said this I understood. 'Lema thinks I'm her mother when you cover me with the skin.'

'Yes. But Lema can't be with her mother forever, child. A daughter grows to leave her mother.'

'Can't she stay? I like her.'

'No. She needs to be with her kind, to have her own family. We must help her learn to kill. Next year we'll return her to the Chitral.'

'May I come to say goodbye?'

'You must come. I can't do it without you.'

"The marmot wriggled to get away. Sakhi caught it in the field. I held it by its tail, then dropped it inside the cage before closing the gate. Village children stood watching.

"I warned them. 'Don't come too close. She is learning to kill.' Lema toyed with her marmot, holding it down under one paw then gripping it between two paws after chasing it around the pen. At last she put her needle teeth deep into the back of the creature's neck. Then she carried it proudly to a corner and ate it. Weeks later, with even more visitors, I dropped a fat chicken into her cage. She killed it, making a fountain of feathers. When she grew bigger, *baba* had me lead a lamb into the pen. Lema's jaws held its throat tight until life left.

"*Baba* asked me to help with the final task. 'We must make a travelling cage. She'll lie in it when we return to Chitral.'

'I can still come?'

'Still.'

"Two trucks filled with villagers followed us on the day Lema left us. *Baba* hadn't explained everything to me.

'Why didn't we feed Lema today? Why did we bring the old ram?'
'You'll see child.'

Father's friend, Baseer, helped him wrestle the ram down from the truck bed. It struggled against the ropes tying its legs. I held the ram's rope while the men lowered Lema's cage. Then I gave the rope to *Baba*. 'You must pull up on Lema's door after I cut the ram's hobble. Say goodbye now to your friend.'

"I knelt on the cage's top. I whispered 'God go with you, Lema.' The ram bolted when father cut its restraints. Moments later, he signalled to me, and I pulled the cord on the sliding door. Lema bounded off as fast as a stone from a slingshot. She caught the ram below on a gravel bed in the middle of a fast river. The struggle took no time. My hands clapped and I shouted for her. I was happy.

"After, in our village, children questioned me. 'My father calls your father Mehmoud Prraang. Is he magic? Is that how he trained the *prraang*?'

'No. I helped him. She was Lema. We played.'

Their eyes grew wide. 'You played with the leopard? You are the Leopard's Daughter.'

Shahay's eyes rose to her audience. 'This is how I came by my *takhalus*.'

The women murmured thanks. Shahay's eyes swept her audience and caught Mohammed's swallow. His eyes shone, then fell. He excused himself, nodding to Bibi.

Shahay looked into her lap. He could not mean... her eyes rose, following him toward the *hujra*. Quickly, so no one would see, she mopped a tear. She was a mother with a son and older. He was *Daktar*. He would leave and forget. He was for someone younger.

***

In the *hujra* Mohammed busied himself unnecessarily with his pack, uncomfortable, sensible to an inner disquiet. He sat alone, yearning and denying, and closed his eyes ...

Before dinner he returned to the *kor*. He would examine her a last time before arranging the return. "Wife of Mehmoud, since your daughter has risen, may I check her wound once more?"

"Of course, *Sahib*." Bibi stayed.

He draped her wound carefully and commented to Bibi, but loud enough to all nearby. "The wound is clean, with good colour and no redness or puffiness. Please daughter of Mehmoud, touch around the wound. Do you feel any pain?"

"A little, but it's less than yesterday, *Sahib*."

He straightened, turned away, and deadpanned. "The patient is so improved, it's no longer necessary to consider shooting her."

Everyone in the *kor* chuckled save the patient. Shahay bridled, caught between the flush of Mohammed's attention and the chance his humour might be at her expense. On instinct she waited.

"Is this a common remedy for wounded daughters in America?" Mehmoud asked.

"No. But it's often the fate of lame horses."

More laughter. Shahay flushed, affecting a pout. "It's wrong that I'm compared to a horse."

Mohammed overheard. "But an Arabian with the finest bloodlines."

Shahay turned away to hide her smile. The household women broke into giggling squabbles on the adequacy of Mohammed's emendation, settling on praise of family bloodlines as redemptive.

Scents of roasted chicken fragrant with coriander and ginger wafted from the kitchen. Lunch was served simply with rice, *wriji*, and bread, *dodai*.

"Your meeting with Baseer?" Ayub asked.

"Friendly but cautious. We meet again tomorrow."

Chapter 14

Shifts

Bibi accompanied Mohammed after breakfast.

Baseer greeted them, conversed politely about health and families, and offered *kava*. Bibi whispered that it was time to visit Gul Sanga and her baby.

"With your permission I should first go with the wife of Mehmoud to check on mother and baby."

Baseer nodded. "Please, return when you're ready."

Even as Mohammed sat, Baseer's pallid skin and laboured breathing were evident. He sorted through routine questions. *Has your appetite changed? How? How is your energy level? Have you experienced diarrhea? Is this continuing?*

Gul Lakhta, sitting with her husband, sometimes corrected Baseer. On their face his symptoms indicated anaemia – pallor, shortness of breath, flat thin nails, the corners of his mouth cracked with open sores.

"My question will seem strange, *kaka*. Have you ever found yourself wanting to taste the earth here?" He pointed to the dirt outside the *hujra*.

Gul Lakhta tried unsuccessfully to stifle her giggle with her hand.

"The soil? Eating dirt? I've not lost my senses, *Sahib*. But ..." Gul Lakhta's eyes widened. "I've plucked carrots from the garden to eat without washing them."

Gul Lakhta's chin agreed.

Precision in diagnosis would be difficult without a lab test. Except – he recalled the family of dogs at his uncle's Denver veterinary clinic.

"Please *baba*, may I touch beneath your *kameez.*" Palpating Baseer's paunch he found it flanked by love handles which, both to appearance and touch, seemed filled with water. "You have dogs, *spayan*, and puppies, *kootray*, in the *qila*?"

"Yes."

"Their health?"

"They're sick" Gul Lakhta said. "They eat always, but are weak and losing weight. One pup died."

"Please, bring them." He confirmed that both bitch and pups had pale gums.

"You have anaemia likely brought on from a parasitic infection, hookworm. A medicine, mebendazole, will eliminate the worms and the anaemia will vanish. All members of the household, dogs too, should take the drug. I don't have these pills now. I'll get them to you. For now, please forgive me, my instructions are unpleasant. For hygiene, dig an oil drum into the ground. Dispose of all faecal material, canine and human, into it. Pour in old motor oil or gasoline every day and fire it. Boil drinking water. Wash raw vegetables in boiled water before eating them. Wash your hands in boiled water both before eating and prayer."

He turned to Gul Lakhta. "Until I provide mebendazole, *kaka* should eat liver once each day, no matter whether beef, chicken, or lamb. Please put a water pail out for the dogs. Don't allow them near household water intake." Baseer and Gul Lakhta reacted with fleeting expressions of revulsion. Mohammed regretted their embarrassment.

"This illness is world-wide, in every country including mine. The medicine will eliminate the problem. You'll recover full health, *Enshaallah.*"

"May Allah confer blessings on you" Baseer murmured.

***

Baseer quietly asked that Gul Lakhta stay for the next part of their conversation.

"You've asked my help. You wish my son shouldn't be your enemy."

"Yes."

"Your remedy is simple. Convince me he shouldn't be."

Mohammed straightened and nodded. "As a believer, I don't take the lives of women, children or old men. So far as possible, I'll prevent my platoon from taking innocent lives. I'll act against a believer only if my life or the life of an innocent is threatened."

"Let me understand. You ask my son not be your enemy, even if he's the enemy of Americans who kill civilians?"

"That's ... that's a start. My men aren't enemies of the Pukhtun. We fight those who claim Islam's authority to threaten and assassinate women, *malakan*, village elders, children and other noncombatants. Our enemies are only those who kill civilians as they did in Batmalai."

"You promise as you should, *Sahib*. But you acknowledge we have enemies amongst *Amreekunee faujayeen*. Some Americans kill civilians. So, *if they* harm Pukhtun villagers my son will fight them in our country, and wherever he encounters them. So will I. Doing less is to be without honour." Baseer went silent, fingers ran patiently through his beard.

"That said, we've suffered the insult of massacre from *takfiri* madmen. I'll speak with my son. He won't be your enemy. I'll leave to him, how he judges your actions. Your Islam is as I understand it. A great man brought it to us. He didn't seek war, but knew when to fight. I think you follow the Prophet's example. The *takfiri*, and many American soldiers, do not."

***

Bibi turned to him as they walked back. "Are you well, Mohammed? Your mind isn't here."

"I apologize. Yes, my mind wanders. I must return to my unit."

He felt bruised but relieved. Mehmoud chastised him, now Baseer. Both spoke hard truths because they accepted his friendship.

***

Mohammed's mind tossed in the darkness. Batmalai's land was green, alive with wild flowers, gardens, trees, well tilled crops and streams of clean water. For much of his adult life he'd dreamt of Laila. Their short conversation ended his hopes. Then, the mountain trail. Shahay was a widow with a son. Mehmoud might be scandalized. *Nya* warned him. 'Marry or have your throat cut.' Idiot! The war was blood, wounds, death and lies. He had to finish with it. Batmalai was family, friends, *dastarkhwan.*

His eyes closed. "Stop!" His shout jolted him awake. Their hands had stretched out for his. A slithering soup of veins, blood and brains had swamped his feet. He hadn't been able to reach.

Slowly, he dozed again. He dreamt of Shahay's eyes and saw in them pools of sadness. She murmured words he couldn't make out. *Louder.* He couldn't hear. What was it?

***

Shahay perked her ears to hear her parent's words.

"You walked with Mohammed from Baseer's *qila.* Did he say when he returns to his war?"

"Soon. His mind was elsewhere."

She lay awake. He was tall, foreign. Why did he look at her? He was *daktar.* She'd felt envy that his hands helped Bangar's wife. She wanted to be the only one he saved. She asked Allah to forgive her. His glances ... He thought of her.

She dreamt his hand stroked her cheek. She sat up startled, alarmed by thoughts of his touch. Her mind stewed. No man had spoken to her as he did, directly, smiling. He teased – a lame mare – yet respected her modesty. She set her jaw. It was foolish. He would forget.

Impatient, she wiped her eyes again.

Chapter 15

Badraga

Shahay walked beside Gulalai. Her limp slowed her pace. But nothing could prevent her *khadi,* the celebratory visit for Bangar's new son. She found Gul Sanga nursing in the courtyard sun, back against a low wall of Baseer's *hujra.*

"I needed the warmth" Gul Sanga said.

Shahay returned her smile. "You must be proud, wife of Bangar. He's nursing well. He looks like his father. And how are your stitches?"

"My wound heals well. And the boy suckles like a horse." Gul Sanga basked in the interest and attention of the women of Mehmoud's household. *Khadi* visits, celebratory social communion, were conventional, expected and reassuring.

Shahay couldn't help but hear the conversation of Baseer and Bangar in the *hujra* behind.

***

Baseer recognized his son's wrinkled brow. Still, Bangar listened attentively.

"You're right to want heathens gone from *Pukhtunkhwa.* But Mohammed isn't *kaafir.* He's a believer who's helped our family and Mehmoud's. He promises help for my illness. I accept his explanation for coming to our lands. So does Mehmoud."

"You believe he helped my wife without thought of reward?"

"I do."

Bangar rested in stony silence "And the help he promises you, without thought of reward?"

"Yes. He asked merely one thing."

Bangar's voice rasped. "Hah! So he *did* want something. Money? Gold?"

"No. Something different. He asked that you not be his enemy."

Bangar's forehead smoothed. "That ... that's not a reward."

"No."

"Then Ayub and Sakhi were right."

"What did they say?"

"That he's honourable."

"*Aw*, my son. But he must leave soon. He's a soldier with no choice. News of his presence may have reached the *Tehreek-e-Taleban* assassins. You've a Mamund acquaintance. *Sahib* must pass near their lands. They haven't forgotten those slaughtered by Americans' drone strikes in Damadola and Chenagai. After Chenagai they collected the discontented like bruised windfalls."

"You wish me to..."

"*Aw.* Meet your friend in Khar. I'll ask when Mohammed means to return. He'll need an escort. He helped our family. Go with his *badraga*."

"I could drive him to the Ghakhi checkpoint. But, road attacks are common driving through Mamund lands. Many would kill an American on sight. And guards at the pass would make difficulties for an illegal American. Better the *badraga*."

"Yes, be discreet. Your conversations will be remembered. So will the the names of members of the *badraga*."

***

At the pre-appointed time, Mohammed engaged SATCOM and pulsed an encrypted message for Montoya:

ETD 19:25 tmrw. We r 12. Prpre pckge Mbndazle for 20 pers. GPS on. Rqst firepwr 1 mile W. Batmalai.

In morning's early light, he thanked God for a night without nightmares, and for Shahay's recovery. She was in the *kor* during breakfast. Custom and modesty permitted no conversation. He defaulted to asking about her wound.

"My wound is well. But you seem worried. Is something wrong?"

He shook his head and retreated silently, fearing to speak and burdened with the unspoken.

***

Ayub and Sakhi led him to meet the *badraga* and made introductions. Ayub then took him aside.

"Baseer volunteered the services of Bangar and a Mamund friend. I confirmed this with Bangar this morning. He insists. In all, we have twelve as we agreed, all familiar with trouble." Ayub pawed his beard. "It's a good sign his father volunteered his name. He is a friend. But his sympathies have changed rather quickly. We don't know his Mamund friend."

***

In late afternoon they assembled within the *qila* walls.

The men wore Peshawari *chapal*, sandals, not boots, *partoog-ka-meez*, not body armour, *pakol*, not helmets. Their weapons, mostly dusted off AK47s smelling of fresh oil, knock-offs from the gunsmiths of Darra Adam Khel, were neither as reliable as Russian originals, nor as accurate as modern M4s. They were farmers, shopkeepers, labourers, not seasoned, disciplined soldiers. Still, Ayub vouched for them.

Mohammed sniffed their cumin and conceded the aroma was an improvement on his platoon's. Tradition invited Pukhtuns to defend a neighbour's *guest* with their lives. His platoon consisted of soldiers trained and paid to kill.

Ayub had them wait on a latecomer. Mohammed's shirt was already drenched as the sun began its descent behind the western mountains. His rucksack alone weighed sixty pounds. The village men sported light bandoliers of ammunition and small shoulder-slung pokes.

He waved to curious village children who peeked in excitedly through Mehmoud's open gates. Wives and family members looked in from the road beyond. His arrival went unnoticed. His departure lacked only a brass band.

He embraced Mehmoud. Right hand to heart he turned to Bibi Rokhana, her son's wives and Shahay. His throat went dry, his eyes fell to his boots. He checked his M4, then risked a glance. Her eyes were full and riveted on him. Beside her, Bibi's mouth gaped. She'd followed his eyes to her daughter's.

Shahay's face coloured, caught out. He read Bibi's lips. "We'll speak." He cursed himself. Bibi knew. He would give Ayub a message. He'd be back when his deployment ended. He prayed Shahay would understand.

The *qila* chorused *Khuday pa Aman*, Farewell, May God go with you.

Once on the move Mohammed pulsed a final SAT message: *Cnfrm 12. GPS on.*

Ayub said a few words to the men as gates opened. Mohammed didn't hear. Ayub took point and led them – *eastwards toward Pashat*. But the Ghakhi base was west. Mohammed held his tongue. Bangar's aside clarified the intent. "This is good. Watchers will be confused."

All right. Perhaps Ayub's test for Bangar. Shortly, Ayub turned them north to skirt the village toward old trails resolving west south-west. The sounds of barking dogs diminished, along with the perfume of warm fresh *dodai*. The route took them on pathways between fields of growing fruits and grains, and through the reeky mists of ripe animal pens. In clumsy combat boots, he descended to ford a boulder-strewn torrent-bed, before ascending into a scattered line of scrub bush interspersed with the beginning of pine forests. Mohammed's pack, rifle, helmet and other gear amounted altogether to eighty pounds. Keeping up with light footed, swift moving *badraga* villagers with their spare loads and long strides, flooded his clothes with sweat.

Through his PVS-14 night scope, he spotted a rabbit moving uphill. An owl floated silently in upon it. A squeal. Silence. After his second scan he tapped Ayub's shoulder, a prearranged signal to stop. He waved. A lone figure waved back.

"Friends ahead." Ayub alerted the men.

He'd expected *badraga* amateurs, civilians. Four were Utmankhel, Bangar's Mamund friend, and six Salarazai. Moving quietly with good intervals and sure tread, they were married to their rifles. Though forewarned, one instinctively raised his Kalashnikov's barrel when two face-blackened *angrezaan* stepped apparently out of thin air into their midst. Ayub quickly motioned the barrel lower.

"Good to see you, Tony, Henry. Warm bodies besides ours?"

"Yes, a group of twenty flanking the main trail below. Three pairs of spotters above. Haven't seen any more ... We've set surprises in the creek bed above the main group's choke point. With your escort we have good firepower. Montoya's up ahead."

He translated. Tony took point.

Two miles farther on, with his eyes fixed ahead, he almost stumbled over Tony, suddenly on a knee. He signalled the *badraga* behind. Tony murmured into his MBITR, hand signing to Mohammed. One shadow covered their six. Another, flanking uphill, made urgent contact.

Tony relayed the message in a whisper. "Two hostiles are on the move toward their lookouts. Our guys couldn't follow. They should be in our scopes within a thousand yards. It's unlikely they've spotted us. But ..."

He passed the message. Bangar stepped forward. "The lookouts may be well hidden" he whispered. "They dig to make caves into warrens. I know where boulders cover entrances. Shall I take others to check these places?"

"We'll come." Ayub volunteered himself and Sakhi. "You lead, son of Baseer." Bangar's white teeth showed through his grin.

Mohammed shivered. Putting Bangar on point meant Ayub would kill him first if he deceived them. The three moved quickly, noiselessly uphill.

***

Mohammed pulled down his night goggles. They moved cautiously now, sweeping for movement. Tony, on a knee again, signalled halt. Two hundred yards ahead figures descended. Mohammed held his breath. Three men waved. He exhaled. The escort moved up quietly. Ayub said nothing. A spray of dark liquid showed on his forehead. Blood wiped from his knife stained his sleeve.

Salty sweat drained into Mohammed's eyes. He cursed his ruck, his boots and the smell of his own ripeness. A further mile along, Montoya grinned and held out his hand. He greeted Ayub's group and signalled a summary move out. They paced steadily due west.

Tony hissed suddenly and dropped flat. "Cover!"

Mohammed dove to his belly. Two short AK47 bursts brought up dirt from the low bank above his head. He wrestled to release his ruck. A slug ripped the bulging pack now beside him. Damn. Hostile spotters eluded the screen. Flashes gave away four weapons above, two below. Increased fire slammed into the turf above. Ayub raised his rifle.

Mohammed instantly shouted in *Pukhto*. "Stop! Hold fire." They were already vulnerable to crossfire. Muzzle flashes would locate them precisely. The ancient trail had sunk into the terrain, providing a small vertical bank protecting against downhill fire. Fire from below could pick them off if they lifted so much as a few inches from their bellies. They'd take casualties unless they continued to hug the ground. They were pinned.

He left his pack behind to belly forward to Montoya. "The main group of hostiles below, they'll be on their way." Behind, on cue, a sudden crackle. M4s on auto fire. Loud explosions, screams. He traded thumbs up with Tony and Montoya. Their IEDs had hit the attackers' choke point. Two more of the rearguard caught up.

Montoya gave orders. "Hostiles up and down. We need to clear them. Seven belly back a hundred yards. Four up. Use scree to flank. Take them out or flush them down toward the trail. Three more down."

"Okay, Cap." He sent up Stoski with Vargas, Ayub and Bangar's Mamund ally. Tony, Bangar and Sakhi crept downhill toward the shooters below. Incoming bursts continued to tear into the shallow bank above their trail.

"*Wayee!*" Mohammed quick-bellied back dragging his kit. Two rounds whizzed over his head. Itbar Gul grimaced, muttering prayers. Bloody mess. Ricochet through his *pakol*. A trough of missing flesh and hair. Skull creased. *Pakol* cap soaked. Superficial head lac. Showering blood. He distracted Itbar. "A story for your children."

Itbar's teeth chattered ... shock setting in. "Too much blood. Speak the t – truth *sahib*. I don't f – fear death."

"Not today. Keep your head down. You'll have a story for your children and a scar, proof of your courage. This will sting." Betadine. "Put your hand here and hold it on the wound." Combat Gauze. Good. "Now move your hand away." Compressive wrap. "Finished. Better than ever. Suck on this." Fentanyl lollipop.

He wrung the blood out of Itbar's *pakol*. The liquid washed out a clump of fleshy hair entraining the smashed bullet. "A prize for you and your children. Proof that a Pukhtun head is harder than a bullet."

Itbar Gul's chattering teeth glowed white. "*Manana, Daktar Sahib.*"

"It's my honour to treat a brave man's wounds."

The sounds changed. Left flank firing stopped. He raised his night scope cautiously over the bank. High right, above, mixed arms rapid fire. M4s picking up return fire from AKs. No downhill AK fire. Ayub's four had found the hostiles. Ahead his scope caught Tony and Montoya. Night scopes on. Looking toward two boulders where flashes located the uphill firefight. Twenty seconds on, they fired simultaneously. Two AK47s fell as they were flushed from screening boulders.

Silence. A minute on, Tony mounted the trail with Sakhi and Bangar. Bangar shook his head at Mohammed. "His pistol killed without sound. One was dead, the other had only begun to turn when the pistol clicked again to kill him. What is this?"

"Special bullets. I'll explain later."

Behind, their rearguard's M4's auto staccato reduced to semi-auto spitting. He breathed deep. Montoya either planned well or was pretty handy when surprised. Anticipated hostile interception, lookouts, crossfires. Few of the main hostile group from below would risk pursuit after their IED casualties. They'd discover their lookouts' fate by morning.

Mohammed walked behind a wobbly Itbar. Pukhtun endurance, *bur'dasht,* was no myth. His proximity probably helped. The wound caused blinding pain. At camp he'd anaesthetize, stitch the scalp and stick him with fentanyl.

***

Montoya and Tony led the platoon and *badraga* through camp gates. Montoya ordered the mess to prepare lightly boiled eggs, tea and toast for the escort. Meanwhile Mohammed treated Itbar, then showed the *badraga* members to sleeping quarters consisting of communal cots in a separate tent to one side of the main square.

"If America's president visited, he would sleep here. Tonight, more important guests." Laughter. Latrines and washstands were over the way.

Mohammed noted the Colonel glowering at them from the door of his quarters.

Platoon and *badraga* ate together. Sakhi was curious. "In America what do you eat, Mohammed? Do you cook American food here?"

He caught Sakhi's drift. "You eat like a Clydesdale Sakhi. I'll have the mess make up more food, beef burgers with cheese and onions."

Sakhi worried. "What is a Clydesdale? I don't know these foods. Are they *ha'lal*?"

"A Clydesdale is the biggest warhorse I know. The foods are *ha'lal*. We have them with a sweet drink called Coke. Like to try that too?"

***

The Colonel summoned Montoya.

"If I find that his negligence contributed to the deaths of his two platoon mates, I'll deal with him all right. And now you squire a group of ragtag Pukhtuns into my camp. I want a complete account, the names of each of the people with whom Karram had contact. A physical description of them, info about their allegiances, names of family members, the whole story. It's your own damned fault. You let him go. Get it done."

With Montoya dismissed, the Colonel called in his senior operative.

"Frank, I imagine your nose is healed from the dustup you had with Karram. He's back and brought some dirty damned Pukhtuns with him. We all need to work out our hostilities. You have my permission to address any problems you might have with Karram at any time. If it were me, I'd look to do it while his bloody Pukhtun friends are present."

***

In the morning, Mohammed conversed easily with Ayub as they followed a vaguely familiar broad shouldered man preceding them to the latrine and its washstands. The man wheeled suddenly to throw a hard shoulder into Ayub.

Mohammed stepped forward. "Ah, the asshole with the grenade." Ayub's hand was on his shoulder.

"Please, I'm your guest. The man certainly offended me most."

The grenadier crouched, face like a Cheshire cat, waiting. "I'll deal with this big prick first. Then it's you and me, Karram."

Ayub stood expressionless, then feinted. His lightning retreat avoided a vicious kick at his groin. Rambo spun out and crouched again, sneer intact. Ayub swiftly reprised the feint. His opponent closed instantly anticipating a retreat. Ayub pounced inside the kicker's strike point and pivoted, simultaneously intercepting the kicking ankle in his massive left hand. The grenadier bent forward, swinging his fist and grazing Ayub's temple. Unperturbed, Ayub seized the exposed belt buckle in his right hand, using his opponent's momentum to spin twice, faster each time. Ankle and belt buckle in hand Ayub released his human discus headfirst into the side door of the nearest Humvee.

Mohammed stood above the crumpled body. "Never seen a man fly. Bet you surprised yourself." Frank's lungs screamed for breath.

Ayub's hand was on the hilt of his *charre*. Mohammed waved him off. "Please no. The idiot won't be a problem now."

The onlooking Pukhtuns walked on, smiling. Mohammed toasted Ayub with breakfast orange juice. The platoon joined in. Four of Frank's colleagues shook Ayub's hand.

Tony interpolated a consolation. "Alas, a *ninja* becomes one with mother earth."

After breakfast Montoya went to the CO to report. "Colonel, your man assaulted one of our new contacts, a valuable one. Fortunately, no one was seriously hurt. I leave discipline to you."

***

Mohammed translated Montoya's address to the *badraga*.

"You've defended us. *Manana*. If you wish to visit Asadabad, we'll transport you today to the *bazar*." He distributed five thousand *afghani* to each man.

Ayub and Sakhi approached Mohammed fingering their currency, an earnest toward the services of the *badraga*. "We'll surprise our sister Farikhta and her husband Ghorzang instead of the market."

"Please give her my name. I spoke with *baba* about threats. Are Bangar and his Mamund friend going with you?"

"No. They're going to the *bazar*. Bangar knows one of the merchants."

He briefed Montoya. "The suicide bombing cemented them against the *takfiri*. But the villagers aren't sympathetic to us either. They don't want us here. Mehmoud told another story known to the community." Reluctantly he related the Persian's tale.

Montoya groaned. "Jesus! No wonder selling ourselves to locals is tough."

***

The camp doc provided Mohammed with the Mebendazole for Baseer. "You'll instruct his son on the meds?"

"Of course."

He was overdue calling home. Communications emailed then timed the Skype connection for the Sabbath, Saturday at 9am mountain standard time. His sisters mugged in the background.

"Hi Mom and Dad. Hi Fariyal and Sabryya. How's the weather?"

They all spoke at once."The weather is fine, warm and sunny. How are you?" (Ali and Ayesha).

"You look tired." (Ayesha).

"When did you grow a beard? Why is your hair so long? Why are you calling?" (Fariyal, Sabryya).

"Are you safe?" (Ayesha)

"Safe and sound. I've had some adventures, made some local friends, visited some places. I'll tell you about all of it. I'm just phoning to say hello. Tell *Nya* I wouldn't be much help here without *Pukhto*."

"We'll tell her. Still can't tell us where you are?" (Ali)

"Sorry. No."

"Remind us – when's your deployment up?" (Ayesha)

"Soon. Then, what did Arnold say?

His sisters brightened and joined his mime. "I'll be baackkk!"

***

The Colonel read and reread Montoya's concise account of Mohammed's supposed intelligence probe into Bajaur. He added the names of two Batmalai patriarchs to the Foreign Others Watch List (FOWL). Karram's captain, the bastard Montoya, was holding back.

OWL: Subject: Karram, M.Y. Appended FOWL:

Further investigation/interrogation attached Bajauri contacts required. Ongoing questions about Karram's loyalties. Participation in unprovoked physical assault on senior camp operative. Return to base protected by suspect Pukhtuns. Unresolved issues of allegiance, loyalty. Recommend interrogate Batmalai family members contacted by Karram.

Chapter 16

Cautions

Shahay feared the questions. "You've said nothing to father?"

Her mother's face had gone cold. "I saw your eyes. What is between you? What happened when you met."

"Nothing happened against honour. We met as Ayub told. The Arab's knife slashed my leg. A bullet knocked him down as he came for my throat. A soldier ran toward me. I didn't know him. I'd fallen. Blood spurted from my thigh. A soldier came and reached toward my wound. I raised my knife. Then I saw only black..."

Her mother's eyes narrowed. "His hands, they didn't..."

Shahay flushed. "My senses had left me. Zarhawar stood by me. Ayub watched. He wouldn't have permitted... My wound took all of Sahib's attention."

Mor spoke more softly. "And afterwards, did you have private words with him?"

Shahay shook her head hesitantly. His eyes looked at her improperly for a moment. But eyes weren't words.

"After I was wounded, I wanted to walk to our home. Ayub argued with me over this. Zarhawar stood with us when *Daktar* took Ayub's side. He begged me to ride the mule home. Then, he spoke boldly. The words stopped my breath. He didn't want my stitches to open. He spoke of my wound as *ours*. He had repaired it. Until

125

it healed it was *his too*. I'd never heard such words. I don't know whether he spoke properly. He didn't mean to insult my modesty, my *sharm*. So I rode as he asked. My brother lifted me onto the mule, not *Daktar Sahib*. When he helped with Gul Sanga's *zoi*, I thanked him for helping her. You were near, as was father, my brothers and their wives."

Her mother's expression remained flat. "Your face when he left..?"

Shahay's chin fell, then rose. She met her mother's eyes. "He was a brother, yet not a brother. When I saw him help Gul Sanga, I wanted to be like him. I was happy when he was in our home, as our guest, eating with us, bringing laughter. He gave new life. I know he's gone and won't return. As God wills."

Bibi stared into the distance. "You know little of men."

Shahay bridled. "You don't think my marriage to Zarhawar's father taught me of men's ways? I've said little of *his* cruelty. I was young and understood nothing. He beat me as he wished. Mohammed is like my father and brothers. He isn't cruel."

A smile traced across her mother's lips. "No, he isn't. *Enshaallah*."

***

Bangar returned alone. Mohammed filled small brown plastic container with pills in the field hospital.

"You're face wears worry, son of Baseer. Is it these pills, *golai*? I promised them for your father. Everyone takes two pills a day for three days. All human and dog waste must continue to be burned. The dogs take one pill a day for three days. Questions?»

"These *golai*, they're good medicine, good *duwa'ee*? They'll make *Baba* well?"

"*Enshaallah*. He'll be well after three days. He'll hunt with you again."

"I didn't think he could recover. To hunt with him again... May Allah grant it. *Manana* for this medicine."

Bangar remained motionless. "May I ask your opinion about an important matter? I ask as a favour."

Mohammed went on alert. "My advice is no favour for one who guarded my return." He sat silent, waiting. Bangar shifted uncomfortably, eyes lowered, fingers mowing his black beard.

A diversion. "Let's go into the doctors' office. He's away. We can make tea there."

Bangar followed, wordless, and sat facing the desk. The kettle whistled into the cramped room's curious mix of bottles, electronics, paper-littered shelves and clipboards. Mohammed abided the silence, letting the tea steep before passing a steaming mug into Bangar's hands. Their eyes met over their tea.

"I took you for an invader, an enemy. I sympathized with resisters."

"Yes."

"But you help as you can. Not like an enemy. Because of this, and another thing, I've changed."

"I see that. You mention 'another thing.' What do you mean?"

"Ayub said your sisters will be teachers. I don't murder elders, children or teachers."

"We're as one on this. Why mention murdering teachers and children?"

Bangar released a deep breath. "The Kunari *takfiri* will act against the sister of Ayub and Sakhi. What shall I do? If I tell them, they'll stay to protect her. The attackers will see and wait for another time. The brothers are my friends. I don't know what's best."

Mohammed stood and paced. "Where did you hear this?"

"Ahmad and I went to the *bazar*. A fighter recognized me. He thought I'd come to assassinate a teacher, the woman Farikhta. He said they warned twice. Now her death would be an example."

Mohammed stopped his pacing. "When will they attack? Will they kill both her and her husband? Did he give details? How will they do it?"

"He said they'd come by motorcycle to shoot them. It's soon.

They watch them now. That's all I know."

"Thank you, son of Baseer. You're right. The brothers' presence would alert the assassins. I promise you, we'll protect Farikhta and her husband. No one will know our source."

Bangar hesitated, his face drained. "If you fail, I'll be guilty in the eyes of the brothers. They'll show no mercy."

"I will then share your guilt, son of Baseer. Pray Allah is with us."

***

Montoya paced. "You're right. He's an asset. He should be careful. Word will soon enough get to the *takfiri*. Agreed, this isn't for the brothers. What are you thinking?"

"I could take Tony. Farikhta should know my name already from her brothers' visit. Maybe four of our guys could go native into A'bad, drink tea and watch. Tony and I can play locals to shadow Farikhta and her husband to school and back. We may not have much time." Montoya nodded.

***

The escort banqueted before leaving. Cheeseburgers, fries and cheese pizzas – riders of caramelized onions, roasted red peppers, and *halal* beef with cumin and black pepper. Another surprise awaited. Montoya adopted Mohammed's plan. The base Supply NCO, aka the Blue Ribbon Scrounger, purloined cases destined for German ISAF stores. The theft served two purposes. Pukhtuns esteemed German equipment. *Badraga* firepower would also be much improved for any hot encounter.

Mohammed watched his escort stir. Muttering intensified as cases opened. Blue cracked open the first case of HK G36 dual scoped German assault rifles. Mohammed called out each name, and handed one to each man. The Pukhtuns' jaws dropped. The Master

Weapons Sergeant slowly took apart the HK G36, with *badraga* members mirroring step by step, each one fondling his G36 as if an intimate body part. His hand stayed Ayub's reach for one of the weapons.

"The *badraga* leader may wish an alternative."

He brought out a HK G28 with a twenty-inch barrel and a 3-20x50mm Schmidt & Bender scope. Ayub's eyes shone.

"This is a hunter's weapon, Ayub. It can bring down an ibex at 1000 meters. It's yours. Please take a G28 back to *baba* as my gift. I've included match grade ammunition for both of you."

The MWS disassembled the G28, eyes closed. Ayub watched transfixed. The longer barrelled rifle suited hunting. Sakhi preferred the G36, opining its rate of fire would provide greater firepower. Ayub clasped Mohammed's shoulders with his giant hands, thanking him profusely.

"Please, no need for thanks. You killed the two assassins of my friends. Now you've guarded my return."

Ayub nodded. "We'll remember you and your men."

He sensed an unintended implication. "No need. Please tell *Baba* I'll return to Batmalai. *Enshaallah.*"

"*Enshaallah*" Ayub echoed.

He stood side by side with Montoya at the gates to see them off. "*Du Khoday pa Aman*" – May God protect you. The escort, laden with extra rifles and ample ammo, walked out.

Impulsively, Mohammed took a remaining scoped G28 and more match grade ammo and caught up with Bangar. "Please give this to your father – to rediscover hunting, *enshaallah*. He helped me. A token of thanks."

Bangar took point, double bandoliered, his father's G28 strapped over his back, his old rifle now in his left hand, the G36 in his right. He looked back shaking his head, grinning.

***

Mohammed brooded to Montoya. "Maybe I was stupid. Guarding Farikhta's a gamble. If we fail, it might cost everything, not just friendship with Mehmoud's family, but any trust between us and the Salarzai."

"Yep. But it's the right gamble. The brothers' odds of protecting her weren't as good as ours."

"I asked Ayub to give my name to her. Bad manners to meet without prior introduction. Bangar said she was watched already. Have we got any details about her?"

"Some. She teaches at the Salabagh School. Her husband, Ghorzang Salahuddin, is assistant principal. Got a street map. Here's their home and their likely daily route, maybe a half mile. Early tomorrow we'll post four along the way. Head in later today. Sidearms only."

"Good. I'll take two small Beretta Tomcats for them."

"All right. Light, easily concealed. Take extra clips."

Chapter 17

Farikhta

Toward dusk on the outskirts of Marah Warah village, Mohammed and Tony, done up as bearded locals, hitched a ride from a local farmer with a load of apricots. Mohammed chatted amiably.

"Are you getting good prices for apricots this year? Is it a good crop?"

"The best in a few years. The prices are too low. How much do you pay in your village? I haven't seen you before. Do you come from a village nearby?"

"I'm from Batmalai" he fibbed. "Our crop isn't in the Pashat *bazar* yet."

The driver nodded. "I thought you were from Bajaur. An honourable people, the Salarzai. I am Safi."

"If you'd stop just ahead. Our friend's home is nearby. *Manana* for driving us. May your day be prosperous."

"You're welcome, friend. *Khoday pa aman.*"

***

Mohammed led, meandering, gesticulating, lazily absorbed in conversation with his companion. *Yak Qadam Pesh* echoed in the winding lane from an open window above. He mimed a few steps of an *attan*. Tony grinned. They paused to cheer five boys and one girl playing soccer on a street off the lane. Two dusty dogs lay sleepily against dirt-stained mud brick walls bordering the presumptive soccer pitch. Farikhta's corner home came into view at the next street junction.

A *burqa*-clad woman with a teenage boy neared, carrying groceries. Mohammed went on an inner alert: beyond, two fierce-eyed beards receded, flicking successive glances toward the home. Once past it, the fierce-eyes lit cigarettes, lazing in the falling sun at a crossroads within view. Mohammed's gaze returned to the children's soccer. He coughed. Tony took the message. His hand went as if to steady himself to Mohammed's shoulder. He removed a sandal with his other hand, shook it out, and took in the watchers' faces.

The scent of lamb and fresh *dodai* married with onion, cinnamon and ginger of a *kabuli korma* as they approached. At the home's corner, within sight of the beards, they affected indecision, fingers and arms noiselessly arguing direction. Tony's shrug conceded Mohammed's choice of route. They turned right, into a side street and out of the watchers' sight.

Mohammed casually scanned overlooking windows and facing doors. "Clear." He interlaced his fingers, cupping his hands at waist height. Tony's right foot pushed off the cup onto the sidewall's crest. He lowered his arm to Mohammed, pulled him up, and they popped down into the tiny garden.

Mohammed moved silently to put his ear to the rear door. Within, voices conversed intermittently. Now the woman sang, her lullaby interspersed with a tired baby's cry. For an instant, the voice was her sister's. The baby's dismissive cry woke him. Moments later the house quieted to susurration.

They needed safe entry. Watchers too might scale the garden wall. Alarmed owners might in turn alert neighbours. He whispered to Tony and chanced a soft knock. Nothing. A second knock. The house quieted. The woman's voice asked what the noise was. A man's voice, nervous, replied. "Someone is at our garden door." His voice rose. "Who knocks please?"

"My name is Mohammed Yousf. I'm with a friend. We must speak to you. May we enter?"

Hurried whispers. "Perhaps we know this name," the woman said. "You may know my sister, my brothers, my father and mother?"

"Your father is Mehmoud Prraang. Your mother is Bibi Rokhana. Your brothers are Ayub and Sakhi. Your sister is Shahay."

The home released its breath. "Please come in with your friend, *Daktar Sahib*" the man said.

He entered the kitchen's fragrances. A simple wood table, bleached with age, scarred by cuts, sat as a working counter opposite two white-washed mud brick stub walls spanned by an electric two burner hot plate. A gently bubbling *korma* stirred his nostrils and made his mouth water. In the doorway to the next room, a bespectacled young man, thin and smiling, extended his hand.

"Welcome *Daktar Sahib*. We know of you. Please, introduce your friend and sit to tea. We're surprised you come by such a strange route. Was our front door so difficult to find?"

"Forgive our unusual entrance. My friend is Tony Mitchell." Tony shook hands. "We'd love tea. I wish our visit were social. We came like thieves because we have urgent information. May we speak of this first?"

"Of course, *Sahib*. First, please greet my wife, mother of our daughter, Maryam."

He bowed slightly to Farikhta. Tony followed. Mohammed's eyes dwelt an instant too long. She had the calm elegance and unfathomably beautiful eyes of her sister. She drew her veil. He'd done it again.

"You have *urgent* information?" Ghorzang asked.

"I'm afraid we've learned an assassination attempt will be made on you. The information comes from a former hostile. Your home is being watched as we speak. That's why we came through your garden."

Their eyes grew. Farikhta slumped. "They've threatened before. We're at their mercy. I wish my father and brothers were nearby."

He winced. "I hope you will forgive me. Our informant knows your family. Together we decided not to inform your brothers."

Farikhta sat back, jaw open.

"Your brothers are fine men. Their presence would have been obvious. Enemies would simply have waited until they left. We'll act as locals, near but unseen. Please allow us to escort you to and from school. Without obvious protectors your enemies will be confident. *Enshaallah.* May we offer a gift?" He presented the Berettas.

Ghorzhang blanched. "Gifts? But we don't ... How? We've never used weapons."

"May I show you? Tony will keep a lookout."

"The pistols aren't loaded. This safety – here – prevents firing. Your thumb pushes the safety off. Right. It's off. Now point the pistol toward the door. Pretend it's the assassin's chest. Pull the trigger. Good. Yes. That lever? It flips the barrel up. Watch. The first bullet goes in here. Seven more go in a clip in here. We'll load bullets each day."

Mohammed held Maryam, while her parents practised.

"Now for *sinama*, Hollywood. Turn your backs to the door, eyes closed. I'll be the assassin's motorcycle. When it stops, open your eyes, turn and find your door. The door will be the assassin. Point the pistol and pull the trigger."

Mohammed sounded the motorcycle with risible imperfection. The baby stared at the strange noise. Her mouth turned down. He stopped. Ghorzang turned colliding with Farikhta, obstructing both his and her aims. Neither pulled the trigger. Embarrassed, they wanted a repeat.

Tony, oblivious to the hosts' tensions, used his sleeve to wipe his tears. "Please do motorcycle again? Can you shift gears? O for a tape recorder! Montoya should hear this."

Ghorzang and Farikhta witnessed Tony's mirth warily. They

looked quizzically to Mohammed. Surely Tony wouldn't laugh at them?

Mohammed surrendered to parody. "Tony dared to laugh at my brilliant motorcycle."

Farikhta, modestly averted her face, put her hand over her mouth and giggled. Ghorzang followed. Soon he joined. All four parodied a motorcycle symphony. A roused Maryam added her own wail.

He hadn't counted on laughter's effect. Farikhta resumed her pistol manoeuvres with unexpectedly streaming eyes. Ghorzang mishandled his pistol to send it clanging off the floor.

Suddenly, Tony raised his hand for quiet. Men's voices outside! Ghorzang picked up his pistol and pushed in front of Farikhta. She took Maryam from Mohammed and knelt behind Ghorzang holding her baby. The voices passed by and Tony's hand fell.

Mohammed's hand went to Ghorzang's shoulder. "They want publicity. They'll come in the street, not to your home. We're here. Rest easy. Tomorrow we'll guard you."

Ghorzhang settled and nodded. "Yes. Tomorrow, we'll worry enough. Please, join us for *korma*."

Mohammed assumed the couple's small appetites spoke of their tension. "In the morning we'll load your pistols and help you conceal them," he said. "Your routines won't change. We have more men on route. We'll slip over the back wall. Tony will lead. I'll be behind. Walk at your usual pace. We're locals going about our business, but alert. You'll be safe. *Enshaallah*."

The home's constrained living space presented a problem. "With your permission, we'll sleep on your floor overnight."

Farikhta and Ghorzhang exchanged furtive glances.

"Please, have I said something wrong? Please tell me."

Ghorzang shrugged. "You're guests. You must have our bed."

Mohammed demurred. "But, the wife of Ghorzang is a new mother. We can't ask mother and baby to give up their comfort."

The modest cultural war ended, to no one's complete satisfaction, with the guests' acceptance of the marital mattress on the floor. Their hosts managed with a blanket-covered slung frame.

Mohammed dreamt. Farikhta's eyes were Shahay's.

In morning's early light, he rose to muffled stirrings in the kitchen and the fragrance of *kajoorey*, fresh baked biscuits. Over *chai* he spoke with deliberate calm.

"We should ignore speeding motorcycles. If one slows or stops nearby, particularly one with pillion, hands on your weapons. Assassins expect surprise. We'll turn the tables on them. Conceal your pistols until the last moment. If either motorcyclist or rider approaches, point at his chest and pull the trigger. Safety catches are off during the walk. I'll shout 'Now' as I shoot."

***

Mohammed trailed the first day. Tony, bearded, darkened by months of Afghan sun, walked thirty paces ahead of the couple toward the school. They ignored friendly beards at cross streets and noted two friendlies wandering through the bazar. Ghorzang's pistol lay between two books, Farikhta's in her sleeve.

Over four days, Mohammed affected calm while his concerns grew. Bangar's intelligence was sparse: 'They'll come by motorcycle between home and school.' But motorcycles were popular. Thirty or forty passed innocently each morning. Returning, even more were on the road.

He bounced his worry off Tony. "Bangar's intel made sense. Targets wouldn't know what was happening until it was too late, because motorcycles are just scenery. But assassins don't fly by spraying bullets. Too uncertain. They'll stop, get off and fire. We'll have a chance..."

Tony nodded. "We saw watchers. They wouldn't be here unless it was on."

Mohammed's untroubled demeanour provided his hosts an edgy

confidence, confirmed by their concealed pistols. Silently he prayed his preparations warranted their trust.

***

Emir, Salafi Taliban, Kunar
Asadabad

Caution and planning allowed him to survive and become commander. Twice he'd warned her. Cease teaching Asadabad's girls. Her defiance encouraged others. She ignored him. Today, her husband would die with her.

His men killed as he ordered. He'd chosen two, young followers, fodder. He provided a motorcycle and weapons. They'd had ample time to prepare. It was unlikely unimportant teachers would be protected. The assassination would have maximum impact near the market. No one dared defy his warnings. If she were guarded, and the assassination failed, he'd know immediately. Those who guarded her wouldn't anticipate the response.

Paid police and military informers said no one protected her. If they were wrong – almost certainly they weren't – her protection would have to be the crusaders. His men watched the Puchi Ghar American base outside the city. No men came from there. If *Amriki* prevented the assassination, they would be their vaunted special soldiers from the mountain base. Their confidence returning to base would make them vulnerable. They'd travel in numbers.

He met his assassins, Salaar and Haji Faqeer, only once. While their devotion to ridding the land of invaders was weak, their appreciation of weapons and a motorcycle was strong. Five days before, he'd warned them against any contact before they completed their task. He smiled to himself. Even their failure would offer opportunity.

He'd learned from experience. Three years before, when Camp Karzai was being built they'd attacked several times. The hill top construction proved too difficult to assault. Better to draw them out.

Where better than between Asadabad and their base?

***

Mohammed shook his head. It was day five. Nothing. Had they been spotted? Had the assassination been called off? Delayed? He suppressed his grin. Tony wore a *burqa* today. Few Afghan women combined Tony's height and heft. But assassins focused on targets, not bystanders.

He led toward school. His loose stride affected someone bent on business. Tony, thirty paces behind, mimed a feminine tread, practised imperfectly in the garden. The motorcycle flow was unremarkable. Most pairs of riders were familiar.

A hundred yards ahead, an unfamiliar pair approached unhurriedly. The hair on his neck stiffened. The engine's coarse throat spat slow, too slow for a dirt bike intent on getting somewhere. As it passed, he stooped as if to remove a pebble from his sandal. A quick peek over his shoulder caught the pillion passenger's sidewise glance marking Farikhta, his mouth contorted in a sneer.

Rising, he snatched a second look beneath his arm. Tony's pace had picked up. Mohammed strode on. Behind, the marble throated cycle u-turned. The rattle closed, winding down.

Mohammed stooped, flashed a peek beneath his arm, hands once more toying with his troublesome sandal. His breath stopped. Praise Allah. Farikhta's pace was steady, eyes lowered. Ghorzang's eyes were on his feet. Tony closed swiftly, flanking to the left, right hand already in the *burqa* sleeve.

The engine burped down five paces ahead of Farikhta, six behind Mohammed. The tail-gunner dismounted and drew a Tokarev unhurriedly from his belt. He ignored the local tending his sandal.

Mohammed rose, as if to saunter on, knowing the assassin's eyes needed to fix on his targets. The Tokarev's barrel rose.

"Now!" Mohammed turned.

Farikhta's Beretta spat first. Her shot struck the assassin's shoulder, spinning him. Three following shots cracked simultaneously, Ghorzang's missing, Mohammed's hitting his chest, Tony's his right side, knocking him off his feet, dead or dying.

The motorcyclist's engine revved. Mohammed lunged for the biker's collar, pulled him from his seat and threw him to his back. His pistol centred between the assassin's eyes.

"*Asalaamu alaikum.*"

"Crusader, American dog! You dare greet me as a Muslim!"

"You know better. We reply '*Wa alaikum salaam.*' Is politeness too much between Muslims? I'm no crusader."

The prisoner scowled. "If you're a believer, what is your name?'

"My name is Mohammed Yousf. Yours?"

"I am Salaar. You speak our language. You're Pukhtun?"

"Close enough. What was your friend's name?"

"Haji Faqeer. Peace on him! You're no Muslim. You're an enemy. You killed Haji and interfered. Why fight against brethren? You are apostate, *kaafir* I think."

"No. I don't murder teachers and I don't obey some *ghalat mullah.*" The words 'false mullah' were deliberate.

Salaar's mouth twisted to a snarl. "Perhaps today you'll find out whether you're a real believer or *kaafir.*"

"Ah, we're in danger? Will you harm us? Will friends rescue you?" He laughed and turned away feigning disinterest.

"If I die today I'll be *shahid,* a martyr who gains paradise. You won't." Salaar wore a sneer.

He turned back. "So I'm to die today? Let's see what happens." The prisoner clenched his teeth.

***

Mohammed handed Salaar off to Tony. "Let's face him away from the *bazar.*"

He followed Montoya's eyes roving across the square, doubtless searching for someone who'd fixed directly on Farikhta as the motorcycle approached. Witnesses to the assassination attempt had gone back to their shopping. Montoya's gaze settled on a cleanshaven man at a tea shop table opposite.

Montoya's muttered orders came over his ear bud. "Subject sitting alone. Spice shop. Seal exits. Hold positions. I'll take him."

As Montoya sauntered nonchalantly across the square, his eyes swept by Mohammed's prisoner. At a fruit stall adjacent to the spice shop, he lingered over apricots and examined early apples. Unnoticed, he slipped over to the target's table, sat and faced him. The sitter stiffened, only to meet the hooded eyes of an unsmiling stranger. Montoya motioned. The target's shoulders slumped. Montoya's HK 23 was directed into his midsection. The barrel prompted the prisoner up and toward the northwest corner of the square. Three platoon members fell in to flanked them.

Mohammed's curiosity peaked. He knew the names, but not the faces of Kunar's leaders. Who had Montoya taken?

***

Mohammed muttered an instruction to Tony. Salaar hadn't witnessed Montoya's capture. Tony blindfolded Salaar.

He led his prisoner toward Montoya's group. When he reached Montoya he removed Salaar's blindfold and observed. Salaar's eyes widened at Montoya's detainee and immediately fell.

Montoya saw it. "Diagnosis?"

Mohammed nodded. "Maybe a commander watching his hit-men do their work?"

"Makes sense. Saw you chatting your biker up. Anything?"

"Name's Salaar. Gave something away. Not sure what. Thinks he might be off to paradise. I'm destined for a hotter location, maybe today. Yours..?"

"Nothing yet. Have a go at him. Something maybe dovetails. He turned away fast when he saw the assassination was blown. On his phone double quick, bit of a smile."

"Fits." He wouldn't be smiling unless... "Keep Salaar out of earshot. I'll work on rattling your mystery man's chain."

He approached the older man. "*Asalaamu alaikum.* I'm Mohammed. Your name?"

The older man studied him. "My name is unimportant. Nawaz Shahid will do."

"You say '*shahid.*' But you aren't a martyr yet. Will death come soon?"

Silence.

"Salaar over there said your friends will ambush us as we return to base. When they recognize you, won't they call off their attack?"

Nawaz's faced paled. "You lie. He knows nothing."

"Knows nothing? He doesn't, but you do? He suggested we tie you to the hood of our lead vehicle where everyone will see you coming."

"Salaar is an idiot. Tie him to the vehicle!"

He returned to Montoya. "Easier than expected. They know each other. Your guy is boss man. I lied. Told him Salaar said we'd be ambushed going back. He didn't deny it. I suggested Salaar wanted your guy on our point vehicle's hood. What do you think? Perching one of theirs on a lead hood might make hostiles hesitate? You going to talk to base?"

"Have to. Hmm. On the lead hood...? That sounds like fun. The rest makes sense. Hit us heading back, on a victory lap. If they're smart enough to prepare a backup, maybe they're even counting on us calling in the cavalry from the base? If that's the plan, they'll be ready on two separate fronts."

"It's a solid plan."

Montoya contacted base and relayed Command's words aloud. "Assume they're watching. Our copters go off eastwards in twenty minutes, heading across the line out of sight ..."

Montoya rang off scowling. "We'll be on our own no more than three minutes ..."

"So?"

"I don't trust the SOB. We could be cut to pieces. It's *our* intelligence, and we're left to drive ourselves into an ambush. Sounds fair doesn't it. Classic FUBAR. Okay. Martyr on the hood. Pass the word. Get them ready."

Mohammed gathered the men. "Looks like some real action. Full battle rattle. Sit Shahid – yes, this one – on the lead hood. Tie each foot to an end of the bumper, arms back to side mirrors. Let him sit upright. If it's an ambush, *his* ambush, let him enjoy it."

He prepared his med pack. His body armour and helmet were uncomfortable, hot and heavy, his stomach near his ankles. His platoon mates were a mile high, necks tense, breathing fast, tongues licking lips. The platoon's hood ornament drew mocking grins.

•••

Inside the lead Humvee, Mohammed's eyes scanned across the river for anomalies. Shahid blocked his forward view. The seats were uncomfortable. Behind him, their 50 cal gunner's feet, just below nose level, smelled like decaying meat. In the back, Salaar sat low, sweating, fidgeting.

His hands trembled. The deceptively tough looking Humvees were targets, traps when IED's exploded under them or RPG's hit weak spots. He wanted his feet on the ground. They crawled ahead. Was it slow enough? Had they been spotted? They left FOB Rooster Road and turned right over the Marawara bridge crossing the Kunar River. At Marah Warah village, they would slow to turn east uphill toward base, onto the Kunar-Bajaur road. It was the point of maximum danger.

Chapter 18

Marah Warah

The Colonel ordered the base helicopters to make ready, then quickly assembled two platoons. "Looks like an imminent situation in Marah Warah below. Copters will take you over the ridge Pak side. Montoya's platoon is returning from A'bad with prisoners. They may have trouble. I'm in radio contact with them. If and when they hit trouble I'll bring you in. Questions? Captain?"

"What's the timing Colonel?"

"You'll be there in plenty of time. Montoya may have his hands full for a few minutes."

He grunted a chuckle to himself. Maybe a difference between three and six or seven minutes could teach Montoya and his platoon a lesson.

***

Field Commander, Salafi Taliban,
Kunar

His son met death in *Amriki* custody. Today he would avenge Omar. The crusaders would count their dead. His fingers whitened on his weapon. The men wouldn't see them twitch. The assassination's failure was regrettable. But the failure beckoned the invaders. Emir

Jan had planned well. Americans *had* guarded the teacher. They wouldn't suspect... Why hadn't the Emir called again?

He'd taken precautions. No word would come from Marah Warah village. He had two throats slit in the past month. Remaining villagers were cowed. Two wolves, his scouts, watched the base above. Helicopters headed away, to the northeast. He prayed they didn't carry too many away from the deaths his men would grant them when they drove down the road to help the ambushed Asadabad column.

A growing murmur amongst his men drew his attention toward four vehicles crossing the bridge below. He signalled for quiet and fingered the first detonator. Two village boys played with a soccer ball near the IED. They would be martyred. *Enshaallah.*

But... Why were the vehicles moving so slowly? His men's discipline, their voices... What? His breath stopped. His eyes followed his fighters' to a clean-shaven man astride the lead vehicle's hood. His hands and ankles tied? He stared as the vehicles closed to two hundred and fifty yards. The man on the hood..!

An elapid hiss escaped his lips. He sucked in his breath through clenched teeth. "Ignore our Emir. Fire on my signal. Kill them even if the leader is martyred."

***

Mohammed's throat tightened. Nawaz Shahid tore at his ropes. Ahead a villager pulled two boys back into the village, running, abandoning a soccer ball. Mohammed shouted into his Falcon. "Stop! Pull over! Right shoulder! Right shoulder!"

The platoon spilled from the Humvees looking uphill. Nothing. Quiet. The river was behind them. Nothing there. His gunner looked down at him, palms upturned.

He signalled to cut engines. He fingered his M4 and scanned the slope. Silence. Was he wrong? The kids. No birds! "Everybody out!

Cover! Cover!" He screamed to Montoya and sprinted to the road's shoulder below the Humvee.

As he hit the ground his ears exploded. Forty yards ahead the road erupted. Dust and dirt blinded him, chunks of road and rock pelted down. His 50 cal gunner, blown off his feet, crawled and bellied to find cover. Montoya's 50 began firing uphill then quickly jammed. Deafening AK47 fire rattled off metal. Rounds struck beneath the Hummers kicking up more dust into his eyes.

"Incoming! Incoming!"

The tail Humvee blew. Flames shot into the sky. An RPG hissed overhead blasting into the river. Shouts.

"Down! Down!"

He pushed his face into the dirt, pulling his helmet into his shoulders. The whoosh of the RPG crashed into his protecting Hummer. Another RPG. Then another. Metal screamed and tore. Man-sized vehicle pieces blew past overhead, clanged off river boulders behind, hissing hell as they hit the water. He raised his head. Bullets threw shards of stone across his forehead. Dirt kicked up into his eyes. Incoming and return fire deafened him. America's Special Forces taught locals these tactics in the Soviet war. Massive incoming fire, controlled, short bursts, well directed, all around. Heavy fire first. Then flanking attempts.

He yelled to Tony on SAW "Hold off auto!" Tony kept the M249g on short bursts. Montoya caught his eyes and pointed to both flanks. Something hissed into the ground beneath the second Hummer, lifting it off the ground. The blast tore Tony's helmet off and threw him into the open. He was trying to sit up.

Mohammed sprinted toward him. Montoya converged from Tony's far side. An RPG cracked above Montoya, crushing him face down into the dirt beside Tony. An axe blow into his Kevlar jacket dropped Mohammed mid-stride. He fell beside an unconscious Montoya. Rounds flew by his ears, smacking the ground. No blood. Ribs screaming. No cover. A bullet whizzed past his right eye. He took Tony's ankle in one hand, Montoya's collar in the other and pulled. Pain ripped his ribs beneath the IOTV Kevlar. *Pull. Again. Allah, help me.* Dust sprayed into his eyes from rounds hitting all round. *Cover. Pull. Cover. Thank God.* Spikes drove into his chest. He ripped his med pack open.

Don't even think you're dying, Chris. Allah, help me! Help me! Anti-hemo sponges. Tony. Sponge. Shoulder. Marcaine block. Pulp. Tourniquet. Higher. Higher. Chris. Breathe. Base copters! *Where are they!*

His ear went to Montoya's mouth, listening for breath. Tony groaned, shocked, shuddering. His own hands trembled. Two down. Where were their reinforcements? A scream. "Incoming!" The ground heaved. He tasted the dirt. The RPG erupted, bucked the Humvee into the air. It crashed down in place. Another RPG hissed. A tank ruptured. The heat, his face. Fire. More incoming – close! He leapt on top of Tony and Chris. Something cracked above and behind him.

His hands covered his ears. No sound. What happened? Were his eyes closed? Open? He couldn't focus. A smell, something burning. His head wouldn't turn? From the corner of his eye someone ran toward him. Vargas? Vargas's mouth was moving. No sound.

He tried to push himself off Tony and Chris. His arms wouldn't work. His finger touched the back of his neck and returned black and red. Burning? Vargas's face lowered into view, at his side. His hand ... tweezers? Aaghh! Burning – neck. The tweezers showed him a smoking, bloody metal shard. Arms pulled him off Montoya and Tony. Tony's mouth, groaning, swearing, again, again. Hands held his face into the dirt. He couldn't roll his body over. Vargas? Vargas's face again appeared beside his, mouthing words – SHRAPNEL! YOU! BAGRAM!

The corner of his eye caught Vargas starting IVs, monitoring Montoya's breathing. Tony continued to curse. Vargas injected him. Mohammed shook, somehow cold.

The sound of his own voice returned, distant, slurred. A thick tongue, not his own, was in his mouth. "Montoya – eyes moving? Neck brace? Tony? Loosen tourniq..."

RPG explosions stopped. Heavy firing. Close. Thunder? Copters! Autofire masking copters. Two of our platoons, high, flanking? Fire from below, picked off from above. He needed to warn them: they'll try, through us to the river!

The M249g pulsed at 650rpm and cut down two attackers rushing toward them.

More copters. Two. Above. Who?

***

A dust storm from blade wash obscured them. Second platoon Charlie company's Blackhawk UH60 was above, twenty feet up, taking fire. A Blue Max A64 Apache chase copter covered. Mohammed's peripheral vision caught someone roping down.

Syringe! "No!" His neck shattered pain as his hand warded the injection off. "No. Not yet. Not yet. No more meds."

Vargas recapped. Mohammed's eyes closed. He listened. Bagram. Must stay alert. He could hear some of the words.

"The neck and the shoulder will need surgery. The captain … unconscious since he was hit?"

"Yes. The RPG hit close. Chief, our medic – the neck – covered the two wounded during the RPG attack. Took out one piece of hot shrapnel. Second piece still embedded. Lucky. Maybe bounced off his helmet. Used tweezers. He's our top D. How long to Bagram?"

"Fifty minutes, tops."

***

Hands rolled Mohammed to his side, then to the stretcher face down. He gasped as his stretcher met the UH 60's floor. Thank God for the vest. Ribs broken?

"Go! Three wounded. Radio ahead. Double time."

"Montoya?" He heard Tony moaning, swearing.

"Still with us" said the chopper medic.

"Bagram, Bagram. Dustoff inbound. Count three stretchers. Confirm three. One, query, blast TBI, unconscious; Two, GS, ortho shoulder, conscious; Three, query, blast concussion, conscious. Neck, embedded shrapnel, burns, query ribs?"

Mohammed drifted in and out of black. The noise... helicopter. Someone muttered to him. He couldn't make out the words.

Chapter 19

Craig O.R.

The neurosurgeon met the first stretcher at the entrance, muttering into his PDA.

"Captain C Montoya presenting ... blast injuries, unconscious ... distal shrapnel penetration, cerebellar base, blood mixed with clear fluid exiting wound. Query ICH? Left front temporal contusion. Eyes symmetrical, pupils reactive. Chest clear. Competent bilateral Babinski."

He signalled the surgical group to prepare. Montoya's gurney rushed toward radiology for a CT. Mohammed's and Tony's trailed.

Lt Sharon Verity headed the OR staff. She prepped her team for Dr Randy McAllister's surgery on Montoya. McCallister laid it out.

"Face him down. Rebound left temporal bleed. Penetration wound impinging the cerebellar dura. Penetration first. We'll burr hole and deal with the bleed next. Let's go ..."

***

Outside the OR Mohammed groaned, shaking at the fire in the nape of his neck. He shooed away the injection. "Not yet!"

"It'll stop the pain, soldier."

"No. Montoya... Captain... my patient. Surgeon?"

"Our neurosurgeon? Name's McAllister. Why're you asking?"

"When he's finished Montoya. I need ... speak."

"Sorry buddy, it's against –"

"Please. I have to... meds. Neck's burning. First... speak to Dr –"

"*McCallister.* I can't make that decision."

Frustration energized his voice. "Get me... McCall..! I'm Captain's medic. Now or I'll go ... myself!"

"You can't do that."

He heard his voice snarl. "Get me McCallister or someone who can!"

"Okay. Okay, soldier. First, your CT scan. I'll get our OR Head Nurse."

***

A frowning Lt Sharon Verity stood outside the OR vestibule. She'd been on her feet fifteen hours.

"So, a pain in the butt. Who is he? Looks like a local."

"Drago says he's ours. SOF 18D. Covered a couple of his wounded against RPG rounds. Not local. Comes from your home town."

Sharon shrugged. His scan was up. The exposed shrapnel sat between C4 and C5, barely missing spinal column impingement. With care, no complications. Neurosurgery would see him next. Orthopods already worked on Mitchell.

McAllister made short work of Montoya, cleared the OR, scrubbed and regloved.

Sharon readied the team for the second patient. Her pre-surgical routine of withdrawing unobserved to vomit, shiver and shake went unnoticed. Her sobriquet, Gibraltar, marked her deception's success. Three years ago she left stateside surgical nursing. She wanted testing service but underestimated the test. Young soldiers arrived mangled, monstrously altered, in pieces. She thanked God the young dark skinned man on the operating table remained whole.

She looked at him again. Strange, something familiar...

"I'm told you want to talk to Dr McCallister. That's not protocol. You'll need morphine before he sees you."

He rolled to his side and met her eyes. "Lieutenant, Ma'am Montoya, my Captain... I'm his medic. TBI?"

"Yes."

"Please, I want your neuro... inject etanercept..."

"Pardon me. You..?"

He grimaced and tried to rise. "No. Wait. Don't try to get up. I'll wheel you in to see him myself."

She delivered him to an already gowned and masked McCallister. "Your next patient – 18D. Says he needs to speak with you about his Captain."

"Son, I'm Dr McCallister. You're a medic. We have a TBI protocol. You know about post-op care for TBIs?"

"Still unconscious?"

"Yes. But ..."

The young man gritted his teeth."No time. I'm ... medic. Your protocol ... cool head ... reverse Trendelenburg." Mohammed fought to open his eyes fully. "Before that ...enbrel into Batson's plexus, between C6 and C7... then *Trendelenburg* five minutes. Same ... every twelve hours until inflammatory markers stabilize ... Pupils? Babinski?"

McCallister listened mouth open. He hesitated ... "Good bilateral Babinski ... Protocol is *reverse* Trendelenburg."

Mohammed's neck muscles tightened. His fixed glare caught McCallister wide-eyed. "After enbrel, *Trendelenburg* five minutes – *after that your protocol.*"

"You know enbrel is for arthritis... You're not a neurosurgeon?"

He heard his voice rise. "No. *My Captain! My patient! Enbrel!*"

McCallister hesitated, then nodded with a slight grin.

Mohammed's tongue wouldn't work. "Now please, fent... fentanyl."

McCallister signalled her. Sharon injected him.

***

"Bossy bugger" McCallister said quietly. "Who the hell is he. Sharon?"

"Let's see the chart... Oh Lord love a duck! No wonder he's familiar. He's the son of Denver surgeons I knew. Ali and Ayesha Karram. I was assistant head, Surgical Nursing. Our patient is Mohammed. He'd come in with them to watch surgeries. Haven't seen him for years. He'd be through med school by now."

McAllister reflected as he worked. Enbrel was an anti-inflammatory used for arthritis. While it wasn't TBI protocol it made sense. Crippling TBI damage came from brain inflammation. Somewhere a research piece touted enbrel injection into the cerebrospinal venous system, Batson's Plexus. True, enbrel mitigated neuroinflammation. Wasn't it for Alzheimers' patients?

"Sharon, you ready to go? Bow out if you want."

"No. I'm good."

McAllister chatted as he worked. "A California researcher – name escapes me – worked on neuroinflammation. It's a killer with TBIs. Enbrel might help. Problem is the BBB."

"What do you mean?" Sharon asked.

"Enbrel molecules are giants. The blood, brain barrier is tight – prevents big molecules getting to the inflammation. The researcher found the neck injection followed by the five minutes in Trendelenburg reduced inflammation."

Sharon's brow framed a question above her mask. "Mohammed thinks it will help?"

"Maybe it's for arthritis" McCallister said

"Oh sure" her eyes smiled above her mask.

"You must be bagged. But if you can, give me a hand with Montoya's injection. After the injection we use standard Trendelenburg for five minutes. We'll follow with our protocol after that

– cooling, reverse Trendelenburg. Then, since you know his parents, please set up a call to them. We owe them that."

Sharon nodded and smiled beneath under her mask.

***

Ali looked at his watch ... 7am Mountain Standard Time on a lazy Saturday. He'd wound the old desk clock to Kabul time, 21 hours. Ayesha yawned aloud from bed. He turned off his electric toothbrush just as the house phone rang. He frowned, curious. Who amongst hospital staff would call at this hour of the Sabbath? The private house phone?

"Dr. Karram?" the voice asked over line crackle.

He suppressed his testiness. "Yes. Who's calling please?" The voice... I've heard...

"Ali, it's Sharon Verity. I'm phoning from Bagram Air Force Base Hospital. We're phoning about Mohammed. He's been injured. Dr. McAllister is our neurosurgeon. May I put him on?"

Ali lowered himself to the bathroom floor. His breath stopped... The phone shook in his hand. A neurosurgeon!

"Dr Karram?"

"Sharon! Yes. I remember. You're in Afghanistan? It's been so long. Thank you for calling. I'm grateful you're with him. I'll get Ayesha."

Ayesha, alerted by the ring and Ali's tone, had already picked up.

"Go ahead please. Ayesha is on with me."

"Please forgive my informality, Ali and Ayesha. It's Randy. Our team just operated on Mohammed ... Sharon can detail what happened.

Ali waited until McAllister finished. "Sharon, can you tell us..?"

Sharon's voice was calm. "His platoon was in a firefight. He's something of a hero. He covered two of his wounded against incoming rocket propelled grenades."

Ayesha gulped her question. "His injuries aren't going to cause permanent..? I know I shouldn't ask..."

"Early days" McCallister said. "His hearing was affected, temporarily at a guess. He was lucky with the shrapnel. It left neck burns that'll be pretty painful for a while and may leave some scars. He was disoriented when he arrived, not so much that he forgot his wounded." Ali heard McAllister's quiet chuckle.

"How so?"

"His captain came in with neurological blast trauma – loss of consciousness, penetration and percussive wave injury. Your son directed an off-protocol post-op treatment."

Ayesha broke in. "He trained with an emergency doc in Phoenix. They covered some research for TBIs. I hope he didn't presume –"

"No, no, he wasn't out of line. Sharon will update you when he wakes. She's watching him."

Ali thanked them. Ayesha shook, fumbling the bedside phone into its cradle through blurred eyes. Ali's hand went to her cheek. "He's in good hands. Sharon is there when he wakes. He'll be all right. *Inshaallah.*"

She responded through clenched teeth. "He came close. Let's be sure. Please, let's not tell the girls until we are."

***

Lieutenant Verity watched wearily. After eighteen hours in the Operating Theatre and a further three at bedside she nodded off.

She jerked awake to a fleeting movement in his face. His eyes tried to open, then stilled. Seconds later, more flutters.

She spoke softly. "You're in Bagram, Mohammed. You've been injured. No need to talk. You're sedated. Open and close your eyes twice if you understand."

Groggily, his eyelids opened and closed twice. She kissed his forehead bandages. She sent her newest recruit to fetch McAllister and ran to communications. She could tell the Karrams he was awake. The next day, they'd send him on to Germany's Landstuhl.

Fighting for alertness, Mohammed's eyes met McAllister's.

"Chris? Montoya?"

"I injected Chris with 8mg of etanercept – enbrel – post-op, six hours ago. For his arthritis."

"Trendelenburg?"

McCallister nodded. "With every injection."

"Same" Mohammed said. "Twelve hours post op."

"Okay kid."

Chapter 20

Strangers

Shahay felt the sun's warmth. She scarcely noticed her leg on the walk to Pashat. The buzz of the crowded market energized her. Colourful fruit stalls competed with the even more brilliant *partoog-kameez* of young girls. Faridun and Sakhi accompanied the household women. They'd walked on ahead. She was alone with Zarhawar, her boy-man who guarded her for the second time. He straggled along behind, aiming his AK at a field mouse running across their path, trying to catch a butterfly in his hand. Now he stopped to remove a pebble from his sandal. She waited, musing.

She wouldn't scold him just now. Later, she'd remind him never to put his rifle aside when he guarded. No matter. The *qila* gates were near, left open for them. Bees buzzed over the blossoms of the blackberry bushes bordering the field corn. Corn sheaves rustled in... What breeze... Why?

She turned and froze. A scream died in her throat, her hand on her knife.

A yellow-beard's hand sealed Zarhawar's mouth, a blade at his windpipe. Squirming from steel's death, her son trembled, eyes bulging. A movement behind her. She spun into a crouch. A barrel was pointed into her chest. A finger at the stranger's lips warned silence. The stranger fixed his eyes on hers. His *Pukhto* was foreign.

156

He pointed. "Move, or your son will die."

She swallowed her fear. Zarhawar mustn't see it. She glanced toward the *qila*. The towers were unmanned. She clenched her teeth. Her hand left her knife's hilt. She walked as the foreigner directed, along a sunken path through high corn stalks, invisible to *qila* and village. Two Afghans fell in ahead. The second foreigner picked up Zarhawar's weapon. The village, already behind, was screened by a copse of walnut trees.

A dog's urgent bark carried on the wind. Two chuffs dipped and swirled above them.

***

Faridun couldn't find his cousin. The gate was open. He closed it and went to find his father.

"Zarhawar walked behind with *thror*, my aunt. Where is he?"

"Isn't he in the *kor*?"

"No. I left the gate open for them They followed us. I looked in the fields. They aren't there."

Ayub ran to *baba*. "Shahay and Zarhawar haven't returned. Faridun, run to Baseer's *qila*. Ask Bangar to bring his Toyota. We'll drive to Pashat in case she returned to the market." They scanned the Pashat market, found nothing, and informed the Khan.

***

Mehmoud fixed his lips in granite. He would not surrender to panic. He couldn't meet Bibi's eyes. Three days ago, an official from Khar reported rumours of roaming men... a woman thought she'd seen strangers. Ghosts. Mere rumours. He thought little of rumours. What action could he have taken? Ayub's and Sakhi's impatience, together with the continuous arrival of armed villagers, discomposed him. Did *they* know where to look? By now, they were one hundred.

Time was vital. How much time was already lost? An hour? He spoke to the impromptu *lashkar*.

"They weren't taken toward Pashat, nor to any settled area. They can't use roads. Ayub, Shakhi, take half the men to the north's trails. I'll lead the rest due west through Mamund lands toward the mountains."

Ayub led. Racing, long striding northwest, through five, then ten miles, sweating, confused, furious. Fifty odd men were too cumbersome, too slow. He assembled them at a nexus of trails. "We're too many. There are many paths to follow." He divided them into five groups, setting each ten on separate routes. He was left with Bangar, Itbar and Sakhi. "Come!"

At each village, he enquired. Nothing. No one had seen her. The dogs hadn't barked. Nothing was missing to signal thieving passersby. His legs grew heavy. When at last darkness forced their halt, he thanked the village *malik* for *hujra* cots.

***

The Afghans avoided Shahay's stolen glances. They weren't her captors. They knew what kidnapping a woman meant, but were cowed by the two others, men who smelled of sweat and filth. She felt her captors' stinking eyes pollute her beneath her garments. A shiver ran through her. She wanted to retch but could not. Zarhawar mustn't see fear. She was his guide. If they survived, *enshaallah*, he couldn't be tormented by cowardice. To endure was to live.

***

Their Afghan guides, Patman and his son Nangial, led toward the large trees on the mountainside. The foreigners spoke between themselves. Patman, who translated, understood their words too well. The tall man and the bearded one walked directly behind him.

"First, we'll find out what she knows. Then we'll have fun with the bitch."

***

Coarse laughter shook in her ears. She shivered. Where were people? Her wounded leg ached. She masked her limp. They'd walked swiftly for hours skirting villages, aiming for tree cover and mountains. Scents of roasting dodai and chicken wafted from the village kitchens as they passed. People must be near. But where?

Her ears picked up a distant dog's greeting. There! Someone was with it. An old woman with a basket stooping, gathering beneath walnut trees. See us! See me! Tell others!

Through lowland trees they ascended onto the mountain's chir-covered talus. A further fifteen hundred meters up she inhaled the turpentine of pines. Her eyes rose to an eagle soaring high above, flat winged, riding free in mountain currents, peering down. A small flurry of green and blue chuffs curled, swooped and turned.

***

Predawn's cold seeped into Ayub's legs. He rose before dawn, jostled Sakhi and others and mumbled words of prayer. The sky's stars were lost to a bluing light. The *malik* brought eggs, *dodai* and tea and wished them well.

He remained impassive at each village. His fists strangled his rifle, wringing life from it. Nothing. Late in the day, a glimmer.

"Our dog barked yesterday late in the afternoon as though someone passed. We didn't see. But an old widow, in Kaga village beyond, she's out with her dog each day. If your sister's come this way, she'll know."

Ayub moved to a fast trot. An old woman, a dog. Kaga. If only she'd seen. Even a glimpse. Another darkness was coming. Shahay with strangers. Alone with Zarhawar.

***

A Widow

She grew Kaga's sweetest squash, a token of her gratitude for her brother. His kindness welcomed her when she was widowed and left alone. The afternoon sun warmed her garden. *Lugay*, Smoke, lay beside her in the sun, eyes closed, stretched out against the black earth, running on his side, paws flicking his stride, small yelps signalling his hunt. She weeded the bed behind the *qila*. Smoke's head rose, looking south east. A greeting wuffed from his throat. She raised her head, wiped her brow and took note. Strange, yesterday a group of armed men. Today another. Hunters?

"*Salaam. Starey me she.*" Good. Their greeting was polite.

"*Salaamat osey.*"

"Please, we come in search of someone who may have passed this way, our sister from the house of Mehmoud in Batmalai. Have you seen a woman?"

"Yes, yesterday. Her eyes looked toward me. I was below the walnut trees." She pointed. "There. You see. I gathered walnuts there."

Ayub murmured quickly. "Who was with her, please?"

"Four men and a boy. They didn't see me. She did. She held my eyes. I didn't know what she wished."

"Were the men armed? Did you know them?"

"The men? Armed? Yes. I didn't know them. Two were Afghans. The other two ... foreign I think. One was tall, the other's beard was light, like the falling sun. They walked quickly, following the old path. It sweeps up into mountain slopes south west and then joins the ridge path toward Asadabad."

"We are grateful to you, daughter of Kaga. I am son of Mehmoud Prraang. May Allah favour you for your help."

Chapter 21

Landstuhl

Mohammed wiped away the eye jam glueing his lids. Morning? Where was he? He shook his head, remembering, trying to fling grogginess out through his ears. His teeth ground together by themselves. His neck... white hot. Someone groaned down the hall. His eyes closed again, shutting out the fluorescent light that made them ache.

Outside a burble of people conversed. The voices? No. He started to sit up and stopped himself. Stupid! How could..? He opened his mouth to shout at them to quiet down but hesitated, listening closely again. Crazy. The voices..? Damned drugs making him dopey.

The door... His eyes shot open.

"What're you doing here? Where'd you come from? How did you know —"

His mother ignored the question, walked over to his bed with open arms, held and kissed him. His father surrounded Mohammed's shoulders.

"Ooooh! Careful."

"Sorry son. Serves you right for getting hurt and frightening us half to death."

His mother's eyebrows arched. "Ali!"

"Sorry for scaring you, Mom." Even a weak smile hurt.

They sat on an empty bed next to his. His lungs fully exhaled into the familiar scents of Dettol's pine oil and alcohol. His mother wore a smile below her forehead's worry. "It was spur of the moment. We didn't forewarn you in case our flight changed. We flew Lufthansa direct."

His father smiled. "Wanted to see you were okay. Your nurse, Miss Taylor? She asked us to keep the visit short. We'll come back later. Meantime, what's this about your friends? She says you're concerned about your captain? Chris is it?"

"Yes. Chris Montoya. TBI. You heard about him? Have to ask Judy Taylor how he's doing. Best guess is he'll need rehab. Dad, if it's extensive can we ... can we help him?"

Ali didn't hesitate. "Okay son. If you don't think they'll do enough at Walter Reed. Denver's Craig is first rate. Their rehab for TBIs is up in Colorado Springs. Let us worry about that for now."

"How'd you find out..?"

"Sharon Verity phoned from Bagram."

***

Mohammed punched the call button when they left.

"Judy, for now please hold the meds. Words get confused. I'm jumpy. Maybe after they leave tonight..."

During their evening visit and now without fentanyl he fought scalding pulses from his neck. His eyes closed with each flash of fire. Words spilled out.

"How was I wounded?" He foreshortened the Marah Warah firefight.

"You were protecting teachers?"

"The teacher, Farikhta ... she was the sister of someone I helped on a mountain trail ..."

His voice broke recounting the deaths of two platoon friends. When he told of a woman, Shahay, wounded, an emergency surgery, travelling to her home, his eyes dropped to his lap. His father seemed to ignore the gesture. But he felt his mother's eyes boring into him at each further reference to Shahay.

"... Ayub invited me back to his father's *qila* to ensure his sister's recovery..." His mother remained silent. He was grateful.

They left for lunch, leaving him to his. He'd go back, damned neck or not. His thoughts drifted from the pain. Her mouth, eyes and face filled him. He dozed and dreamt... Shahay's eyes... frightened?

They returned after lunch. By late afternoon he was talked out, tired, hoarse and trembling. Judy saw them out. Fifteen minutes later she returned to inject pain meds. He fell into deep sleep.

Frank sprawled, gurgling, sinews of his neck askew, twitching, open arteries gushing. His arms were without strength, his hands wet with pieces of Barry's jelly brains. "Help me! Help!"

Judy came to settle him. "It's your meds."

He slept and dreamt again. She walked away. Turn around! Turn back! Where was she going? Why couldn't she hear? "Shahay! Watch!"

The cry echoed down the corridors.

***

Judy stood over him in the pre-dawn. He thrashed, eyes half open, amidst drenched sheets. He didn't notice her. His eyes closed again. She thought he'd dozed off. But he muttered, raised his voice, settled, raised it again then sat up, rubbing his eyes.

Judy was at his side. "Good. You're awake. You've had a rough night. Lots of shouting."

She hesitated. Both envelopes were marked 'Urgent'. One from a Sgt Vargas. The other came from Asadabad. She couldn't read the name... Mohammed was already unsteady. But *Urgent. Red ink.* She had to give them to him. Better now while his parents were here... in case...

She left the envelopes reluctantly, closed the door and walked toward the nurses' station. Anguished shouts blew from behind. "Judy! Judy!" She sprinted through the door.

His face was purple, eyes filled.

His voice broke. "Please, find my parents. Please hurry."

***

The Karrams breakfasted at the Pfeffermühle Restaurant. Freed from worry about Mohammed's condition, they'd left cellphones along with their worst fears at the hotel. He'd would be all right. In twelve hours they'd be on their return flight to Denver.

"Cheers. Bless Mohammed. Bless Judy and his doctors. More coffee?"

***

Judy tried their cell phones to no avail. She contacted their hotel. Breakfasting? Where? It was a short drive. She burst into the Pfeffermühle's dining room white faced. "I'm sorry. I tried your cells. It's Mohammed. When I left him to phone you... It's my fault. I gave him the messages. He fell apart. He's gone."

Ali rose from his chair. "Messages? Gone? What do you mean?"

"He's not in his bed. We couldn't find him in the hospital. He left you a note. I should have brought it with me. I'm sorry. It's by his bed."

She told the little she knew as they drove back. Messages, from a soldier named Vargas and from the sister of someone called Shahay. They read the note.

Shahay and her son are missing. I have to help find her.
M.

Ali looked at her. "Where would he go?"

Judy shook her head. "I don't know where it is exactly. He has to be heading back to his base."

Chapter 22

Dread

On the seven and a half hour C17 flight from Ramstein to Kabul he prayed. Voices of other passengers were noise. He prayed for God's mercy, for her life, for her safety, for her rescue, for Zarhawar. Who had taken her? He prayed it wasn't *takfiri*. They'd be angry for his contact with her family. It had to be them. Would they exchange her and Zarhawar for him?

A hand on his shoulder, a woman's. "Sergeant. You're shaking. Your wound's leaked into your dressing. Looks a mess. I'm a medic attached to the 327th. May I redress your wound? Do you need something? I have my pack."

"Thanks. I'm Mohammed. The shakes... coming off meds. A fentanyl patch?"

"Yep. I'll get it and some water. The dressing..?"

He hung his head. "Would you have some saline solution? I'm not up to debriding."

"I have saline solution. Your patch? Special Ops. 'Debriding'... you a medic too?"

He nodded. She looked concerned. "Mind my asking, flying out of Ramstein? Landstuhl didn't discharge you like this. What's going on?"

"I told the duty nurse I needed to walk around. It's... an emergency.

165

I have to get back."

"What emergency gets someone in your condition out of hospital?"

"It's a friend, she and her son. They're missing, probably kidnapped. I dressed and left. Told the gate I needed a stroll."

"God. I'm sorry."

"I need to get to my unit."

"Where are you posted?"

"Kunar. You?"

"Same. A'bad. Above it really, in the mountains."

"Please, your patch, 101st Airborne, tell me you're going to Monti."

"Yeah, we are. How did you –?"

"Can I hitch a ride?"

***

The CH-47F dropped him at 2am at Karzai. He thanked the medic and her CO.

Wakened by the heli's roar, Karzai's medical officer shook his hand. "You shouldn't be here. You look like a whipped dog. Landstuhl alerted us you might be coming our way. They're pissed... Vargas is leading your platoon looking for your friends. Her family has search parties out on the Bajauri side."

"Where are our guys? I'll catch up with them."

"God man, you're nuts. Your neck's affecting your brain. They've had a half day's start. You need sleep and meds."

"Right. Just give me their position and a communications guy. If they're searching, they're moving slowly. I haven't had a long mountain run since Denver. I'll get to them by first light."

"In the dark? Even if you're crazy, no. I'll put you under guard if I have to. There's another way."

"She's like family. Permission or not I'm..."

"Okay. Okay. I get it. You're insane. I'm tight with the CO at the A'bad base. He's got spare copters. You wouldn't make it 'til morning in the dark in any case. Barry owes me. I'll get him on the blower. If he can spare the bird we'll get you to Vargas's bunch by daybreak. They're in the trees. You'll have to rappel down. For now suck on this Fentanyl lolly and bunk down for the night. I'll wake you tomorrow before light."

***

"Vargas has his med pak" the base doc shouted over the thump of the blades. "You won't need yours. He knows you're on your way. Just don't fall when you rappel and break what's left of your ugly neck. The copter guys have your gloves. Here's a helmet and M4. Good luck, soldier."

He backed out of the UH 60 as the sun began to gild the tree tops below. The winch crewman directed. "We've dropped 175 feet of rope Sgt. As far as I can tell through the trees it's hitting the ground. We're as low as we can go. You know the drill – if the gloves get hot, slow down."

Half way down he took a deep breath. His arms and shoulders burned. A pitchfork stabbed into his ribs. Tree branches, deceptively soft from above, tore into and ripped away his neck's scabs as he scraped through. Twenty feet above ground, Vargas's shout refocused him.

"Mohammed, you look like something the cat dragged in. Get down before you fall down... Good to see. Jesus! Let me clean up whatever you call this thing that's supposed to support your head. Your dressing's hanging off the branch twenty feet up. Wound looks like raw hamburger."

"Never would have guessed. Feels like a wire brush worked on it for a half hour. Any Ty 3 and water? I'm out."

"Here's your water and pills. Sit still while I work... Ayub's bunch are converging from Kaga direction. A sighting had four men with a woman and boy coming east from there, following an old trail that came up into the hills. Shahay and her son should be between us and Ayub if they're still… Sorry."

Mohammed rose from his knees. "The neck feels better. Thanks. I'll take an energy bar if you have one. Let's go."

Chapter 23

Cedars

Nangial, Patman's son, saw them first. He pointed above to two giant deodar cedars framed against the lowering sun. Nangial turned to the foreigners.

"These are the great cedars. They mark the *ghar*, the cave we spoke of."

***

Shahay hid her fear. They posted the younger Afghan outside the cave to guard Zarhawar, trussed up with ankles roped and wrists tied behind. The foreigners lit a fire. They spoke through Patman. Their questions stupefied her and steeled her anger.

"Who is Mohammed Karram? What information did your father and brothers give him? Are your brothers and father *taliban*? Who's their leader?"

She remained silent. One held her upright by her hair. The other began with hard knuckled backhand slaps across cheeks and forehead. Her blood stained his knuckles. Fingers gripping her neck choked her to blackness. A hand pulled her by the hair up from darkness. Fists hammered her breasts, liver and stomach. The blows knocked her to her knees. Boots crunched into her stomach and chest. They asked about the *taliban* again and again. She spat blood and saliva at their feet. After two hours the foreigners directed the older Afghan to leave, posting him with the younger one outside. They spoke now between themselves in the foreign tongue.

***

At the cave's entrance Patman listened to their words.

"You were first with the little Afghan bitch. This cunt is mine. I'll soften her up for you. She'll be screaming in no time."

***

The yellow haired man left and returned, dragging Zarhawar. He held the knife to his throat, grinning. Sneering, he pointed into the cave's darkness. The tall one tore her up from the ground by her hair. His rifle jabbed violently into her buttocks and pressed into her back, forcing her into the cave's depths. Her hand hovered by her knife. She let it fall away. Zarhawar would die if she used it.

Dizzy from the beating, the dimming light of the cave's mouth lost, she could no longer see. In the black, she felt for the cave's wall. A sudden blow cracked into the back of her head, knocking her face first into the earth. She coughed to clear the dirt from her mouth. An iron knee pressed into her back. A hand removed her knife and threw it aside.

Powerful arms tore hers violently backwards and pinned them beneath knees. Hands bound ankles to wrists. A fist-sized rock pounded metal tent pegs into the cave's floor. Fingers gripped her hair and belt, lifted her into the air then slammed her onto her back. In her side something cracked. Blackness, then flashes of stars, replaced the darkness. Her breath wouldn't come.

Hands freed her wrists one by one and bound them to the pegs. She raised her feet to kick. A fist smashed into her solar plexus, emptying her lungs, forcing her to draw her knees up. Iron hands tore her knees apart. A body thrust between them to release her belt. A knife slit open her clothing.

She tried to breathe against the urgency and weight. The body became the man who beat her senseless and attacked her on her wedding night. Fingers held her jaw in a steel grip so she couldn't turn away. Foul breath burnt her nostrils. Her stomach started into her throat. She would vomit on him. It would be her weapon.

But her throat had closed. He rose, grinning. He stood, leering and suddenly fell on her again. His fingers bit savagely, tearing her haunches. He pulled her hips high. She bit into her lip and tasted its blood.

The yellow-haired man came outlined against the cave entrance's faint glow. She waited until he came close to kick at him. He feinted at her legs. His fist hammered into her cheek, stunning her. He caught her feet in mid-thrash. His fingers found her red healing wound. His left hand gripped her thigh, the thumb digging fiercely into her wound. Stars raced across her eyes. She clenched her teeth, silent save for a gasp. His knee rammed through hers, fetid breath suffocating her. His right hand tore her hair into a ball. He shouted sounds she did not understand into her face. "*Fukubich. Fukutiludye.*"

The pig's knife's was no longer at her boy's throat. Yellow-hair didn't leave. He took a cord from a pocket. She closed her eyes as it slipped around her neck and tightened. He snarled more angry foreign sounds.

Tighter. Choking. Eyes bursting. No breath. Darkness... Her eyes opened. He sneered down at her, kneeling over her chest, pushing into her throat, a stone in his hand threatening her teeth. Her hands didn't feel. Her body wasn't hers.

Filth with my blood. What of it? A mother dies for her cub. Feeling left her body. She listened to her breath, closed her eyes and saw Lema chase down the ram, grip it by the neck to kill, to eat. Wait... a growl?

The blackness of the cave's night gave way to morning's dull grey. They came and went. Each man choked her with the rope, sneering as blackness came, sniggering as her eyes opened. They left it round her neck.

They meant to strangle her with it.

***

Outside the cave Patman spoke quietly to his son. "They have paid us half. They're savages. She's a mother of our people. When they sleep, we leave." He hesitated, fearing the foreigners' wanton, skilled cruelty. Now he cupped his ear for the cave's words.

"She's been the best yet. Tough bitch. I can't make her scream. I worked that scar on her leg until she fainted. I wanted the sour cunt to squeal. We should celebrate this one. Any booze left? Good. Let's finish it. My turn next. Ha. Ha. We'll finish her and the kid in the morning after one more good go. I'm fucked out right now. A coin flip for who does her and the kid? Or just one each?"

"Good by me. Any whiskey left?"

***

Patman and Nangali moved into a shaft of afternoon sunlight streaming through the trees. Nangali cocked his ear. His father stood close by the cave's entrance. The laughter and chatter from within had stopped. Patman moved closer. Sounds of snoring spilled out.

Carefully they peered in, then moved away from the cave's entrance. They conversed, quietly animated. Nangali spoke for leaving immediately. Patman shook his head. "No."

***

Zarhawar tried again. He couldn't loosen his bonds. He'd heard sounds of the men fighting his mother. They shouted angry foreign sounds. He sneered. She wouldn't yield. His feet and wrists were too tightly bound. The knife in his belt was beyond his reach. Somehow he'd help her. At first, they'd been careful to check his ropes. But the stinking men's vigilance was weakening. He might have the chance. *Mor* was brave. Why did they move her away into the cave?

His ears caught stirring at the entrance. The Afghan grey beard crept quietly toward him, knife in his right hand. Zarhawar's back stiffened as he faced the knife. If he was to die by the blade he would not show fear. Why... the grey beard's finger was at his lips?

The blade cut his ropes. The finger went again to the greybeard's lips as he withdrew. Zarhawar stared after the retreating man. He twisted, slipped his knife from its sheath and cut the ropes at his ankles. His AK47 lay beside the snoring men. He crawled to it noiselessly. He could shoot them now while they slept. It would be easy. He raised the barrel, and hesitated. Who first? He wanted to see their blood. What if the tall one attacked while he shot yellow beard? He would wait. First, *mor...* She would know best how to kill them. He moved silently, cautiously through the gloom toward the back of the cave. It was black. He couldn't see, and didn't dare call out. His hand felt along the cave's walls, slowly, carefully lest his rifle scrape against the surface.

Don't stumble. Praise *Khuday*.

***

Rustling
Shahay's eyes opened. She raised her head. A shape came toward her, backlit by the glow of the fire's embers. She trembled, eyes filling, seeing, unable to believe. Her beloved *zoi* almost tripped over her outstretched legs. She heard her voice whisper, rasping, hoarse.

"I've waited for you."

"*Mor?* Are you whole?"

"Yes. Feel my face. Now, move to my hands. Cut the ropes."

She gasped as her wrists released from the pegs. Her hands were numb. She shook them, again, again... Slowly feeling returned, shoulder to bicep, elbow to wrist. She tried to curl her fingers. They wouldn't move. Again. Again. *Khuday* help me... Aah. Ahh. She rolled to face away from her son. He couldn't see in the black. He mustn't see her clothes.

She wiped her eyes, massaged her wrists and closed her *kameez* with her belt. Rolling to her knees, she balanced carefully and crawled uncertainly toward her knife. She stood, steadying herself again the cave wall, testing her battered body's weakness. Would her legs hold? She drew a deep breath, and another...

With each breath she straightened. She drew her shoulders back and the pain of breathing lessened. Her limbs were stronger. She felt a flood of feral energy. She shook herself, once, twice, placed her hands on Zarhawar's shoulders, put her mouth to his ear. They had lived.

She purred cautions, encouragement and instructions. He nodded. Her hands left his shoulders as she turned away, toward the cave's mouth.

She trembled with excitement. They would feel her teeth and claws. They would know *badal.* She would be on them before they woke to see her son freed.

She padded silently toward the snoring men, and moved their weapons beyond their reach. Licking her lips she readied her knife for the bearded one's throat. She motioned to Zarhawar to be ready for tall one.

The embers of the fire glimmered on the cave's grey recesses. A flame flickered momentarily in an intruding draft. She added two sticks to the coals. She stared open eyed at the sleeping men and contemplated. Tall-one stirred at the crackle of the first stick. She nodded to Zarhawar.

He prodded the waking man's leg with his rifle barrel, stepped back and waited to see the eyes open fully. The eyes moved frantically side to side, looking for a rifle, a pistol, a rock. He started up...

Zarhawar's first bullets slapped into knees. Screams. He retreated just beyond the victim's reach and fired into each shoulder. Blood and tissue splashed onto the cave's walls and ceiling. Screams gave way to helpless wailing.

"Aaahh. Aaahh ..."

At the first crack the bearded one sat bolt upright in front of Shahay. His hand shot blindly toward where his weapon had been. She slashed instantly, opening his right forearm to the bone. He recoiled but failed to guard his face. Her blade raked his left cheek staining his beard with spurting blood. She held his eyes and muttered.

"Please. Move again. My knife is ready. You're angry, yet you quake. Are you afraid?"

She moved behind the bloody beard. He held the hand of the slashed arm to his face, the other hand to his bloody arm, working to staunch the flow. Her blade pressed into his carotid, inviting his anger. She held back striking again. A deep snarl from her belly curled through her teeth.

Shahay rose and stepped away in one motion. Zarhawar fired short bursts into the sitting beard's knees, then into each shoulder. The beard blubbered roars as rounds smacked flesh and shattered bone. His screams gathered with his mate's and became wet moans. They wept.

She cocked her head, ignoring their foreign sounds. A growl, low, snarling, rippled from her throat. Her tongue found salty blood on her lips. A marbled purr rumbled from her belly. She scanned their bodies, trying to focus, trembling before prey.

Their hands ... *Their fingers and thumbs insulted and tortured her.* She emptied their packs, examining each item, found a whetstone and prepared her knife. Zarhawar stood near, waiting.

"Bring a limb of wood. This size." She made a circle with her fingers. Zarhawar hurried back. She placed the limb on the ground next to yellow-beard. His right hand lay limp at the end of his flaccid arm. She drew it onto the wood, ice-eyed, muttering, purring.

The prey man's eyes widened, loud shouts came from his mouth, screams...

"Yes, it is my bite. See how easily it takes your fingers, now your thumb. And your other hand, see how your blood spurts. Bright like a chicken's. Have you seen a chicken's blood?"

Zarhawar wobbled.

She wagged her chin. "Don't shiver. They fear as they should."

She turned now to tall one. "Ah you're shaking, wetting yourself. Easier if my foot's on your neck. There. Yes. Better I chop than saw. It's quicker and I've much to do. These fingers insulted me. My *charre* has punished them. Cruel thumbs aren't for you."

She gathered the offending pieces, studying them, cocking her head. *If they lived to speak of her?*

"Where is your tongue? No. Don't role away. If I force this limb deep into your throat, does that help? Ah, you gag but show your tongue. I'll pull it to make it easier to sever. You struggle so... Ah, there..."

Her eyes widened at the gurgled howls spewing from the blooded mouth. A strange sound. With her next stroke, gore surged into the beard of the second attacker.

"Your tongues won't speak of me."

She studied them. If they survived and their story were known, she would have to find them once more... She severed their ears. "If I learn of men without fingers and tongues, I'll find you. *You won't hear me come.*"

And what if people confused their wounds with those honoured by battle?

"People should know you." She severed their noses.

"Wherever you go, your dishonour will be seen."

***

Zarhawar's knees shook. His mother was drenched in blood, her eyes empty, her voice deep as a man's. She was a devil, a leopard *shaytan*. Her face was blank, covered in blood, her hair crimson. She licked the blood from her lips, eyes closed. A deep purring growl rattled from her lips. She licked again and blinked. Her finger pointed him to the cave opening.

He moved toward the cave's entrance, and hesitated, looking back. Her glare and point confirmed her command. He sat outside, with arms wrapping his knees.

***

She dropped to her knees beside the bloody beard.

"Yes, I kneel. You think for prayer? No. My claws have more work. *You cut through my clothing to dishonour me.* I'll do the same for you. Do you know we do this with vicious dogs? Ah there they are, your treasures. Are these pieces dear to you? Your eyes bulge? Are you frightened? Panicked? No need. It's quicker to pull as I cut. Is the noise that comes from your belly your terror? It won't help to squirm... You see. It's done."

Deaf to his howls, she discarded the pieces into the fire. From deep within she sounded a peeling snarl.

"Less work than fingers and thumbs. So easy. Once they were yours, now they roast. If your hunger grows, you may find your *saamaan* in the fire to enjoy one last time..."

She knelt again by tall one. He whimpered, screamed, and bellowed as her claws bit. She heard only a nearby voice mumbling amidst a leopard's snarls. Urine mixed with his blood. *Saamaan* into the fire.

"Thank you Allah for sending Lema to me."

She stood above them, licking her lips and hands, savouring the blood, her voice a hoarse rumble.

"Pity you must lie in your own blood and filth. You gloated over me, abusing me and my cub, meaning to slaughter us. Now you've felt our teeth and claws. Your blood has nourished me. I've repaid you. It's *badal*. You're welcome."

She took a pack for herself, another for Zarhawar, and led toward the settling sun. The M4 on her shoulder might reinforce Zarhawar's AK47, if needed. A poke dripping blood looped over her left shoulder.

Imperceptibly, the intensity she'd needed to survive began to evaporate. Within the hour, unnoticed, her energy began to wane. Her body trod on, foot on foot, its weakness seeping into her spirit. Her sense of foreboding grew. Sapped by the mountain's descending chill, trembling with pain and shock, her gait began to falter, her eyes to lose focus. From her mouth quick breaths pushed puffs of steam into the frosting air.

Drying blood caked and darkened, painting her head to toe, hair, face, clothing, feet and sandals. By her side, Zarhawar was cloaked in a layer of the cave's grime. They moved quietly, without talk.

***

Daylight was done. Ayub struck camp just into the tree line. The men ate hastily and divided into the gloom. Ayub and Sakhi looked for signs south west. Bangar led his friend Ahmad directly uphill, toward two sky high cedars, black giants outlined against a moonlit sky.

He recalled a distant remark about the trees. What was it? He mounted a small rise onto what seemed a path. He moved cautiously, low to the ground, peering first ahead, then at his feet to avoid dry twigs that might snap. The path ended a few feet ahead at a faintly glowing arched opening into the base of the cliffside. He dropped to one knee and signalled to Ahmad. He dared not breathe. Through the opening wavering light flickered orange against the inner cheeks of the cave's mouth. He sniffed. Burning wood. He cupped his hand to his ear. Unearthly, muted sounds. Animals?

Silently he crept nearer. Something, a half dried liquid, stuck to his sandal. In the moonlight, he found more stains in the earth. He dabbed and tasted. Blood. He signalled to Ahmad to cover. Barrel levelled, he entered quietly. The shapes of men, the backs of two huddled whimpering, moaning forms, surrounded a fire flickering onto walls stained blood-red and dripping with gore.

He fronted them and recoiled. Illuminated by dying flames, masks rose slowly to reveal mouths burbling blood, earless, nose-less. He sucked in breath. The masks sat above raw-meat shoulders extending to limp arms and hands without thumbs or fingers. His eyes took in blood-soaked *partoog* with butchered groins, and faces without noses, and earless heads. A choked groan from the bloodred face of the bearded man escaped a mouth with no tongue. He placed the muzzle of his rifle on the monster's chest. With his foot he drew the unmistakable outline of a woman and a smaller figure. The demon's chin motioned toward the entrance.

Now its eyes fixed on Bangar's. It lowered its forehead to the business end of his HK36. The eyes closed. Bangar pulled the trigger. A second creature, taller, offered his forehead and closed his eyes. Bangar used a second bullet.

He explored, added wood to the fire, dropped ropes from the back of the cave into the flames. He and Ahmad dug two shallow graves, tossed in the pegs and placed the bodies on them. They covered the dead with earth, rocks and pine staw leaving only their monstrous faces showing. Ahmad remained silent.

Bangar noted their footwear. They were *Amriki*.

By midnight Ayub and Sakhi returned. Bangar gave the news.

"She and Zarhawar are alive and on foot. Two foreigners, *Amriki* barely alive, sat in the cave. I shot them. Ahmad and I buried them, but left their faces exposed so you might see her blade's work. She defeated them and left. You'll see. There was no sign of Afghans. We can follow her trail in the morning."

Chapter 24

Search

Mohammed shuddered. Sharp breaths came in gasps. His neck throbbed with fire. On point, he worked the teams quietly along the faint *Lakro Sar's* ridge-line trail as the sun began its descent. He shivered in the rapidly cooling, nine thousand feet air. Dusk's stillness settled slowly through the hillside trees. Waning sunlight and gentle breezes filtered through long needled pine, casting spidery shadows onto the forest floor.

Above a long-eared owl cocked his head, eyes fixed on a fat thrush below bobbing amidst a host of twittering sparrows. The owl leaned gently forward, readying his silent glide. The floor dwellers suddenly ceased their chatter. Thrush and sparrows flurried into higher branches and huddled, mute. The owl held, talons digging deep into his branch. Higher up, waxwings quieted. A nearby woodpecker's knocking alone ignored the silence.

Mohammed's hand signalled a halt. He scanned ahead, cocking his ear. Birds chirping... now silence save the woodpecker. He motioned his searchers to drop. From behind trees, he looked forward into mottling shadows and shouldered his M4.

Two figures. Both carried weapons, one a bag. The taller, a slim midnight wraith, stumbled momentarily, staggering under its load. Shaded beneath the forest's limbs, it wore a satanic mask, blackened as if by fire. Recovering its tread, the spectre slipped into a last beam of dimming afternoon light to reveal its true colour, a dark ruby red. Its smaller companion stopped, peering ahead, sniffing for danger. It dropped flat and raised its weapon. A child's voice caromed through the forest's silence.

"Who's there? I'm Zarhawar of the house of Mehmoud Prraang. Show yourself or we'll kill you!"

"Zarhawar!" he shouted. "It's Mohammed!" Is she with him? Allah, please let her be with him. "Friends are with me. Soldiers. *Dhost! Dhost! Amreekunee faujeeyaan.* Don't shoot. We're here."

Zarhawar lowered his rifle and stood. "Mohammed? Help us! *Mor* needs you."

Mohammed saw her blackened face turn to her boy. He dropped his rifle and ran. He barely heard her slurred words.

"What did you say? Mohammed? Here? O *Khuday,* help me. I can't feel my legs. Where are you? Am I dying?"

She dropped as a wounded tree releasing life. The pine-straw of the forest floor cushioned her fall. Mohammed lifted her bodily onto a makeshift stretcher. He found her pulse. Her breath snuffled through a smashed and swollen face. *Alhamdulillah. Alhamdulillah.* He wiped his eyes.

Vargas contacted base – too dark to hazard copters. They'd carry her in shifts without letup until they reached camp.

***

Ayub prayed thanks at sunrise with the others. He covered the coals of their fire and walked uphill. He stood with Sakhi and Bangar over the exposed masks of what had been men. He concurred with Bangar's description. *Amriki.* "You're right son of Baseer. Little work was left for bullets." Bangar nodded.

Ayub led following drops of blood leading south west, through trees shrouded in early morning fog. The trail grew fainter. An hour along he signalled a halt and cupped his hands to his ears, motioning for silence. Voices, nearby. He lowered behind a tree, rifle ready. Movement amongst the trees below. He sighted along the barrel, watched and listened.

"Father! Father!"

He lowered the barrel. "Faridun! We're above." Mehmoud, Faridun and four Pashat men. Mehmoud embraced Ayub and Sakhi.

"They've been found. Mohammed and his soldiers have them. They've taken her to a doctor."

"Are they wounded? We've seen blood."

"They didn't say. They're both alive. We'll learn more soon enough."

"We found two men. Dead. Her knife destroyed them."

Chapter 25

Sisters

Mohammed's grip failed. He off-loaded his corner of the improvised stretcher to Vargas. His mates took over. He peered down at his feet, dragging from legs that had lost their strength. Despite mountain-crisp air sweat somehow poured from his forehead and body. He'd begun to stumble.

Vargas looked at him. "Mohammed, are you all right?"

Mohammed ignored him. "Not Karzai. To her sister's home. My friend, Laila Sayyed, a doctor at the Maui Clinic. We need her."

Mohammed directed the Hummer from Karzai to Farikhta's home. Vargas and the men carried the stretcher in to Farikhta's cot. He stumbled behind the stretcher. Laila had already arrived. She stared at him, mouth ajar.

"Mohammed, what's going on? Your eyes. Your face is like a ghost. Why – your clothes are dripping wet.

"Dizzy... hot..." Below was a black hole. He felt himself falling into it.

***

Vargas's quick hand caught Mohammed's head before it crashed into the floor with the rest of him. He'd crumpled, his eyes rolling up before closing.

Vargas felt his forehead. "He's burning up." He rolled Mohammed to his stomach. "His neck! Shit! It's infected." Laila knelt beside him, eyes wide.

"Get him to your base. Fluids, antibiotics. Quick."

Vargas grabbed Mohammed's shoulders. "Ghorzang, help me lift him. I've got to Humvee him back to base and hook him up."

***

Farikhta looked down at her sister and sucked in her breath. Shahay's eyes stared vacantly out of a swollen, blood-crusted face. Her clothing was slit, held together by her belt, pasted to her skin by gore. She was unrecognizable, alien.

Ghorzang's eyes dropped as he addressed Laila. "Please, what do you need, *Daktara Sahiba*?"

"Hot water. Clean bedding. Please, hang sheets for privacy. *Daera manana.*"

Farikhta spoke quietly, uncertain Shahay heard or understood. "*Khor jannay*, dear sister, Laila is Mohammed's friend. He asked her to come. She is *daktara*. We'll bathe you and see to your wounds."

Farikhta saw her sister recoil and shiver at Mohammed's name. Her eyes first looked away, closing only to reopen to stare absently. She gazed absently at the needle entering her arm and mumbled incoherently.

"Who is..? What is the needle? Why does fire burn in me? Spears are hurting inside my chest and belly. Flames ... my throat. My ribs? What's happened..? Farikhta? Is it you? Who is with you? Why am I so tired?" Shahay sighed and closed her eyes.

Farikhta's eyes streamed. "Please *Sahiba*, how may I help?"

"Please, begin by bathing her face and hair with warm water. I'll start at her feet and examine as we bathe her. First, I'll start a line..."

***

Beyond the curtain, Ghorzang sat with Zarhawar. They drank tea. Zarhawar looked to him hopefully.

"Laila is *daktara* like Mohammed?"

"Yes."

"She'll help *mor*?"

"Yes. Are you all right, son of Shahay?"

"Yes. But I worry for her. They were big men. She fought them and wouldn't give in. I heard them fighting. They hurt her, but I don't know how. She took revenge."

***

Farikhta stood by Shahay's head as Laila gloved and began to remove Shahay's clothing piece by piece to examine her minutely. Caked blood and grime yielded to warm water, slowly revealing skin beneath. Farikhta shuddered as crusted blood gave way. Massive bruises had swollen her sister's face to a grotesque blue mask. Red rope burns encircled her neck and wrists. Her tears fell on her sister. She replaced the grisly garments, stiff with blood, with fresh pieces from her own wardrobe, as Laila finished each stage of her examination.

"Please, I must remove her *partoog* to examine her. You may wish to look away." Farikhta shook her head and gritted her teeth.

"Please no. I will not look away when she could not."

Laila used the body of a large bore syringe to perform painstaking mild vinegar and warm water lavages to rinse Shahay internally. "Please, wife of Ghorzhang, help me wash her loins and legs. Then we must roll her to attend to her back."

Farikhta oversaw Laila's progress silently. Shudders rolled through her. Laila applied ointment to Shahay's groin. When they finished, with Laila's help, she changed the bedding and left Shahay to sleep. She whispered to Ghorzang who took the imbrued clothing to the garden to burn.

Farikhta's rimmed eyes begged Laila's counsel.

"She's been horribly beaten. You've seen massive bruising to her chest and face. Those are bite marks on her breasts. Two teeth are loose but she won't lose them. She's badly bruised and torn everywhere internally. Those are rope burns on her neck and wrists. One or two ribs are certainly cracked but not splintered. I've wrapped her chest for a little comfort, but each breath will be painful for weeks. She has a recent surgical wound on her leg. It shows deep bruising all around. It's as if a thumb repeatedly attempted to penetrate the flesh. The pain would have been agonizing."

Farikhta nodded, wet-eyed. "My brother Ayub told of this. Mohammed and Ayub fought dacoits in the mountains. My sisters artery was slashed by one of the criminals. Mohammed cut a piece from inside the leg and sewed it over the wound."

Laila shook her head. "That's... it's astonishing. It's difficult surgery in a good operating theatre. He's a gifted surgeon. It's clear her kidnappers used the wound to torture her. If the stitches had ruptured, she would have died."

"But she endured," Farikhta muttered. "Bless you for your help, *Sahiba*. You are Khoday's mercy." Laila held Farikhta's shoulders.

"Mohammed is my friend from university. Even if he'd been able, he shouldn't have treated your sister now. I'm so sorry for your beloved sister, and glad I could help. I've given her one injection so she'll sleep, and another with antibiotics. I've taken a blood sample in case her attackers infected her. I'm at the Maui Clinic. I'll return every day to see her."

"*Daera manana, Sahiba.*"

***

Slowly, Zarhawar recounted events. A man had appeared silently and unseen. "He put his hand over my mouth and held a knife at my throat. Three more joined us. Two were Afghans. We walked for hours to a cave on a mountainside. They tied my hands. One Afghan guarded me outside. Two men took *mor* into the cave. She showed no fear."

"Then what happened?"

"I don't know. I think they beat her. She did not speak. Then they dragged me into the cave and held the knife at my throat again. The other man put a rifle in her back and pushed her away."

"Did she cry out?"

"No. I heard sounds of fighting. She wouldn't give in. They shouted at her. They were angry. On the second day, they were careless. They slept after drinking something with a strange smell. The Afghan grey beard cut my ropes and left. I took my weapon and went to her. She was waiting. We planned what to do. She told me where to shoot them. They screamed."

"Sergeant Vargas said she carried a bloody sack. Where is it? What was in it?"

"Their fingers, ears, tongues and noses. After I shot their knees and shoulders she sharpened her knife. She took *badal*. We left the bag of their pieces when Mohammed found us."

He smiled, shoulders squared, tremulous.

Ghorzang nodded. "She did well. So did you."

Chapter 26

Wounds

His eyes flickered open. Someone... Vargas sat holding an IV. Travelling? Where am I?

"Henry, what..?"

"We're in a Humvee heading to base."

Mohammed's lids drooped only immediately to rise again. "Shahay?"

"She's in one piece. Torn up, bruised, cracked ribs. She'll heal. Time you looked after yourself. You keeled over, out like a light."

"Haven't slept since early yesterday. Thirsty."

Henry shook his head. Mohammed mumbled incomprehensibly, then let out a deep sigh. Eyes closed.

***

Mohammed heard a voice before opening his eyes. Vargas. Ah, it's so bright.

"Mohammed! About time you woke up."

He tried to shake his head only to be stopped by pain. His tongue was covered in fur. An IV and... a catheter? "Henry... Wazzup? Did I sleep? What's going on? Who? I have a catheter?"

Henry spoke quietly. "You've been out eight days. You picked up a doozy of an infection. Doc's kicking himself he let you come after us. We've debrided your neck twice. Just as well you were out of it. You were a bloody pus-filled mess."

He turned his head to reply and instantly needed to throw up, choking back what was in his throat. Dizzy. "What's... the bag?" He pointed to the IV.

"Isotonic saline now. Started with Ringer's. We've been sticking you with Daptomycin. You were massively dehydrated. With the wrong meds, they would've been serving up your kidneys for brekky in a UK mess. Ready for some other news?"

"News?"

"Your parents are frantic, wondering if you're okay. They've gone through channels to find out where you are. We've put them off. But–"

"But what?"

"Looks like they're flying into Pakistan. Last contact was from Dubai."

"Pakistan? What are they thinking? What the hell?"

"You went AWOL from Landstuhl and left a note. What could they think when they heard nothing for a week? What did the note say?"

Talking tired him. He wanted to close his eyes. "I can't... I think... had to go help find Shahay. Farikhta? How... Shahay?"

"I've spoken to Farikhta. Shahay is coming along but quiet, maybe still in shock."

He closed his eyes. "Ah... have to see her..." He heard a long sigh. "Get better first, man."

***

Shahay didn't want to hear Farikhta's worries. "Assassins will come again. We can't stay."

"But, I'm not ready."

"It's been ten days. I know you're not healed. But if we don't leave we may all die. I've arranged it."

She could do nothing. Farikhta was in charge. A local, a student's merchant father, would take them up the Kunar-Bajaur Road to the checkpoint at Ghakhi to meet Bangar's truck. Ghorzang, her brothers and Zarhawar were consigned to the truck's bed. Shahay and Farikhta with her baby would be more comfortable in the cab.

**

Mohammed's new Captain, Jerry Richards, was cheery. "Good to see you putting your boots back on, son. Don't worry about looking like a walking skeleton. I'm told it's an improvement."

"Yeah. I didn't recognize the guy shaving in my mirror. Listen, last time I was awake Vargas told me my parents might be coming to Pakistan? Was I dreaming?"

Richards grinned."Nope. That was a week ago. They worried – maybe panicked – when you disappeared. I caught them in Dubai, explained some things. Vargas filled me in on your Bajauri friends. I told your parents when you finished malingering, I'd put you on leave and expected you'd be off to Batmalai. They headed there. Your grandmother's with them. My guess is they're already there."

"*Nya* Shazia too? But Shahay is..?"

"Vargas hasn't told you? She's not here. Her sister took her, her son and her own family to their father's home. In case you're inter-ested, we've located a local trucker with a load of apricots for Pashat's market." Mohammed turned quickly.

"When?"

"He's leaving tomorrow morning. Up for it?"

"Sure am. Thanks..."

**

Mohammed thanked his driver at Pashat's market, and closed the truck's door. He turned to see Bangar standing by his truck, grinning ear to ear.

"You're a welcome sight, son of Baseer. I haven't been well. Don't know if I could make the walk to Batmalai." Bangar's hand found his.

"*Sahib,* please don't thank me. My father is *recovered.* My wife and son are well. Come, come to see your family, and mine and Mehmoud's."

He'd hadn't ever driven with Bangar. But Ayub said Bangar sped like a madman. Now Baseer's son drove as though he carried the weight of Bajaur on his shoulders. The truck moped along in first gear.

"What is it, son of Baseer?"

"I... I found them and killed them both."

"Who?"

"The men who kidnapped the daughter of Mehmoud. Her knife took their fingers, thumbs, tongues, noses, ears and... *saamaan.* She'd been tied. There were ropes and metal stakes in the cave. I burnt the ropes and buried the pegs in the two men's graves. They were *Amriki.* Ayub and Sakhi came next morning. They didn't see the ropes and stakes. I didn't tell them. We buried the bodies leaving only the faces to see."

Mohammed looked away shaking his head before finding a deep breath. "Thank you, son of Baseer. They deserved what they got. If I were treated as she likely was, I'd relieve them of their packages too. Thank you for your kindness to the daughter of Mehmoud."

"Yes, *Sahib.*"

Chapter 27

Maimoonai

Nya Shazia's eyes rose to steps on the porch, and fell to her knees. Mohammed pulled her up by her hands and hugged her.

"Oh Mohammed. I've worried. You're a skeleton. I almost didn't know you. Thank God you are well and you've come." She called into the *kor*. "Ali, Ayesha come see who's here."

His parents' faces fell. He preempted. "Never fear. It's just me. This is my lighter, leaner look. I've been on a diet. I gave up whiskey, cake and chocolate. Now look, Omar Sharif!"

"You're so thin. Give your mother a kiss, Omar" His mother grinned. His father embraced him.

"Whose *qila* is this, *Nya*? Where's the owner?"

"It belongs to a widow. Her children live in Peshawar. She wanted to visit with them. Baseer suggested we help her do so. He wanted us as his guests, but his *hujra* wasn't large enough to accommodate all of us. He arranged for us to rent while we waited for you."

***

Mohammed's parents tidied up the dishes. He squirmed against the stiffness in his knees. His eyes were met by Shazia's.

"You're restless. Didn't you enjoy dinner?"

"Yes. It was delicious. My mind was... I haven't seen Shahay since we found her."

"Nor she, you. And?"

"I have to see her..."

Shazia frowned. "Whoa! You've been ill. Please, remember where you are and your manners. Have you forgotten everything?"

Her lips had gone thin. "Please, *Nya jannay* remind me."

"Perhaps you recall the story of Sher Alam and Maimoonai? It frightened you as a child. "

"Not much. Someone was killed. That's what frightened me."

His parents rejoined them. "You told me that story too," his father said. "They married and ... some kind of tragedy. Near here... Nawagai?"

Nya nodded. "Yes. Ayesha won't know the tale. Mohammed says 'He has to see Shahay.'

She took a breath. "The story is of Maimoonai, the beauty, who married Sher Alam, the overgenerous. They loved one another. He entertained friends daily in his *hujra* with gambling, food and drink. A guest was envious. Hasan was once fond of Maimoonai and thought Sher Alam a fool, a door-mat. When he overheard Maimoonai scolding her husband for being freehanded, he grew angry the largesse might end.

Ali broke in. "I remember. Sher Alam went off, *hujra* festivities continued. Hasan knocked on the host's door to borrow tobacco, pretending he'd forgotten his. Maimoonai slid Sher Alam's tobacco pouch under the door."

Nya nodded. "Hasan flaunted the pouch in the village. Everyone knew its owner. Stories began. Maimoonai opened her door to another man in her man's absence. Sher Alam's initial doubt turned to humiliation. His honour was at stake. Soon, anger replaced his sorrow... In a rage, he cut her throat."

Nya found Mohammed's eyes. "His cruelty frightened you... The story didn't end there. A friend returned from travels and told

Sher Alam he'd accompanied Hasan on the fateful day. Maimoonai refused to open the door, instead slid the pouch beneath it. She was blameless. Sher Alam went mad."

His mother's face was beet red. "It's a horrible tale! You told that story to a child? It's nothing to do with Shahay! It's as though you want to cause trouble. Shahay has no husband to harm her."

Nya stared through his mother. "True. Yet, she lives in her father's *qila* and has brothers..."

"You're not suggesting Mehmoud or his sons would harm her!" his father said.

Nya wagged her head. "I said nothing about what her father and brothers might do. You've missed what's important." She left and went outside on the porch. Mohammed followed without observing that his mother trailed.

Nya spoke without looking at him, slowly, distracted. "Women tell it differently. Maimoonai asked Sher Alam what troubled him. He told her of the taunts, the *peghore*. She said she'd not opened the door. Instead, she pushed the pouch beneath the door to protect his reputation for generosity... But Sher Alam's head remained low. She drew a knife and offered it to him.

"It is easier to stop a caravan than to stop people's tongues" she said. "I know honour's demands." He shook his head without raising his eyes." His weakness broke her spirit. "'No taunt shall stain your honour' she said, and with that opened her throat."

Ayesha listened unseen behind them. Her voice cracked. "Unforgivable! We know nothing of what happened to Shahay! Whatever happened is no one's business but hers."

Shazia shook her head. "You miss the point again, daughter. Here, taunts are everyone's business."

"You can't mean that!" his mother hissed. His father's hand went to her shoulder.

"My grandson listens, daughter" *Nya* said. "What does the story speak of, Mohammed?"

"Mother, please. *Nya* has told us how Pukhtuns may see what's happened. Please grandma, go on."

"We haven't visited Shahay yet. Before you came, Mehmoud and his family greeted us politely. We met Farikhta and Ghorzang. Years ago, a woman's kidnap meant rape. If the kidnapper was known, the couple were forced to marry. If either refused, both were slaughtered. Even if such times are past, Mehmoud's daughter may feel profound dishonour, not so much from what happened, but for what's imagined. Taunts may come. If they did Mehmoud's family would suffer disgrace."

Mohammed cheeks flushed. "That's why you were angry. I spoke of my needs..."

"And forgot hers..." Mohammed rose to walk a few paces into the courtyard.

His father wagged his head. "It's a different culture, *mor*."

Nya turned on him, eyes sparking. "'*Different*'? *Different*, my son! So, our lawyers never argue 'You claim rape but didn't you have an orgasm, madam.' Half-wits never speculate a victim might have enjoyed it, might have struggled more, might have consumed less alcohol? No one asserts that her clothing, her smile or her words encouraged the attack? Witless men and women never snigger that she should have kept her knees together? No one implies she asked for it? Morons never speculate and gossip about the awful thing that happened to this victim? Thank God *we* are better than those who taunt."

His mother turned and stamped into the house. His father followed.

Mohammed returned to sit beside *Nya*. "Are you still cross with me?"

"No. It's your parents. They wish Denver on Batmalai."

"Umm. *Nya*, something you should know..."

Nya met his eyes. "What do you imagine I don't know?"

Chapter 28

Walls

Shahay gasped. Instinct again caught her unawares. A careless deep breath speared her ribs. Her thighs still throbbed lying down, sitting or taking steps. Fire still scorched through her using the *koza*. She trembled conversing with her mother and sister, wary of tongues brimming with unuttered questions. Though her appetite had re-emerged, her jaw healed slowly. Laila had said no bones were broken.

Zarhawar popped in unceremoniously with news.

"Mohammed's come. He's staying with his family in the widow's *qila*."

Her eyes welled. No. No. Why did he come? He mustn't be here. She couldn't see him. She dozed fitfully, dreaming, trying to run to him, restrained by powerful hands.

***

Nya brought good news. Mehmoud invited the son of Ali and his father after lunch. Bibi would entertain *Nya* and his mother.

En route Mohammed greeted Baseer, Bangar and four of the *badraga*, with three elders, all presumptive self-invited companions. Mehmoud greeted them at the *hujra* while Bibi led his mother and *Nya* into the *kor*.

Mehmoud extended his hand while the others sat. "You're thin, my friend. We were told you were very ill. It's good to see you recovered. We're pleased to meet *Nya* and your parents... but your eyes are elsewhere."

His words stumbled. "How... the daughter of Mehmoud?"

"Thank you for asking. She's recovering. The cowards beat her. But you... you've helped my family again. *Manana*. Let's sit with the others. I was sorry to hear of your illness. What happened?"

"It's a long story. We'd come from Asadabad, twelve of us with prisoners. *Takfiri* attacked in the outskirts of Marah Warah."

Mehmoud cocked his head. "What happened to give you prisoners?"

Mohammed looked to Ghorzang.

"I'm sorry, *Baba*. I've waited for the right time to tell the whole story. You knew assassins threatened us twice before. When the son of Ali returned from Batmalai he learned of a plan for our assassination. With his help and Allah's grace, we survived. He took two prisoners."

Mehmoud turned to Mohammed. "Again, I'm indebted to you. I'm curious. How did you learn of the threat? When did this happen?"

Mohammed hesitated. If he explained, he'd implicate...

Bangar's voice rose uncertainly. "In Asadabad's *bazar*, men asked if I'd come to help assassinate the daughter of Mehmoud and her husband."

Mehmoud and his sons glared at Bangar. "At the time of the *badraga*? Why didn't you inform my sons immediately, son of Baseer?" The tone was iron, lethal.

"Please forgive me, *baba*. I asked Mohammed's advice."

Mohammed nodded to Mehmoud. "Please, son of Baseer, give *baba* the rest of our conversation."

Reinforced, Bangar's voice steadied. "We agreed. With your sons at her side, the assassins would wait for another time. Mohammed could make all seem routine, so Farikhta and her husband would seem to be easy targets. He'd guard her. It's what he did. I trusted him."

Mehmoud stroked his beard, his gaze fixed on Bangar. His face was expressionless. Bangar's head sank into his shoulders.

"*Khuday* graced our friends with wisdom and granted Baseer's son his father's common sense. It's true my sons couldn't remain forever protecting Farikhta. *Daktar Sahib* saved our youngest daughter. He's been our guest and friend. That he should protect our older daughter was right. We spoke of it when he was our guest. Did we not, son of Ali?"

"We did. But I played a small role, *baba*. Ghorzang and your daughter defended themselves. After the attack, I spoke with our prisoners. They seemed strangely content after the assassination's failure. It suggested trouble returning to base..."

The Salarzai men listened: the *takfiri* commander tied to the hood, the IEDs, the ambush, the heavy RPG bombardment.

Ayub's face took on a sly smile. "That's a bad burn on the back of your neck, *Sahib*."

Mohammed caught Ayub's drift. "Keeping my head below bullets and explosions secures it on my shoulders. I fell on two wounded instead of burying my face in the dirt."

Ayub grinned. "Ah, those clumsy feet, once again tripping and happening to land on friends as once you tripped and accidentally shot a man about to slaughter my sister. Did your friends survive your stumble?"

"Both did, my friend. I must learn to tighten my laces."

"No need. I hope if I'm at risk you're nearby. You stumble well."

Baseer frowned. "*Daktar Sahib* has Pukhtun blood."

***

Bibi Rokhana, Farikhta and the brothers' wives embraced first Shazia, then Ayesha. Shazia translated courtesies, welcomes, and questions.

With courtesies exhausted, *Nya* approached her purpose. Behind the curtain Shahay's ears pricked up.

"Please, wife of Mehmoud, remember Mohammed's mother is *Daktara*. I speak for her when I say she'd be honoured to attend your daughter."

Bibi's eyes dropped. "My daughter speaks little of her pain."

Shazia grasped the opening. "She must still be in shock. Anyone would be, taken by cowards, forced to fight for her life and her son's. We honour her courage. Of course, *Sahiba* may speak of a patient's health only to the patient herself. Since we're here, may we meet the daughter of Mehmoud now? Ayesha knows little *Pukhto,* but I'll translate for her."

Bibi's eyebrows rose. Slowly, she nodded, stood and disappeared through the curtains to speak in hushed tones with Shahay. She returned wearing a bemused smile.

"She'll see you. I'm surprised. So far she's seen only family. She apologizes that she's resting."

***

Shahay saw a firm face with sparkling ash green eyes framed by grey-streaked raven hair approach. A handsome younger woman followed. Unasked, the older woman embraced her gently, kissed her on each cheek and sought her hands. She spoke in whispers.

"I'm presumptuous to embrace you, daughter of Mehmoud. My manners are an old woman's. I'm Mohammed's *Nya*. I am Shazia. Please greet Mohammed's mother. The wife of Ali is Ayesha. She is *Daktara Sahiba.* If you wish, she may tend to you. We came to your village because we lost track of Mohammed and feared for him. He fell ill. We learned that when he recovered, he meant to come here."

"He is here? Why? He was ill? I didn't know. What happened?"

"Near Asadabad he was wounded. He and his platoon fought *takfiri.* His wounds became badly infected. He's been in hospital almost two weeks."

"But... but when soldiers found us, I thought –"

"Yes, he found you. You were covered with blood and had fainted. He put you on a stretcher. That's as much as he remembered."

"He knows nothing of... of my wounds?" Why had he come? They *must not* ask her to see him.

"Nothing. He's grateful you survived. He came as soon as the hospital released him. Daughter of Mehmoud, we've come for you. I've said to your mother what is true. *Sahiba* may speak of your wounds to no one but you. May she treat you? Might we return tomorrow? I'd accompany her to translate your concerns. We sorrow for your misfortune. We pray your health will recover. Please, allow us to help."

Shahay closed her eyes. This *Nya*... she trusted her. *Daktara* would say nothing. "Perhaps... if you and *Sahiba* were to return."

"We will..." Shazia embraced her again.

Shahay hesitated. "But I... I needn't see him?"

"No. He's with his father. Like you, he's still recovering."

Shahay nodded. A sigh released from her belly.

***

Shazia brought a stool to Shahay's shoulder, sat, took her hand and held her eyes.

"My eyes are with yours, daughter of Mehmoud. *Daktara* will examine you."

Gloved, Ayesha gently drew bedding and garments aside, and began.

Shazia murmured comforts, while Shahay shuddered, trembling with Ayesha's touch. Her teeth dug into her lip as gentle hands examined her thigh, perineum, and chest. Her body convulsed at the application of ointments. Ayesha spoke softly with foreign words. Shazia whispered in her ear.

"*Sahiba* is sorry for your discomfort. For small infections she's applied an antibiotic ointment and will leave pills, *golai*. One in the morning, another in the evening. They'll tire you but help with the pain. She's finished for now unless you have questions... No? All right. May I stay on to speak with you alone?"

"Please."

Shazia's murmur became a whisper. "I watched your suffering during the examination. You're brave to bear these pains. They surely come from men's evil."

Shahay's eyes flooded. She sat up, silent tears cascading onto her *kameez* and inclined as a child onto Nya's shoulder, gulping her sobs. Slowly, she calmed as *Nya* stroked her hair and murmured reassurance. She helped Shahay to lie back. Household chatter beyond the curtain masked their words. She brought her ear close.

"Two men took us to a cave. One held a knife to Zarhawar's throat, the other pushed me with his weapon...

Shazia nodded."You surely made a final cut."

"Yes, with it ... then I threw them into the fire... It became the cave of their sorrow and of my *badal*. We left and walked south-east along the ridge."

Her eyes met Shahay's. "It's as I thought. Your endurance and *badal* astonish me. You make me proud to be *Pukhtanna*. Mohammed told us of your combat when you first met. But now, may I ask of the pain of your spirit... are your curtains not now a wall? What keeps you behind them? Is it fear of *peghore*, taunts?"

"If my kidnap dishonours *Baba*..." Her head fell.

"Strange... You surely didn't fear death when the criminals used the rope on your neck?"

Shahay scowled. "Death? *You* ask this? I'd gladly have suffered death rather than dishonour. I feared for Zarhawar's life... Why ask what you know?"

"You're quick to anger. Good. I asked only to understand your curtain. You alone know two *Amriki* acted against honour. No curtain stops *peghore*. Even if *taunts* caused your death, you prefer that to dishonour. Perhaps the curtain does little for you. Zarhawar glories in your revenge. He tells everyone."

"He's my son. I'm proud of him. But *Nya*, you won't repeat – ?"

"No, dear girl. Never. Your words are for us alone. Don't worry... Wait! Why? Your face! Are you all right? What's happening?"

Shahay sucked in her breath and sat bolt upright, eyes wide with alarm. "Please *Nya*, bring my sister. I must be alone with her. Come tomorrow..."

Shazia puzzled. She fetched Farikhta as asked, and left. As she walked back she stopped suddenly, clasped her hands in a short prayer, laughed and began to hum.

Shazia entered smiling next day. Shahay's cheeks were suffused. She stumbled over her words.

"I'm sorry I asked for Farikhta. I needed her help for... to–"

Shazia anticipated. "I think I understand, dear girl. What must have worried you so, your *mensez,* paid a visit?

"Mohammed, I must speak privately with your parents. Perhaps you might visit the family of Baseer?"

His face bore evident curiosity. "I don't suppose you'll tell me what you're up to..." She remained silent. "All right, *Nya*. I'll visit with Baseer."

She gathered Ali and Ayesha and began. "I've spoken privately to Shahay. You may not understand why. I know she's not educated as Mohammed's fellow student was. Laila was her name, wasn't it?"

Ayesha paled. "Why..? You can't... Yes. Laila Sayyed. A beautiful young woman, bright, educated, civilized, a doctor like Mohammed. Not a common *villager*... who... who cuts men into pieces."

Shazia's cheeks drew tight. Her voice lowered. "Yes. You know of this only because Zarhawar's boasted of her revenge. And I know of Laila, a lovely woman who prefers women."

"What! Who said..? No. She was my student. I saw no evidence–"

Shazia wagged her chin. "*You* would scarcely have *seen* evidence. In any case, you're mistaken. She revealed herself bravely to Mohammed. While Laila is civilized and educated, she's in love with the woman she lives with in Asadabad. The woman's name is Malalai."

"But living together..."

"No, daughter! Mohammed defended Laila and her girlfriend in Denver. No mistake. Laila has been clear. His hopes cannot be with her."

Ayesha's lips went thin. "Mohammed hasn't said anything to us. I know Shahay was his patient. She... she's not... She comes from a small backward village... She reacted to her awful experience like –"

"'Like a savage?' How kind. Pukhtun honour demands what you think is savagery. Sometimes the obligations of Pukhtun honour are discharged to dissuade future insults."

Ayesha snorted. "Deterrence motivated by honour!"

Shazia's voice remained calm. "Why not? Deterrence for the community's benefit. Does our deterrence differ? You don't deny they deserved her revenge?"

"But her barbaric savagery, the knife..."

"Humph! How ironic coming from a surgeon who believes *her* blade cures. A Pukhtun knife is superior in that it may cure twice – the one who is cut and the one who cuts. It certainly remedied the ailments of Shahay's attackers."

Ayesha's face reddened. "When you speak like this, I don't know you. You smile about ghastly violence. It's Mohammed's life and you're seriously misjudging what kind of person is right for him... for... for his future and the kind of woman he deserves." Flushed, Ayesha's voice trembled. "At least we must take time to weigh matters. We'll see what Mohammed decides, once we've returned to Denver."

Nya set her teeth. "You may wish for time. But then you don't take seriously the lesson of Maimoonai. You may consign Shahay to death for men's honour, an honour with which you doubtless have no patience. There is a second reason to get on with what we must do... I've arranged a meeting through Baseer."

Ayesha's eyes flew open. "With Baseer? What are you up to? Ali, please ask *Nya* what she's doing?"

Nya offered a half-truth. "We must thank Baseer for his kindness before we leave." She turned her back and left in silence before Ali could find words.

***

David Verraeter, hand on chin, head down, paced in his office. The two contractors hadn't checked in. Two weeks. Nothing. Their Afghan helpers were in the wind. Ratcliff, in field communications, had nothing more. He was ex-military. Not one to speculate.

"Did our two even make contact with anyone from the Bajaur family Karram visited?"

"You saw the last text: 'Interview to come.'"

"'Interview.' Right. So they had someone in hand. The Batmalai family was on their task list. Get busy. Find out what happened to them. This may be important."

Next morning his desktop peeped a message.

"For DV OWL:" Agnt: SOLO
Bajaur: Kidnapped villagers (unknown) recovered NE of K. base. No sign contractors. SOLO, Pshawr

Verraeter punched the DDO's number.

"Mary, please tell Bill I'm coming up. I'll be brief. I need information about an OWL listed SOF medic recently serving with your guys... Yes. That's the one."

"What?" Verraeter drew a sharp breath. "They weren't local civilians? SOG contractors? I thought... So, if Karram..? I thought you had local civvy operatives. SOG? Wasn't that overkill?"

"Is this your signature on the assignment, David?"

"Well, yes. But, how could I know—"

"The information was there if you asked. Interrogating unwilling

Pashtuns in Bajaur with civvy operatives wasn't going to happen. Our guys were Americans, but officially private. Gave us deniability. They had other tasks as well. Our manpower isn't unlimited."

"Whatever. My concern is to find out how deep Karram is into their disappearance. SOLO has put out a reward. We need to find our people, above ground or in it."

Verraeter descended to his office buoyed. If they were dead, all the better. Karram was certainly involved. It would be what he needed, proof of concept.

Chapter 29

Chess

Baseer's invitation perplexed Mehmoud. He turned to Bibi.

"What does this mean? He invites us *both* to his *hujra*? It's as though *we* have business with him. But he would not invite my wife for business."

Bibi shook her head. "We've been distracted. Could it be important? Has someone died? Pray it isn't someone we know. It's not too late for a *las niwa* visit to console the family. I'll make enquiries."

She found nothing. Their curiosity grew.

***

Mehmoud masked his surprise. Baseer had other guests. Not only was the wife of Baseer present, but also Ali, Ayesha and Shazia. Ayesha too seemed surprised but unsettled. Baseer took Mehmoud's hand and began polite enquiries.

"We've been concerned with your daughter's health and have forgotten our manners. How is your family? You look well."

The greeting persisted a full five minutes before refreshments were served.

"Ah, all well, my friend. More *chai*? Are the biscuits to your liking? We think of your brave daughter, who Zarhawar tells us fought her captors so fiercely, and meted out revenge. We hope she continues to recover."

Mehmoud smiled and nodded. Bibi responded quietly. "Thank you for your praise. Farikhta says she's recovering. Shahay still says little. We are grateful to the wife of Ali who helps her."

Ayesha listened to Shazia interpret, and replied through her. "She suffered a massive shock. I've given her pills. They help heal at the cost of dulling her pain, but they also lower her spirit."

Mehmoud nodded. "She still has pain. Her injuries mend. *Enshaallah*."

Baseer straightened and directed the conversation elsewhere. "My friend, the mother of Ali, Mohammed's *Nya*, wishes to speak on important matters."

Mehmoud's brows rose with his chin. Bibi dropped her gaze. Mehmoud thought he heard her breath stop. Ali and Ayesha looked sharply toward Shazia.

***

Shazia drew a deep breath, while Ayesha, face livid, hissed. "What are you up to? You said we were to thank Baseer before leaving for home."

She ignored her daughter-in-law, leaving her question untranslated, even while allowing its animus to be seen. Shazia's eyes went directly to Baseer and Mehmoud.

"First, for our family, we will treasure our memories of Mehmoud's and Baseer's hospitality. We've begun to speak of returning home. You have made us guests of your village. We're grateful for fine food, the warmth of your company and your generosity, even amidst difficulties."

Baseer, Mehmoud and their wives flushed and smiled.

Now, she focussed directly on Mehmoud and Bibi. "I ask your patience now, as I speak for Mohammed on a matter of honour.

What I say may surprise not only you, but also surprise my son and his wife. I've guarded from them what I know. Now everyone may hear. Mohammed greatly admires your family. His words are 'There is no one for me but the daughter of Mehmoud.'"

Ali paled, then translated for an open-mouthed Ayesha. Her cheeks flamed and quivered.

Mehmoud held his breath while Bibi trembled, chin on chest. They remained silent and alert.

"Of course, the daughter of Mehmoud does not wish to see the son of Ali just now. There are other reasons for patience. Wounds need to heal. But I ask, even if these two wished to marry, would it be wise to support them? In America divorce is common. It's uncommon and discouraged here."

Ali muttered translations for Ayesha.

Mehmoud hesitated. Shazia suspected he'd never sat with women in a *hujra* let alone addressed one. Now he met her eyes and nodded firmly.

"We cannot support a marriage we think won't endure."

Shazia's chin agreed. "I understand, *baba*. Perhaps Mohammed's parents also agree. How could we help the son of Ali and your daughter if they're destined for one another? They have different cultures. Mohammed will be a physician. Years of training remain. In America modern women seek education. They are doctors, like Ayesha, teachers like Farikhta. Few stay in their homes once their children enter school. Would the daughter of Mehmoud grow to resent Mohammed's education? Even if she could have it, would *she want* more education? She would speak English if she lived in America. Should she learn that language, if Mehmoud were to support her marriage? There are many questions. Perhaps you too have some."

Mehmoud and Bibi exchanged brief hushed words. He turned back to *Nya*. "You speak then for Mohammed. But his parents seem as surprised as we are. My wife asks what you propose."

"While I speak for Mohammed, he doesn't know of our meeting."

She ignored the collective gasps and subsequent mutterings of four parents, and waited to regain their attention.

"As for Mohammed, I don't doubt him. His words are clear, 'There is no one else.' You are right, *kaka*. His words were unknown to his parents before now. I'll explain what I see. Shahay's parents and Mohammed's may wish to consider my proposals.

"Mohammed's parents must return home. Mohammed should accompany them. With Mehmoud's permission, perhaps his daughter and her son might wish to accompany me to Islamabad. There, they both might learn English if they like. The daughter of Mehmoud may reflect on her future. Her son would continue his school. Mehmoud's daughter and the son of Ali are young. In time, she may be ready to consult with her parents and to consider his interest. As for their expenses, please pay no mind. I'll care for her and Zarhawar in Islamabad. May I add that even putting aside Mohammed's interest I would be happy to have the daughter of Mehmoud and her son as my companions in Islamabad. I have come to know her and greatly admire her spirit and her character."

Bibi whispered in Mehmoud's ear before he spoke. "But to be clear, you take Mohammed's words to mean he wishes to marry our daughter?"

She looked to her son and Ayesha before she answered. Ali's forehead wore a deep crease. Ayesha's face was chalk.

"Mohammed spoke to me about the daughter of Mehmoud. He hadn't yet spoken to his parents. You know his words. He would marry Shahay *tomorrow*. Please understand. I'm *Pukhtanna* and know customs. In America sons don't seek parents' permission to marry. We know my grandson. I take him at his word."

Mehmoud grimaced. He sat stonily for what seemed minutes before surrendering a deep sigh. "Our daughter can't marry one whose parents object."

Nya saw their expressions. Bibi turned sharply toward Mehmoud. From the corner of her eye she saw a trace of a smile flash across

Ayesha's lips and just as quickly vanish. Ali frowned and remained silent.

Nya bobbed understanding. "Of course, Pukhtun custom is wise. But Pukhtun patience is also esteemed. Recall our proverb. *What Allah has ordained will happen. Don't suggest, friend, that we try to escape fate.* The son of Ali's voice is clear, while he voice of Mehmoud's daughter is unheard. My grandson is patient. Meanwhile, I offer her, if she wishes and Mehmoud permits, my friendship, more education if she wishes, and time to heal elsewhere. Her son's education won't suffer... Who knows what fate awaits us? I don't believe my grandson's regard for your daughter will diminish. If she accompanies me, she'll have time to reflect on her future. I ask only one thing. Please, inform her of my proposals. I've said nothing of them to her, nor to the son of Ali."

Mehmoud stared impassively at Shazia. As he began to speak Bibi's whisper intercepted his words. His eyes held Bibi's as she spoke, his fingers pondering his grey beard. He turned back to Shazia. "We'll inform her. She must consent before we can agree."

***

Mohammed returned to find *Nya* with his parents on the verandah. *Nya* smiled while his mother's lips were clam tight, her cheeks rigid. His father sat with his chin cupped in his palms.

"What's going on? Mum, you look upset. Dad? Grandma, why are you smiling?

Nya responded cheerfully. "We've sat with Mehmoud and Bibi."

"Why? What... what was that about?"

"I conveyed your words about Shahay."

Mohammed's breath whistled in through his teeth. "*Nya*... I didn't mean... Mum, Dad, I meant to tell you. When I began to beat around the bush, *Nya* asked the direct question. Shahay won't even see me yet. What... what did they say?"

"Always the right question" *Nya* said. "They asked whether your words meant marriage. Your parents' discomfort was visible. Mehmoud said he couldn't agree to marriage without their consent. I made proposals allowing patience."

His mother's voice went scarlet. "*Nya* took it *upon herself* to propose your marriage to Shahay! As for you, you can't be serious. We understand Laila's a disappointment. But Shahay... she has no background at all, no education or experience of the world. In God's name, she is a *village* peasant, a widow with a child. For all we know she may be pregnant with another! Her culture... She suffered dreadfully but reacted like... like an animal! You've been away. You've felt lonely and rejected. Of course we pity her, as you must. She was your patient, then suffered a horrible kidnap. But setting your sights on a backward villager and mother of someone else's child when any number of suitable women from home would give their eye teeth –" Her voice stopped. "Mohammed, your face... I –"

"Mother, don't even *try* to diminish her. *Nya* spoke honestly for me. I hesitated to do it. You're right. I was infatuated with Laila. Why wouldn't I be? She was beautiful, bright, modest, idealistic. We'll always be friends. Shahay has a woman's beauty and... a spirit like no one I've ever met. Yes, she's poor, has little education, hasn't travelled and yes, she has a child. If... if she's..."

He turned away. Why hadn't he thought..? His stomach convulsed. He wiped his eyes and gritted his teeth to speak again.

Nya's hand went to his shoulder, her voice quiet. "She isn't pregnant. I know this."

He mouthed a silent *Alhamdulillah*. His fingers tightened into fists. He turned back to his mother and summoned ice. "You question her intelligence. I don't, and you have no reason to. You think my feelings come from pity. You're wrong. As for lofty ambitions... she needs room for those. She should have it. I've had time and space to grow. She hasn't. I helped when she was wounded and would have died. Yes, I'm sorry as hell she was kidnapped and attacked." He hesitated, trembling. "I beg you... for my sake and hers, don't ever question her revenge on men who kidnapped, brutalized and meant to murder her and Zarhawar. *Nya* is right. I want to marry her."

His mother turned away, eyes flooding. His father held her and met his eyes. "You're serious?"

"Deadly."

"Well, then listen to *Nya*. She made proposals to Mehmoud."

"*Nya?*"

"If she agrees, I'll take her and Zarhawar under my wing. We'll rent a place in Islamabad. She could relax, take courses if she wished, pick up some English. Zarhawar would continue his schooling. Mehmoud insists she consent."

"So what do I do?"

She smiled and shrugged. "For now, go back with your parents to Denver and be patient."

His heart sank."How can I leave..?"

"She isn't ready."

"But I..."

Shazia stamped her foot."No! Dammit! In God's name not 'I'! Think of her. Remember what taunts do. Your mother mentioned pity. You admired her bravery. But now she's been savaged. Maybe she feels that she's failed, so you *do* pity her. She needs to regain a measure of pride. If you can't match her pluck, you could lose her."

"I saw her kill two attackers with her knife. Pity? Merciful God, please don't let her believe that... I don't want to force her into anything."

"All right. Hesitate out of respect. But remember Maimoonai. If someone taunts her, *peghore warta warki,* they taunt and dishonour her family. Even groundless taunts might mean death. I admire Mehmoud. But I don't know how he'd respond to slander. Nor do I know the lengths *she* might go to to protect her father's honour. She deeply respects and honours Mehmoud."

His mother wagged her chin. "No. I can't believe Mehmoud

would... Shahay is a widow. She didn't elope with a forbidden suitor. She was raped. But it isn't as though she was an innocent child."

Nya's face went purple. "In God's name daughter," she said bitterly, "when will you understand! Perhaps Mehmoud wouldn't act. But others might. As for Shahay, she's no less innocent than a child or Maimoonai, whose innocence didn't matter a tinker's *damn*. Do you think I told Maimoonai's story for our amusement? Shahay might well consider using her knife on herself to defend her father's honour."

Her grimace fell away. "As a widow Shahay may decide for herself. But she'll respect her father's wishes. Refusing dishonours him. Mehmoud won't support marriage now because of your parents' disapproval. Moving her to Islamabad limits the danger of taunts.

"Removing you from Islamabad eliminates her parents' worry about illicit romance. As for being forced, neither of you wants that. Mind... even if she were forced, it wouldn't mean she'd had no choice. Pray she accepts my proposals."

Chapter 30

Precipice

Farikhta's news startled her. *Baba* and *Mor* visited Baseer? Was it taunts? What had her father learned? Farikhta would say nothing. Surely *Mor* suspected. If *Baba* were dishonoured... She felt for the hilt of her knife. Better she deal with it... Her stomach churned.

Farikhta placed Maryam beside her on the cot and sang gently. The baby cooed. Shahay stirred, moaned and looked to Maryam, then her sister. Farikhta smiled down continuing her lullaby.

Shahay awoke from a nap and sat up. Farikhta stood near, gently swaying with her baby. Without thinking Farikhta placed Maryam in her lap, eliciting Shahay's gasp.

"I'm so sorry. I didn't think, sister. I wanted you to hold her."

"*Manana.*" Shahay moved the baby to the crook of her arm and rocked her.

That evening she ate fresh *dodai* and chicken *biryani*, her first solid food since returning. Her jaw had begun to unlock. Her night-time pill with water deepened a dream-filled sleep.

In the black a hand rested on her shoulder. Her eyes struggled to open. Someone whispered.

"Tomorrow we'll sit with you. We spoke with Mohammed's family... Listen to your father." Silence.

Mor? Who spoke? Has his family learned? Did he insist... What

215

if *he* has learned? Praise Allah, no one must speak. No. No. The wife of Ali promised not to say... He mustn't know. In the blackness, a shape.

"Trust your heart, not your fear."

Was it a dream? His family didn't know her. Who speaks with *him*? Why would they sit together? She slept fitfully, dozing and stirring, reimagining a dream in which *Mor* spoke of Mohammed's family.

She awoke bolt upright, stifling a scream, gripping her knees tight, clawing at a faceless nightmare man kneeling between her legs, grinning, plunging his knife into her. She tasted her tongue's blood, trembled and settled only as early light coloured the sky.

***

Baba summoned her before midday. It wasn't a dream. *Mor had* visited. She sat, squirming against the yellowing bruises of her haunches, leg, chest and face, clenching her teeth against searing scars.

"It pleases me to see you up" her father began. "Do your injuries heal, daughter?"

"Yes, *baba.*"

"We have news." Her father's voice was flat, non-committal. "We met with our guests. Mohammed's *Nya* spoke his words... 'There is none for him but the daughter of Mehmoud.'"

Shahay shook, rattled as if by a *jinni.* Her throat closed and shuddered. She'd thought of him since they met. He speaks without *knowing...*

Baba stared at her with open mouth."Are you all right, daughter?"

She covered her face with her hands, excused herself, rose and turned away. When her shoulders settled she sat again, eyes rimmed. She bowed her head, silent.

Baba lowered his head to match hers. His hand beneath her chin gently raised her gaze. "You're dear to me, daughter. While the son of

Ali wants marriage, his parents hesitate. His *Nya* proposed patience. We're weighing her proposal. Patience may bring clarity."

Her mind galloped... His parents hesitated? Why? *Nya* spoke for patience. What did it mean?

"She would care for you and Zarhawar for a time. If you accompany her to Islamabad' you and Zarhawar may learn *inglisi*. *Nya* offers friendship. She –

Shahay unbottled a geyser of anger. "*His parents? They* hesitate? Have I wronged them? Why do they dislike me?" Her questions gathered in the air, menacing all hope.

Ayub came from the porch. "*Nya* has come."

Bibi left to greet Shazia, and ushered her in.

Baba exhaled a welcome. "Thank you for coming, mother of Ali. It's a good time. We've informed our daughter of our conversation. We've told her the parents of *Daktar Sahib* hesitate. She asks why they dislike her? Has she offended them?"

Shazia shrugged, palms up. "It must seem so. This is why I came. Like many parents, they visit prejudices and illusions on their children. His mother imagined he would marry another doctor, an Afghani named Laila."

Shahay's mind raced back. Her *daktara*! "*Laila,* who tended me in Asadabad?"

Nya nodded. "Yes, the same. But that won't happen. Laila keeps company with another woman. My grandson went to university with Laila. They remain friends. His heart is with the daughter of Mehmoud. His mother fantasizes about another Laila."

Shahay felt her eyes well. "But I'll never... I'm a mother. It's too late. I'm not a doctor..."

Nya smiled and held Shahay's eyes. "Would you even want that, dear girl?"

"What Mohammed does, I admire more than anything. If I were young..."

Nya grinned. "We each live many lives, daughter of Mehmoud.

Perhaps, if you accept my proposals, we'll have time to speak of doctors and their training. For now, I'll leave you to your discussion. I apologize for interrupting. I meant only to clarify the confusions of my grandson's parents."

Shahay suppressed her grin. *Their confusions! Hah!*

Baba continued to stroke his beard after *Nya* had taken her leave. "*Nya* is a friend." His tone gathered steam. "She's also Mohammed's *Nya*. She proposes well for you. But what of his interest? His parents doubt the marriage. They don't imagine *we* may refuse. He isn't Pukhtun. He is *angrezay.* If you don't want marriage, we'll deny him!"

Shahay's hands covered her face again. Tears from helpless eyes became sobs, sobs she couldn't swallow ... *Baba* tested her. Mohammed's parents insulted him. But Mohammed *did not know.* She could not marry under a lie. She would not bring her dishonour to him.

Her mother's eyes sought her face. "*Nya* offers you rest and opportunity. You'll have time to weigh and reflect." *Mor* glanced fleetingly at her father. "*Baba* admires *Daktar Sahib.*" Her gaze fixed on Shahay. "Perhaps the fog in his parent's eyes will clear. Then marriage may be possible."

She trembled, unable to think, heart wild. "It's up to you, my parents. If you think I should go with *Nya*..."

She gulped for air. If she went, taunts wouldn't start.

"It's agreed then" *Baba* said.

She forced a smile to answer the grin tracing within her father's greying beard. Her parents wanted a new life for her, an end to troubles. Tears rolled down her cheeks into her lap. Mohammed's hands had saved her. He knew nothing of her dishonour. She couldn't deceive him. Waves from her belly wailed relief, horror, happiness, frustration and resignation. The household converged to see what was amiss.

Bibi clucked through her own tears and comforted her daughter. *Baba* recovered cheer. He rose chuckling.

"Our daughter will go to visit with Mohammed's *Nya* in

Islamabad. Everyone who wants his *kameez* washed should embrace her. Her tears fall like monsoon rains."

***

Zarhawar listened in a tizzy.

Mor might marry the *angrezay Daktar?* It was true he'd helped *Mor*. But what if he was cruel? He wasn't as strong as Ayub. No one was. He was *daktar*. But was he wise like grandfather? He came from *Amrika*. It was far away. Would they live there? He was happy in Batmalai with Faridun. If they went far away, they'd travel. By truck? They wouldn't go by mule. He rode in Baseer's truck once. The wind blew his hair. He liked it. They wouldn't walk. That would take many days. There might be dangers. Beyond the village there were enemies. He would need his rifle.

Chapter 31

Spaces

Shahay was grateful when Shazia explained.

"First, I must see Mohammed and his parents off in Islamabad. Then I'll be free to look for an apartment for us three. I'll also need a vehicle. When all's done, I'll return to fetch you and Zarhawar."

Already five days passed with no word. She knew she'd worn a path on the porch. Had *Nya* forgotten her promise? What if she'd fallen ill, or been the victim of thieves? How would they find her if she were lost or, God forbid, kidnapped? Farikhta said Islamabad was even greater in size than Peshawar.

Next day at noon the *qila* dogs barked alerts. Momentarily, a car's horn sounded outside the gates. A white Vitara entered with Shazia grinning behind the wheel. Shahay's heart seemed to rise into her throat. Her son ran to *Nya*, embraced her, then jumped behind the Vitara's steering wheel.

***

Zarhawar's questions spilled like floodwater as they drove. "What is the smell inside the car? How long will we travel? Is it many days? Is it all right that I take my rifle, *Nya*? What will we eat?"

"It's the smell of a new car. Our trip will take six hours or so.

220

We'll stop in Mardan for tea and lunch. Will that be all right? Thank you for bringing your rifle to protect your mother and me. Please, leave it in the car while we have lunch. It's impolite to lunch with a rifle by your side."

He puzzled. "How did you learn to drive?"

"Do you know I've forgotten how I learned. But your mother will learn to drive too. When you are of age, you too can drive."

Mor looked at *Nya.* "I'll drive? Why?"

"Ah, when we reach Islamabad you'll see. It's a large city. We can't walk everywhere we'll wish to go."

"Where will we live?"

"In our apartment. We'll have to stay in a hotel until it's ready. Two days, I think. It's being painted. I've ordered desks and computers for each of you."

Zarhawar pressed forward from the back seat. "A computer? I saw one in Pashat. It had pictures."

Nya smiled. "You may use it for school homework. Perhaps *mor* too will do the same. All in good time."

***

Nya could have sworn Shahay's brow smoothed with each kilometer travelled. Over lunch of *chapli kabab, naan* and tea Shahay smiled and, for the first time Nya could remember, allowed her curiosity to emerge.

"We will live near schools?"

"Yes, we'll live near schools. A tutor will teach us Urdu. Would that be all right?"

"What is a tutor? You wish to learn Urdu?"

"Yes, I do. I know a little, perhaps like you. A tutor is a teacher, one who comes to our home."

Shahay's expression clouded. "But not a man."

"No, an accomplished *Pukhtanna.* She's expecting a baby in six months and isn't working. She teaches Urdu, English and much more. She has advanced degrees. Her name is Amineh."

Shahay stared. "You haven't met her yet? I know some Urdu words."

"I've spoken with her only on the phone. I'll call to ask her to join us for breakfast at our hotel."

"So quickly?"

Shazia looked into the rearview mirror. "Here is a puzzle, Zarhawar. Every day I do something I would rather not do. Do you know what it is?"

He shook his head.

"I grow *older*. So, no time to lose meeting Amineh."

"I *want* to grow older" Zarhawar said firmly.

***

Shahay followed Nya's gaze. Across the hotel's restaurant a handsome pregnant woman came toward them. Her glistening black hair, without *hijab*, fell freely on her shoulders. In public? Her shawl..! Her arms were *uncovered* beneath it! The woman greeted *Nya* Shazia warmly, and extended her hand to Shahay.

She caught Nya's nod, took Amineh's hand and listened closely to their *Pukhto* conversation. Each morning Amineh would teach two hours of Urdu followed by an hour of English. She would bring books. *Nya* would reimburse her. Amineh asked if there were other subjects she might help with.

Nya speculated politely. "It's possible. Once Shahay's son has his primary education and if he wishes to pursue medicine, would he first need English and Urdu, and after that biology, chemistry, physics and mathematics?"

Amineh smiled holding Shazia's eyes. "Yes. That's the order of march. Languages first, then the rest. The science subjects prepare students either for engineering or medicine. They're my subjects. My doctorate is in physics. Shall I bring some sample GCSE material to look at?"

"Yes, thank you. GCSE? British?"

"Yes. It's a pre-university level of study. To attend a top-ranked university, you would first finish GCSE, then A levels. The student must be prepared to work very hard."

"Thank you. As we go along, perhaps we may discuss this more."

***

In their hotel room Shahay tried unsuccessfully to stifle her yawn.

Shazia stopped unpacking. "Dear girl, little wonder you're weary. A bath will help your pains. Come. I'll show you. The hotel gives us little bottles for us to use."

"Thank you for thinking of me. You'll show me the bath?"

"Of course, follow me. Here, these taps mix hot and cold water to fill the bath. This bottle sweetens the water. This one is shampoo. Call out if you need me. You frown. A question?"

"In the bath, no clothing is worn?"

"No. No clothing. A moment..."

Nya returned to place a new powder blue *partoog-kameez* on the counter and closed the door.

Shahay hesitated. She'd never... without clothing... But warm water might bring comfort. She locked the door. Taps..? Ow! too hot... too cold... All right. She grimaced in the mirror at her fading bruises. Was her face lopsided? Wait! The taps! She turned them off, staring at the water's expanse. So much waste. Her hand hesitated at the drain. It was soothing, warm. To be immersed in water... Perhaps... She sniffed the bottle with a sweet smell and poured it in. Eyes shut, she undressed.

Feeling for the tub's edge, she lowered herself sucking in a breath as the water stung. As her hands moved through sweet bubbles they burst. Momentarily the stings relented and warmth suffused her...

She woke with a start, blubbering on swallowed water and spitting it out. *Nya* hadn't warned against falling asleep! The water tasted of roses. She washed and rinsed her hair using a fennel-scented liquid in a tiny bottle.

Refreshed, eyes closed, she felt for the edge of the tube, stepped out and opened them. She gasped. "*Who are..?*"

A naked woman opposite stared directly at her through a steam-filled window! Her hands moved instantly to cover – then to her open mouth. *A window?* Oh! It wasn't... she recognized herself in the mirror's frame... Momentarily, she turned away with colouring cheeks. She had allowed her eyes to linger.

A huge white towel soaked the drops from her skin. She donned the soft white belted coat hung on the back of the door and looked in the mirror. It didn't *cover*! She quickly rehung it and dressed in the clean *partoog-kameez*. She would thank *Nya*.

Shazia napped on the giant hotel bed. Shahay joined her.

***

Shazia was pleased with the pale sage green she'd chosen to soften and lighten the apartment's walls. Shahay and Zarhawar wandered, distracted, testing cosy beds in their rooms, each with an adjoining full bathroom. They shared an office with desks and computers. Zarhawar found bollywood videos and showed *Mor*.

She took the opportunity to email Mohammed. The note was deliberately spare of detail.

We're in. Spacious. Living room, kitchen, three bathrooms, four bedrooms, one converted to a study. Rent reasonable. Well situated. Nya

***

David Verraeter read the email. Unlikely Karram had seen it. He'd just landed at Dulles after a stopover in Ankara. He'd have no internet in the small windowless room he'd be taken to in Langley.

A JAG Captain and his assistant would do the interview. Two Americans operating in Bajaur following OWL directives were officially missing, probably dead. Their last known location was the vicinity of Batmalai. Karram just returned from the village where he had contacts. The place and timing of his activities together with his Bajauri contacts left little doubt. His training put him in a command position. Civilian villagers couldn't have handled the contractors. They were former Seals. Karram was a different story. He went AWOL from a Landstuhl hospital bed, then heli-dropped into the Pak mountains at just the right time. He'd spread bullshit about a missing friend. If he didn't murder the two operatives personally, he orchestrated it with his Pashtun friends. It was the only thing that made sense.

***

The pug-faced CBP officer fronted him in the waiting room.

"You Mohammed Karram?"

"Yes, officer. What—"

"You're to come with me."

"Me?... Is there a problem, officer?"

Silence. The bull necked turnip ushered him to one of Dulles' small interview rooms. Two grey faced Army JAG officers entered. An MP stood outside the door.

He saluted. "No need for that, Sergeant. This is entirely informal. We'd like your assistance in answering a few questions. We've had your bag offloaded."

"Don't mean to be peevish, but I'm en route to Denver. I've got a connecting flight and I've been travelling for sixteen hours. What's it about?"

"It won't take long. You'll accompany us to an offsite location."

Too fatigued to object, he dozed off in the back seat of the SUV.

He awoke just before the car's doors opened and looked quickly at his watch. An hour already – not long his ass. They entered a nondescript office building in Langley's suburbs. The room had no windows.

"Sergeant, could you tell us where you were over the past week?" Wups. *Nya* always said he had an angry nose. He knew his nostrils flared at the first question. He stared at the questioner and felt the hair on his neck bristling. Calm down.

"After speaking with my captain I left base in Kunar, took a ride with a local to Pashat, then visited Batmalai. Stayed there with family for the past ten days."

The JAG officer opened his briefcase. "Thank you. We'll get back to Batmalai. Do you mind if we record our conversation? Brief us, short version, on the previous two weeks."

His fingers drummed the table. "Not much to report. Most of it was in the base clinic – infected burns. A medic in my platoon looked after me."

"Who was the medic?"

"Sergeant Henry Vargas."

"And before the base clinic?"

"Landstuhl. Picked up some wounds in a firefight."

The senior JAG officer didn't look up as he read from a notepad. "You don't deny you left Landstuhl without authorization."

Mohammed's fingers drummed energetically. He knew he was tired. Maybe that's what made him chortle. "Hmm. 'I don't deny.' Sounds like an accusation. I heard about missing friends. I went to help find them. Landstuhl, searching for friends, base clinic. In that order."

"There's nothing funny here, Sergeant. So you were in contact with friends in Batmalai even while you were at Landstuhl."

What in God's name were they on about? "Let me think. In contact? In contact?" He tried to gather himself. "Two messages came, one from base, another from Asadabad. A daughter of Batmalai friends lived there. Members of her family were missing."

"So you don't deny you kept in contact with your friends in Batmalai through a relative in Asadabad? Then it's 'yes'?"

He stopped his drumming and suppressed a desire to slam down his fist. He fixed his eyes on the JAG officer. "Again, 'I don't deny..?' Hmm. Is that a question? What's your point? I don't have contacts. A message arrived about a missing Batmalai friend. The missing person's sister who lived in Asadabad sent it. That's what happened."

"We'd like the names of your Batmalai friends and acquaintances as well as your Asadabad contact."

He was exhausted. Even so, he shouldn't have laughed. "Hmm. My Asadabad contact..?" Contact? Friends and acquaintances were 'contacts.' Sounded more ominous than friends. What's the worst that could happen? Arrest? At least there'd be a bed... Nope.

He stood, stretched his arms above his head and yawned open-mouthed.

"No, no thanks." His voice lowered and steadied. "I gather I'm not under arrest or detention. I'm off home to Denver. You seem to have lots of time on your hands. I don't. Information from my friends saved lives. Some fought with us. I don't like your questions. As of now I'm eighteen hours into my trip home. I'll take my bag. Catch up with me in Denver if you'd like."

The JAG Captain stood. "I'd like you to stay, Sgt. It 'd be in your interests. We have more questions."

"I bet you do. Before now, I didn't know I'd have questions too. Delighted to hear you're concerned about my interests... Good talk." More questions! Where was this coming from? Karzai's glorious demented commander? Now, JAG junior was on the blower. Who was *he* contacting?

He dialled a cab as he walked away, threw his bag in the back seat and sat up front – the better for the cabbie's ear. He called American Airlines, confirmed he'd missed an earlier flight, and booked the next one to Denver. He paid the cabbie with a credit card, took his luggage inside. At the ATM he withdrew cash. When he saw the cab was gone, he exited and hailed another taxi.

"Where to?"

"Andrews AFB." He paid cash.

The Andrews desk was sympathetic. Given that he'd already been en route eighteen hours they could arrange accommodation at the Presidential Inn. They quickly found him a morning flight – Andrews to Colorado's Buckley AFB.

Mohammed dialled the family lawyer from the Presidental room. Gary Blaine headed the third largest firm in Denver.

"Mohammed, you back stateside? All good?"

"Yes... a few scratches, otherwise fine. Sorry to call late. Just back. Outside DC. Mum and Dad are arriving in Denver an hour or so from now on an American flight. "

"You aren't with them?"

"That's why I've called. JAG people waylayed me at Dulles... Yeah... no idea. You were with JAG before starting your Denver firm? Thought so. Whatever's up, my sense is it's nothing good... Right, I share those worries. I went to 'assist them with some questions'. Yes... their words... Right again, not questions. Look, my Denver recruiter is Jaime Gomez. He can be trusted. Please contact him. I've a bad feeling. He knows some people... Yes. Thanks. I'll come by when I'm back. Please, keep this between us. I'll fill Mum and Dad in when I get there."

At three AM, he jerked awake. The dead operatives... They think they want *me*. When they find out... Oh God! *Shahay and Bangar!*

Next morning he picked up the flight toward Buckley deep in thought, fighting panic.

***

Gary listened intently, making notes. Mohammed avoided names.

"So, they don't know who she is?"

"Unlikely. Not yet. But coming for me, they'll eventually find her. She has information about the dead contractors. She'd have to say what her role was. I don't want that."

Gary scratched his head while Mohammed sat silent, waiting. Gary came around his desk and sat beside him. "You're right to worry. A foreign national can't plead the fifth. But there's a way round this. Find out if *Nya* Shazia knows a lawyer in Islamabad who speaks English, please. There's a chance we may be able to head all this off."

"No language worry" Mohammed said. "Pakistan's official languages are English and Urdu. Lawyers speak both."

***

Verraeter's secretary buzzed: "DDO on the line."

Operations? He picked up. "Verraeter."

"We have news, David. Not good. Two bodies. In Pak side mountains.No. Farther from Karzai. Worse still–"

Verraeter interrupted, rubbing his hands together. "How far from where the search party found the woman?"

"Give or take four miles... I hadn't finished. The bodies were, I'm quoting, 'mutilated'. No details yet. One head shot each, close, powder burns. JAG got nothing out of Karram. Looks like he skipped back to Denver. They tried to track him after he walked out of the interview. He booked on American from Dulles but disappeared – consistent with someone hiding something. We'll take it from here through SOCOM JAG, a Routine Article 32 enquiry. Looks like he either did them himself or put someone else up to it. If so, Article 118..."

Verraeter entered the OWL file database confidently. They were going to nail him.

M Karram: SOCOM JAG Article 32 Enquiry pursuant to prospective (?) Article 118 CM for murder, conspiracy to murder, torture of US citizens.

Chapter 32

Means

Amineh's Urdu lessons vexed Shazia and Shahay for two weeks. Neither *Pukhto* nor English words were permitted. Zarhawar progressed quickest – jabbering more and caring less about mistakes. Today Shahay formed two novel if primitive sentences in Urdu using components of phrases taught earlier. One wasn't quite right. Amineh corrected her. Shahay repeated the corrected sentence. At the lesson's end, loosed from Urdu, Shahay asked if Amineh might begin additional afternoon English lessons.

***

Shazia looked toward their entrance at the knock. She cracked open the apartment's door cautiously. A young man addressed her presumptively in Urdu. Shahay and Zarhawar were in their rooms. Amineh overheard and came to assist. She signed something the man held in exchange for an envelope.

"It's a telegram. Why would... a *telegram?*"

Shazia unfolded the page.

BUY FOUR CHEAP CELL PHONES. PREPAID MINUTES. CASH ONLY. CALL FAR 8AM MDT SAT.

What? No signature. Fariyal? Why would Mohammed have her

230

call his sister?

At 7pm Islamabad time she dialled. Mohammed answered.

"Don't speak. No names. Discard the phone in the street well away from your location after this call. Two dead men were found on the Af-Pak border. Your grandson was questioned. He knew nothing. *No one he knows* does. Find out how to turn off location services on your computers, then do it. Please, your other cell phone numbers..?"

He rang off.

Shazia sat staring at the phone. Her eyes rose at the sound of garments rustling. Shahay stood at the kitchen door.

"You spoke quietly."

"So as not to disturb you."

"To him?"

"Yes."

"Did he ask..?"

Shazia rose to put her hand's on Shahay's shoulders.

"He thinks only of you. He's concerned for your safety. I'll explain."

Shahay sat across the table with her son. "Mohammed worries that others may enquire about missing men." She smiled at Zarhawar. "So if a son spoke of his and his mother's bravery in defeating their attackers, and dangerous people heard by chance of this story..." Zarhawar looked up uncertainly at *mor.*

"But he's spoken of this to all of Batmalai..."

"Yes. I'll contact your *baba.* He can help contain the story. All right?"

"*Baba.* Yes, he will help. I don't understand..."

Shazia weighed whether to add the rest. Without it, Shahay would remain confused.

"It appears authorities in America think Mohammed was involved in the deaths of the two men..."

Shahay's lips trembled. "Mohammed? *Their* soldier is *their* enemy? How could..? Why would they..?"

***

Shahay sensed a burden lifted. Nya's words somehow calmed and steadied her. She sat taller and spoke quietly. "My son, you go to your room now." Her eyes rose to Shazia's. "Thank you *Nya* for your trust. You've explained. It's for me now."

"What do you mean?"

She shook her head. Throughout the next morning's Urdu class she felt a renewal. Amineh stayed for lunch. Additional English lessons began that afternoon.

***

Amineh's eyes grew. Shahay had been a good student, if shy and uncertain about her direction. Overnight, so it seemed, she'd begun to speak of her goals with preternatural self-possession, and to approach her studies with unaffected focus.

"Something has changed. You're so clear about... *Nya* Shazia mentioned your interest in medicine. I'd no idea how serious you were. We're just beginning English. The good thing is *Nya* is fluent and educated. Try speaking English only to her when I'm not here. The key first step is a Cambridge test called the CPE. After that, Cambridge GCSE then A level maths, chemistry, physics and biology..."

Shahay asked quietly. "I'm a mother. I'd rather not sit in school with children."

"Of course. A friend, Asma, works with the British Council. You'll register as an independent student."

Shahay nodded. "One more thing. Do you know a lawyer in Islamabad?"

"We... my husband and I... we know several lawyers."

"Thank you. I will need a name. Soon, I'll explain."

***

Vargas's text message didn't surprise Mohammed.

Who knew you're such an outlaw? The a'holes asked who your Pak contacts are, whether you had us take out some contractors, how many times you disobeyed orders in camp and on missions, etc.etc. Couldn't help them. Said you were a boy scout. They're talking to everybody including T. He gave them the verbal finger. They threatened him with a CM. V.

His father was white-faced. "But you've done nothing, nothing...! You fought for our country!"

His mother crackled to attention. "It's the men who kidnapped Shahay? They've found their bodies... They think you—"

His hand cautioned her. "Please. You know nothing, *nothing*! You're speculating. You've no first hand information about bodies, and know nothing about a kidnapping except gossip. You have to promise not to speculate with anyone, including lawyers or anyone in the military."

His mother wagged her chin. "But what if we're asked? Wouldn't it be easier to tell the truth? Shahay was with the kidnappers. *She's* responsible for anything that happened to them."

Mohammed glared at her. "If asked, in court or elsewhere by lawyers, by anyone, you have no direct knowledge of what happened. You can offer only *gossip*..." He glared at her. "If ... If anything you say implicates her – if I'm of any importance to you, you'll stay mum! You won't mention her name or Zarhawar's. Don't speak of what you think you know to anyone. Do you understand?"

His father paled. His mother's eyes brimmed. He'd never before shown his rooted anger. Her lower lip trembled. Her eyes showed pain and fear.

No one spoke. Mohammed fetched a glass of cold water, drank it and returned.

"I'm sorry for raising my voice. I've kept you in the dark... I've met with Gary Blaine twice. He's investigated through a friend. My name's on a list ... the Others Watch List, OWL for short. It's been there from the time Laila and I went to hear a visiting speaker at U Col. She's on it too. My friend isn't certain about the next bit. Apparently, if my name is on the list, you are both on it as are Fariyal, Sabbryya, even *Nya*."

His mother stared open-mouthed. "What? Why?"

"It doesn't matter. But be careful of new faces in the mosque, and especially of chatty people at medical conferences. Intelligence types go undercover to medical conferences, posing as doctors, nurses, pharmaceutical reps or executives. They mine naïve doctors for any information they can get. Then they bribe, leverage, threaten, and blackmail."

"My immediate concern is my residency. I can't do it here with a hare-brained investigation over my head. I've made an appointment with Dean Klugman to explain, and to ask for his assistance. I've done some research. I'm looking for a neurosurgical residency elsewhere."

His mother's tears began to spill. "You're thinking of Pakistan aren't you? You know it's a third world country. They won't have any programs worth–"

"Mom, please stop. Many foreign hospitals have first rate residency programs. I'll be lucky to be accepted."

She spat the words. "You just want to be near *her!*"

"I do. But I won't crowd her. If foreign residencies are anything like ours, I won't have time."

His father shook his head and faced his mother. "No, Ayesha." His eyes locked on hers. "It's wrong. If Mohammed gets in, he should make time to see her." He turned back to Mohammed. "Make sure they're safe. Make sure of your feelings. Do what's right for you and her. I don't understand – whoever's behind this, I mean. You should see the Dean. You'll need cash..."

***

Dean Klugman welcomed Mohammed. His face paled as Gary Blaine progressed.

"... She's a widow with a son... In spite of his wounds, Mohammed took off back to his base, and parachuted in to search for them. The kidnappers were US contractors. They wound up dead. When Mohammed returned, two JAG officers detained him at Dulles. We've found out Mohammed's been on a secret watch list since his last year in your medical school. He was guilty of attending a talk on Afghanistan with Laila Ahmed. She's on it too. Because Mohammed's name is on that list, all members of his family are likely on it as well."

Klugman shook his head.

"I can't believe – I remember both of you as students. Please understand, I'm sorry to ask – *you* had no hand in the deaths of the two contractors?"

"No, nothing to do with it. But it seems somebody believes I did. I arrived back at my base in time to help find the kidnapped woman and her son. She was beaten to a pulp and covered in blood. Later, I learned they'd tortured and assaulted her. But at the time we were searching for her, I knew nothing about who kidnapped them, why they did it, or what had happened to them."

"You're asking for my help... you have it. I'll get in touch with the right people. You and Laila were our two outstanding medical students in your year. And you've served in our military. Mohammed, I know you and your parents. That's all I need. I'm sorry for your trouble and doubly sorry I had to ask the question. Gary, Mohammed, we'll get this done."

***

His father's face was drawn. "Yes, I've checked. Montoya's currently at Walter Reed. His neuro and rehab specialists are holding their breath. Given the intake prognosis they report his progress is remarkable. They'll allow further rehab at the Craig. We'll visit, I promise. If the army doesn't cover all expenses, don't worry. We'll cover it. Can you tell us your plans? Anything? Can we keep in touch? When will you leave?"

Mohammed shook his head. "Best you know nothing. That's your protection. It'll be soon... This afternoon pay cash for some cheap phones with prepaid minutes. I'll need the numbers."

Jaime Gomez drove him, his parents' burner numbers in hand, to Missoula's bus station.

At dinner time, two JAG officers accompanied by an MP knocked at his parents' door. By then he'd paid cash for the Calgary to Toronto flight, and cash again for a direct flight to Karachi. Gary Blaine had been direct. "Don't wait. A prolonged JAG investigation will delay, even forestall your residency. If you think they won't waste your time, with or without malice, think again. Get lost. Literally. Say nothing to anyone. I don't want to know. I'll handle them here."

Gary was up to speed on burner phones.

***

After six weeks settling in, he was growing used to the hunger and the brutal hours. Nearing midnight, he was famished. He hadn't eaten for eleven hours. With *naan* warming in a little *ghee* in one pan, he lit a second burner, added more *ghee* to a second pan and poured in three eggs whipped with cream. He shaved in cheese and continuously swirled the eggs into a fluffy roll of omelette. Rounds were at seven am. His handwritten letter of thanks to Dean Klugman was brief. Somehow, through contacts at Harvard and the University of British Columbia, Dean Klugman pulled off a neurosurgical residency at Karachi's prestigious Aga Khan University Hospital. So far there was no sign he'd been located. He'd find *Nya* without alerting anyone to her location or his own.

Admittedly his reception had been cautious. Both the Aga Khan's Dean of Medicine and Chair of Neurosurgery greeted him tactfully.

The residency hadn't gone through normal channels. A one off, a courtesy. Minimal Urdu. Former American military. High praise from references, albeit from often hyperbolic American sources, so, skills unknown. They were polite, thorough, helpful and distant.

In the sixth week, he worked an emergency rotation under Amir Khan, a top final year resident. For three days Amir had limited him pretty much to watching. He'd been allowed stitching of minor cuts, intake assessments for English and Pukhto speakers, but invited merely to observe serious trauma. Today, for the first time, Amir asked him to present a teenage girl with blunt force neck injury. Mohammed checked the CT. The scan was inconclusive.

Amir prompted. "So what's next."

"Extensive bruising. I'd hold the heparin and suggest DSA."

Amir smiled. "DSA..?"

"Digital Subtraction Angiography."

"Why?"

"Small pupil – anisocoria, ptosis and miosis, ipsilateral headache. So, beginning signs of Horner Syndrome. A DSA gets us a more definitive vascular picture."

"Good call. Ever managed a case like this."

"Never."

"Good observations. Let's order the DSA. You're right to be cautious. She might have a bleed. If so, what do we watch for?"

"TIA, limb paresis."

"Suppose we find stenosis, pseudo aneurysm?"

"Depends on severity. Hope it isn't Grade 3-4. Worst case, surgery."

Amir smiled again. "But the position of the contusion..?"

"True. It's likely external carotid. Easier to patch a bleed there."

"Okay. Last question: if the indication were rupture, what's the surgical response?"

"Again, worst case, we – well, surgeons patch on a Goretex vein graft."

Amir's grin broke through. "So surgery-wise you're not exactly a virgin. Tell me about your first time..."

He laughed, began with veterinary surgery and ended on a mountain trail in Bajaur and a femoral artery repair. Within the week, the neurosurgery chair and the Dean dropped by for a friendly chat and how-are-you-getting-on.

***

Verraeter' fingers felt for his neck veins. Bulging. Pumping hard. Fucking Janet had booked off early, as if she was the only person who suffered headaches! Why should a dumb-ass secretary get to leave work for the day? He'd hated having to handle the phone himself. As if on cue it rang. He fumbled it as he answered.

"Verraeter."

"Sir, I'm Captain Morrison, JAG. I'm lead on the Karram enquiry. I'm sorry, we've lost him. He's not in Denver. His parents weren't helpful."

Verraeter remained pointedly silent, timing a full sixty second pause on his wrist watch. He pitched his voice lower. He'd read about it. An assured flat, low tone and deliberate pace reflected cool authority, tinged with suppressed anger.

"How would that happen, Captain?"

"Our first objective was to interview members of Karram's platoon. We'd no reason to think he was a flight risk. Unless our enquiry finds grounds warranting an Article 118 court martial, we wouldn't order surveillance, let alone detain him."

His face felt hot. "You're not implying it was *my* job to check Karram didn't fly the coop?" Silence on the other end ... "Right. And Karram's platoon mates?"

"Nothing there. Looks like he was in Landstuhl when the two contractors were in Bajaur."

"He still could have been in touch with his Bajaur contacts!

Have you checked them? Your mandate is to determine how Karram conspired to mutilate and murder two Americans!"

"Please, Mr Verraeter, 'how' is presumptive. It's possible he was involved. We have no evidence on that yet."

He staunched a curse. "Well Captain, our contractors had some Bajauris in hand. We need to find out who. Whoever it was could have turned the tables and killed them. But not without Karram. He had the skills. He ordered an operation that killed our guys. If you can't bother yourself to get those names, I will."

He slammed the phone into its cradle without waiting for Morrison's reply.

Karram had gone AWOL from Landstuhl to find someone who'd been kidnapped. It had to be OWL operatives who did the kidnapping. So, who was kidnapped? He picked up the phone.

"Connect me with Islamabad Head of Station, please."

Chapter 33

Witness

Mohammed took Gary Blaine's update on his third burner phone of the week.

"The Islamabad lawyer is in contact with your grandmother. Separately, as you asked, I raised the subject of immunity from prosecution for witnesses in JAG's investigation. They wanted details, what kind of evidence they'd provide, whether they were domestic or foreign."

"Would the immunity extend to any US court, civilian ones as well?"

"Is the witness civilian?"

"There are three witnesses, all civilian."

"We apply then for blanket immunity, first to the Convening Authority, who will coordinate through the DOD and DOJ to get the Attorney General's approval."

"All three civilians are foreign nationals, one is a minor, a child."

"Hmmm... A child. I'll check whether a minor needs immunity. I have to record your answer to one question. Would any of them testify without immunity?"

"Absolutely not."

"What kind of testimony are we talking about?"

"Two have evidence about the alleged maiming. One has

information on the contractors' deaths."

Gary sucked in loud breath. "Whew! Glad I don't know names. So, these three know *who did* the maiming and killing?"

"Collectively, yes. They'll also provide evidence on conspiracy. If the Advocate General wants to know whether I murdered someone, or formed a conspiracy to maim and murder, evidence from these witnesses will settle it. Other issues?"

"Maybe. I've talked to Jaime Gomez. He doubts the kidnappers were official military. More likely, private contractors. If intelligence contracted them, they might argue national security was involved."

Mohammed remained silent for a full minute. "So, even with immunity, witnesses would be at risk after testifying?"

"Your guess is probably better than mine. Personally, I'd be cautious."

"Right. They can't be at any greater risk than they are right now. So, the witnesses will be available in Pakistan, nowhere else, and then only with blanket immunity. Interviews of witnesses will be at a location we select. National Identity Cards will identify them. The NICs will be shown only to the JAG supervising officer. He alone will interview and take statements from the witnesses. He can neither record nor transmit the identities. That's because the three witnesses have no faith in the word of the American Government."

"Christ! Do you want me to say that?"

"It's what the witnesses and most Pakistanis believe. I'm beginning to share their belief."

He rang off and contacted Batmalai. "Please, alert everyone... beware of visitors with questions about the kidnap. Please, pass the warning to Pashat."

***

Mehmoud's neck stiffened. It was as Mohammed cautioned. An outsider spread money and asked questions about the kidnapping in Pashat's market. His worry receded after reading the rest of the Pashat report.

'We have outsider's picture and license plate. Drove Pashat to US Consulate, Peshawar. Photographs of man (Pakistani) and two Americans exiting consulate together. All followed to residences. Photos of residents include women and children. One of two Americans subsequently followed to Islamabad's Diplomatic Enclave. Same later left enclave with woman (wife?) and children. Visited local market. Photos. Wife (same) later visited same market with two women. Two women (same), accompanied by men (husbands?), photographed outside enclave. Enclave contacts provided addresses and names (back of photos).

Total suspected principals (names and addresses) 40, not including family members. If family members are included 112 photographs of Americans associated with man asking about kidnapping. Additional twenty three photos Pakistanis, (names, address and family members on photo reverse) meeting one or other of 40 American assumed principals outside Diplomatic Enclave.'

***

Mohammed listened to *Nya* laugh describing Shahay's studies.

"She's working hard on her English and making incredible progress. I didn't doubt her intelligence. But Amineh, who doesn't exaggerate, has gone even farther... she says Shahay is evidently brilliant. Amazing. She was quiet as a dormouse leaving Batmalai. When I told her you'd been questioned, and were worried about her, it's as though she suddenly woke up."

"We're seeking immunity for her. If it's granted, she'd speak with the military lawyers who are chasing me and may well end chasing her. Her information will end their pursuit. It's... it's not without risk."

Nya's voice growled. "You want her to answer questions about her experience to a military lawyer? How could *you* ask *this*? She barely knows the Islamabad lawyer. You haven't even visited yet. She says nothing, but must think you've completely forgotten her."

"*Nya*, please understand. By now *I* may be watched. My tracks aren't completely covered. If I talked with her it could look like collusion, conspiring with her, having her make things up. Don't mistake the risks if she *doesn't* testify. Two Americans are dead. They'll track down anyone they think is involved. If she and I don't head this off now, we'll both be hunted down. Please, tell her I think only of her."

"I'll have to consider this. You're asking more of her than you've any right to."

***

Two days later *Nya* sat with Shahay in the evening while Zarhawar played video games in the study. "Mohammed asks that you speak to an American lawyer about the kidnap. He has the name of your lawyer here. I think he's mad. I don't think you should do it."

Shahay's eyes gleamed. "No. I must... It's why I asked Amineh for a lawyer's name."

"What? Do you understand the risks? Please think about this. They may ask about things no one... no one has a right to hear."

"Yes. But... I owe him my life. They won't believe him without hearing the truth. He doesn't deserve this. It's for me. I'll speak to them."

***

Mohammed had Shahay's lawyer arrange to rent a vacant Bani Gala grocery store, closed for renovation. Windows were to be papered over. One day only. Chairs and desks to be set up.

Gary had settled details with the JAG's Captain Morrison. Morrison accepted the stipulations set out by Gary and the Pakistan lawyer: the witness and her son were kidnapped. She'd been beaten, tortured and sexually assaulted. *Nya* Shazia would translate. Mohammed would take Zarhawar for a walk while Shahay testified.

***

Shahay felt no unease. She knew what must be said and would do so, despite her anger at having to speak unveiled before men she did not know.

At 10 am Gary rose to begin the interview using questions Mohammed provided. "I'm Mohammed Karram's American lawyer. Thank you for appearing."

Shahay listened to Nya's translation, then nodded.

"Two Americans kidnapped you and your son?"

"*Aw.*"

"You were present when these two were mutilated, cut with a knife or knives."

"A knife. *Aw.*"

"Do you know who did this?"

"*Aw.*"

"You can identify them?"

"*Aw.*"

"Please do so."

"My son wounded them as I directed. Then I used my knife."

Gary's mouth dropped. He sat down, staring at his notes. Slowly he rose again. "You're saying that you... a Pashtun woman and your eight year old son... you overcame two highly trained–"

"My son freed himself, then me. They slept. As they began to wake, he shot into their limbs."

Blaine dropped his pen and his chin. He sat down white-faced.

"Captain Morrison, your witness."

"Yes, thank you." Morrison rose. "I am Captain Morrison. I'm the lawyer investigating the circumstances of the maiming and death of two Americans."

Shahay attended to Nya's translation.

"Did you speak with Sergeant Karram before directing your son to shoot these two Americans?"

"No. I didn't speak with him after he left Batmalai."

The interrogator's mouth quivered. "There was no contact? You didn't correspond with him through your sister in Asadabad?"

"No contact. I didn't correspond with him. He didn't with me. It's not permitted."

"You directed your son to shoot into the knees and shoulders of these two men?"

"*Aw.*"

"Was this to incapacitate them..? To make them helpless?"

"*Aw.* It made it easier to make them suffer."

Morrison's face went beet red. His voice rose. "When these men were helpless, you cut off their fingers, ears, tongues, noses and genitals?"

"*Aw.*"

"Did you mean to kill them?"

"No. I preferred they suffer."

"Did you not in fact then direct your son to finish them off with a shot to their heads?"

"No. Did you not listen? That would have ended their pain."

"What did you wish to gain by maiming these men so brutally?"

She listened intently to the translation. Her lips curled.

"The custom of these men was rape. My custom is revenge, *badal.* I meant their faces to show dishonour, their bodies to show they lost a battle to a woman they wronged. My knife ensured they would never take pleasure from wickedness again."

"Do you know who killed them?"

"No. No one spoke of this to me. Whoever killed them shortened their suffering. I didn't want that."

"In Pakistan, does the law permit you to act as you did against these two men?"

"I know little of the law."

"So, you don't care about justice?"

Her eyes locked on his. "*Badal* was *my* right. These men acted against *me*, not you, not an *Amriki* woman. America cannot tell Pukhtuns what is just!"

Morrison's face went chalk.

***

After minutes of note taking Captain Morrison's first question for Mohammed was brief.

"Sgt Karram did you conspire with anyone to maim and/or murder two American contractors in Pakistan?"

"No."

"Did you take pride in your service with the US Armed Forces in Afghanistan, Sgt Karram?"

"I was proud of the men in my platoon."

"So you say. But you fought with others during training, disobeyed a superior's command and assaulted him in an Afghan village. You also took it on yourself to threaten and dismiss an Afghan interpreter hired by your superiors."

Gary interrupted smiling broadly. "Captain Morrison, since you're recording, please note our objection. As counsel, you haven't asked my client a question in your recitation of alleged facts. In any case, none of the incidents inaccurately described by you bear on the specific charges that are the subject of this investigation. In short, as counsel you're testifying, rather than acting as an officer of the court."

Morrison grimaced silently, and recorded the objection.

Mohammed nodded toward Gary then addressed Morrison. "You made three points. Three men at Bragg looking for a fight slurred my mother and sisters. I gave them one. They washed out. Secondly, in a raid a fellow soldier having a hissy fit endangered civilians. He shouted toward a village home that showed no hostility, a home in which no one understood him. When he went to throw a grenade through its window, I stopped him. It wasn't clear to me, nor to my ODA Captain, Chris Montoya, that the man in question was anyone's superior officer. No rank was indicated by his uniform, and none was offered by any verbal or written command. He was over-excited and out of control. As for the interpreters dismissal... I witnessed him attempt to blackmail a village headman. I told him to bugger off and not come back. Subsequently, villagers provided more tips about hostiles. I'd no way of knowing our command Colonel hired a blackmailer. My actions solved a problem created by the Colonel's hire."

Morrison bristled. "So you think you have the right to decide which of your superiors' orders you follow!"

"I don't know how you get there Captain."

"Then let me be clear. You disobeyed a superior and attacked him in an Afghan village raid!"

"No, you didn't listen. Without an authorized command structure in the field nothing suggested the man was my superior. What's more, I understand throwing grenades at civilians breaches Geneva Conventions. It is illegal to follow orders breaching International Law, isn't it?"

Morrison's face flamed. "You claiming to be a lawyer?"

Mohammed stared him down. "Please, answer my question first."

Morrison glared. "The witness may step down."

Gary Blaine cleared his throat. Morrison sat silently, the crimson in his cheeks slowly leaving, writing in a notepad.

Morrison's cell phone was in his brief case. He was unaware it revealed his precise location and actively recorded every word spoken.

***

Mohammed's eyes found Shahay, now veiled, outside the enquiry doors with Nya. He embraced first *Nya*, then Zarhawar. He greeted

Shahay and met her eyes.

"*Nya*, Zarhawar and daughter of Mehmoud, you must all continue to be vigilant when you're away from the apartment. I'll be sending gifts. You'll understand once you see them. Learn to use them."

He addressed Shahay. "When I spoke with *Nya*, I explained why I've been unable to visit. It wasn't that I didn't want to. I can't tell you how often I think of you... Today I saw your courage again, in words spoken to defend me. Thank you. Soon, I'll be able to come to speak with you. But now I must go immediately to Batmalai before returning to the hospital."

Shahay shook her head. "Why do you go to Batmalai?"

"To speak with your father. May I leave it at that?"

She flushed and nodded. He hated himself at that moment. He wanted to explain but needed to convince Mehmoud and his sons of the danger she was in.

***

Hashim watched the uniformed American Captain get into a taxi from across the street. He tossed his cigarette aside. The Captain had assisted him without knowing. The same embassy handler who had him follow the Captain also fed the court proceedings live to Hashim's cell phone courtesy of the borrowed Israeli eavesdropping program, Chrysalor. Turned on remotely, the Captain's cell phone had acted as a broadcast centre. The younger Pukhtun woman was the target.

He photographed two women, a boy and a young man as they exited. The man walked away after a short conversation. Hashim followed the women's car. He snapped photos again as they entered their buildings parking area, and exited their car.

***

Verraeter grinned at the photos while he spoke to Islamabad. "Good work. So, I assume we have local operatives who can assist her trip to Paradise?"

"Plenty. It's just a woman. A pair of guys will be enough. What about the older woman and the boy?"

"Do whatever it takes. If they get in the way, they're expendable. Collaterals aren't a problem. The sooner the better."

***

Mehmoud was grateful. "You believe she may be in danger still."

"Yes. I've sent *Nya* two Walther PPKs with loaded clips. That isn't enough. For now three or four men you trust should follow *Nya* and your daughter whenever they leave their apartment. Try not to kill anyone simply following them. Break bones instead. If they mean harm to your daughter, they'll stake out at least one armed watcher, perhaps two, and at least one armed assassin. Give armed killers what they deserve."

***

Nya followed Mohammed's instructions. Her text message, consisting of a single numeral, identified their destination exactly an hour before they left. On the Saturday following the enquiry, she led Zarharwar and Shahay toward their car's parking stall, nodding to a now familiar bearded figure in *partoog-kameez*. It was Shahay's turn to drive. She directed Shahay toward the Islamabad Farmer's Market off Margalla Road.

***

Zarhawar muttered to *Nya*. "A short man behind us in a dirty *kameez*... he isn't looking at the fruits and isn't buying things. He looks at you and *Mor* then looks away."

Nya thanked him and muttered something he didn't hear to *Mor*. He stole another glance back. "He's coming this way on the other side the stalls."

Nya's right hand moved into her left sleeve. "Shahay, please walk ahead with Zarhawar. My boy, you're very observant. I'll speak to him if he comes too close..."

Twenty paces on Zarhawar's head spun round to look toward a scream. Thirty feet behind *Nya* the short man lay howling on the pavement, holding his shattered leg. His pantleg was crooked and bloody. In the distance, a cream coloured *pakol* on the head of a tall grey bearded Pukhtun receded into the busy market crowd. He walked with a sturdy cane and disappeared around a corner.

He looked like *babaji*. But Grandpa lived far away in Batmalai.

***

Late afternoon Friday Verraeter's secretary buzzed. "Overseas. A Mr Banks." Finally. He grinned and reached for the call from Islamabad.

"Verraeter here. Glad you called... Badly? What do you mean *failed*! What the *fuck*! Send someone else! It's a woman! A child and sixty-five year old woman are her only protection for Christ's sake!"

"That's what we thought. The first contractor we sent wound up with a splintered leg in a public Farmer's Market. He'll have a limp for the rest of his life. He can't work for us again. We sent two more, the toughest and most experienced professionals we've worked with. The watcher was triple-teamed. Both his arms were broken and his pistol taken. His right hand was butchered at the wrist. He's finished, done. No hope. When our shooter got within ten yards of the target, he was dropped by blow across the back of his knees. The target whipped around and slashed his wrist. Damned near cut his hand off. A local took our man's Glock and put bullets into his buttocks. His thumb and trigger finger are missing. Our guys were pros. Now

250

they're cripples. Neither of them will ever pull a trigger again.

"That wasn't the end of it. Someone shouted our guys were American agents trying to kill Pakistanis. A crowd stomped the shit out of them – broken ribs, concussions, smashed faces. The police arrived and put our guys under armed guard in hospital. This is long term trouble. We contacted other locals to take the contract. They've all heard what happened. None of them will touch it with a fifty-foot bargepole. They know she's protected and don't know by whom. State is pissed. We're in deep shit on this. We're backing off."

"Look. This bitch cut up two of ours. We need her done. End of story."

"You don't get it... the story is she has more people looking out for her than we can match. We're taking casualties. They didn't kill our people yet. They're sending us a message. 'If you want war we're ready.' You seriously expect us to go up against God knows how many of them there are? We haven't identified one of them! Not one!"

Islamabad's voice soared.

"We don't know who to look for. But they do apparently. We received tens of photographs with a note saying there are more to come. Look I'm a professional... my sense is if we send anyone else they're as good as dead. Send five guys or ten, they're all done. Local cops aren't on our side. Pakistan's ISI, who hate us anyway, can barely hold back laughing in our faces. The story about an attempt on a local woman's life is still in the press. The USA is mentioned in every article as the culprit behind it all. The Embassy isn't just nervous. Our ambassador's been summoned by their Foreign Office. We're scrubbing the op. Sorry. That's it."

The phone went dead. Verraeter threw his phone against the wall, stood and slammed his palm onto his desktop.

***

Three weeks after the enquiry hearing Gary Blaine received the Article 32 report. He read the short version to Mohammed.

"The meat of it is summarized in the possible charge counts. It reads:

"*With respect to prospective charges under UCMJ (1) 81, (2) 118, 119, 134 and (3) 124 which would specify that Sgt M Karram did, with persons unknown, conspire (81) to maim (124) and murder (118-9, 134) US citizens C Murphy and D Prenny in FATA, Pakistan on or about the 30th of June, 2010:*

"*Relevant evidence presented by each of Sgt Karram's platoon members, his commanding officers, treating physicians and staff at Bagram, Landstuhl and his base in Kunar Province, is as follows: Karram was at no time able to contact the kidnapped woman and her son, her sister in Asadabad, nor villagers from Batmalai, Bajaur where the kidnapping originated. Nor was he out of sight of witnesses from his platoon or Landstuhl hospital staff where he was a patient during the times at which maiming and deaths of his alleged victims occurred. Further, the kidnap operation and therefore the existence of the kidnappers could not have been known to him before the kidnap itself.*

Relevant evidence presented in preliminary hearing, from a kidnap and assault victim, [name withheld] was that she alone directed her son to incapacitate her attackers before maiming Murphy and Prenny who had kidnapped, tortured and sexually assaulted her. She had not spoken with Sgt Karram for weeks prior to her actions. Neither she nor he could have known weeks earlier (when they were in contact) that she would later be subjected to kidnap by the deceased Americans. Conspiracy between them was therefore out of the question.

Further, evidence sworn at the US embassy in Islamabad by a Pukhtun villager [name withheld], is that he shot dead the US citizens Murphy and Prenny. Ballistic tests on bullets shot from his HK 36, which he voluntarily brought to the Embassy, confirm that he alone shot the dead men with a single shot to their foreheads.

Accordingly, the investigation not only establishes that no evidence

supports any of the charges proferred under the Article 32 investigation
of Sgt Karram. On the contrary, evidence clearly establishes that Sgt
Karram did not maim or conspire to maim, did not murder or conspire
to murder Murphy and Prenny whose deaths occasioned the enquiry.
More plainly, evidence strongly suggests the original charges arise at best
from unwarranted speculation.

Recommended disposition: Vacate.

"So that, Mohammed, ends that. You smiling as wide as I am?"

"I am, Gary. But will they leave it alone?"

"Good question. But before I answer yours, I have a question
for you. I received a request from Captain Morrison for information about photographs delivered to the Islamabad Embassy. Know
anything about this?"

"What photos?"

"Good, you've answered one question. They wanted to know
if you knew anything about them. Apparently, Shahay's Islamabad
lawyer received a large unmarked envelope with photos of a few
dozen Embassy employees with home addresses noted on the back.
He couriered the envelope to the US Embassy. Jaime Gomez caught
buzz that the Islamabad Head of Station is panicked. The photos
included over three quarters of his CIA personnel and even more
outside contacts. An enclosed note warned against any attempt to
harm members of the Salarzai, male or female. My guess is they've
been well and truly warned off."

***

Verraeter avoided the call for three days. Janet buzzed again just
before lunch.

"It's that same voice. It's a Fort Bragg number."

He picked up. "Verraeter here."

"Thanks for picking up. It's Mick Crowe calling. I imagine you
know who I am?"

"Yes, Admiral."

"I imagine you have some idea why I'm calling?"

"Yes sir. Certainly our office shares what must be your disappointment in the Article 32 result..."

"No. That's not it. I have a different take... I looked into your Karram guy before I was aware of the Article 32 enquiry. Fact is, weeks ago I'd written up a commendation for his actions under fire in a Kunar ambush and firefight. His unit commander recommended a decoration. So, I was surprised when the Article 32 enquiry turned up. Appears he was a burr under the saddle of some of our JSOC cowboys. I wondered why. What do you know – I found Langley had a file on him *even before* he was deployed."

"Yes sir, he was involved in an incident at Fort Bragg and–"

"Hold on. Back up son. I'm the admiral, and it's *my* ship. You opened a file before he ever arrived at Bragg. Looks to me like you listed him when he went to a talk given by Major John Grant. So don't suggest *first* he was a troublemaker, *then* you created a file. It was the other way around."

Verraeter's face felt hot. "But Admiral I'd say the fact that he got into trouble at Bragg shows we had reason to create the file."

He heard the Admiral's chuckle on the other end. "Kinda thought that's how you'd try to play it. But your file reports only that he was written up at Bragg. So, frankly the writeup was pointless. I spoke personally with someone mixed up in the punchup, a Specialist Mitchell, Karram's platoon mate. Karram took on three toughs who'd called him a nigger while insulting his womenfolk and his religion. He showed some spunk. Did you create files on the three guys who tried to tune Karram up?

"Well, no I..."

"The question was rhetorical. Mr Verraeter. Here's how it's going to happen. He doesn't deserve to be on your radar any more. We're going to give Karram an honorable discharge on medical grounds. His neck injury from the Kunar incident almost killed him."

"Not incidentally, for your information, I'm sending a letter up the ladder recommending him for a Medal of Honor. My commendation will note that he risked his life by running through heavy fire to rescue two badly wounded platoon members in the open, dragged them to cover under fire and while wounded. Further, while treating those wounded in the same engagement, he subsequently incurred further wounds when he threw himself over his wounded, sacrificing his body to protect theirs from incoming RPGs. So, after discharge he's likely to receive, without fanfare, a package containing his decoration. It'll be sent to his US address, to his parents' home, so they'll be in no doubt what kind of soldier he was.

"You're quiet Mr Verraeter. That's wise. Because I'm pissed. I'm pissed because we have thousands of guys working in the Muslim world, and none with anything like Karram's skill set. His languages alone gave us a leg up. It turns out he has brilliant surgical skills, repairs an artery on a tribal, then leverages that into a whole village helping us in a key area of Af-Pak. His actions under fire in Kunar probably save his Captain's life. He saves a Kunar village from going hostile because of a crooked Afghan interpreter.

"Well, I don't think the evidence–

"Don't interrupt, David. I'm just warming up. You have him on a bloody list, a 'watch' list, so everything he does raises suspicions, and every fucking suspicion you have is in his ever expanding file. Now I have just one question. Have you ever once, in the shit show you run, looked at his file and found any real evidence *confirming* your suspicions? You have a JSOC Colonel in Kunar go off his nut trying to malign Karram. We believe the colonel was so ginned up by having an OWL listed guy under his command, he arranged an ambush meant to take Karram out. Karram survived, but two of his platoon died. You send two private contractors to interrogate a Batmalai widow without doing a background check to see they'd been booted from the Seals for almost certainly raping and murdering two adolescent Afghan girls. To top it off, you start an Article 32 because you have such a big file on him."

"I–"

"*I said* don't interrupt... One of Karram's defence witnesses testified under oath at our embassy in Islamabad. I have his name. He
killed your operatives, one bullet each. Probably did them a favour.
Four Salarzai came with him. They said if any harm comes to their
guy, to Karram, his girlfriend or her child, any harm anywhere, they'll
respond in kind. You must have seen the dozens of photographs they
brought to the embassy?"

"No. I didn't see–"

"They're photos of dozens of American operatives living, working
undercover for us in Af-Pak. The names and addresses of each one
is written on the back of the pics. So, Mr OWL, my take on your
program is that it's bullshit, and counterproductive. Four of our
people are dead, not because of Karram, but because you think it's
brilliant to have files on successful Muslims. Sorting friends from
enemies takes judgement and perspective. Your list multiplies so
many names you can't identify real enemies. OWL doesn't deserve
to be called an intelligence operation. Start by taking Karram, his
family, his girlfriend's family and anyone in or around Batmalai off
that fucking list. Send me confirmation you've done that today. If
I have to call your boss, I'll make it my business to see you're done.
That's all."

The line went silent

Chapter 34

Nests

Nya could see Shahay was energized. "You won't say who our guests are?"

"No. Then it won't be a surprise. We'll shop after we decide what to prepare... What do you think our meal should be?"

"But custom... you are my elder. It's for you to say..."

Nya shook her head. "Let's forget custom just now. Pakistan has some of the world's best food. We're blessed with guests, yours, ours and mine. Let's help each other."

Shahay's eyes wore her puzzle. 'Yours, ours and mine?' Who..?

***

The fragrances of roasting chickens, fresh *naan*, *chapli kabob* married with a Kabuli lamb korma's fresh onion, ginger, coconut milk, cinnamon and coriander. Shahay answered the first knock with Zarhawar. Amineh, lustrous hair framing her face, introduced her companion, a handsome man bearing a bouquet of yellow tulips.

"Please greet my husband. Salman, this is my brilliant student of whom I'm so proud. This is the son of Shahay. He is Zarhawar. Beyond in the kitchen is *Nya* Shazia."

Shahay felt her cheeks warm."Welcome to you both."

Salman waved hello to *Nya* who waved back. He turned to Shahay. "Please, daughter of Mehmoud, Amineh wishes *Nya* to have these."

Shahay looked to Shazia with Salman's yellow tulips in her hands. What did she do with..?

Nya relieved her confusion. "Zarhawar, please bring the flowers Salman brought for me and put them in water in this vase."

A second knock. *Nya* encouraged her from the kitchen. "Yes Shahay. I'm tasting the *korma*. Please get it."

She opened the door a crack. Her hand went to her mouth, eyes filling.

"Father, mother. Welcome. I'm... I'm... so happy you've come. How did..? I didn't know. Thank you for visiting us."

Nya grinned. "Shahay, please introduce your father and mother to our other guests."

***

Nya led. "How was the harvest in Bajaur wife of Mehmoud? And your sons..? The family of our friend Baseer..? Salman and Amineh, you should meet the sons of Mehmoud, mountains of men... Yes, it's a *korma* you smell. It's good Ayub and Sakhi aren't here. It's said that whole horses have disappeared into cooking pots around Batmalai. I hope our meal pleases you... Yes, since you ask, we await my guest. He's a single man in whom I've long held an interest."

Shazia's arched eyebrows affected mischief. Mehmoud, Bibi and Shahay shared a doubtful frown. Amineh giggled behind her hand. "So *Nya*, you have a secret admirer?"

"You might say so. Someone I'll scold for being tardy."

At a knock Shazia waved Shahay off. "Please. Allow me. It must be my guest – just in time."

She opened the door.

"*Nya*, thank you for inviting me."

"Thanks for coming, dear boy. Come in. Perhaps you know this grey beard." Mehmoud embraced him, hands clasped. His free arm drew Mohammed in. "You look well, my friend, though tired I think."

"Twelve hour shifts. It's my first week without patients."

"Your family is well in Denver?"

"All well, *manana*. Ayub and Sakhi and their wives? Faridun?"

Mohammed greeted Amineh, shook Salman's hand, embraced Zarhawar and Bibi and greeted Shahay.

Shazia and Shahay loaded platters for dinner. Shazia teased.

"It seemed that Shahay had Zarhawar, Mehmoud had Bibi, and Amineh, Salman. I thought I should be allowed a man friend."

Bibi and Amineh laughed behind their hands. Shahay busied herself in the kitchen.

***

Shahay lay awake. Next to her Shazia snored. Mohammed's arrival startled her. His eyes showed fatigue. But he'd spoken freely and easily to her in the company of her parents, asking after her studies and her goals. Like *Nya* he teased.

"Now, I've not met Amineh before. She sings your praises... a brilliant mind, diligent, exacting. Tell me Amineh, did the daughter of Mehmoud pay you once for lessons and a second time for praise?"

Her parents laughed! She'd hidden her happiness, eyes lowered, bursting with his attention. He asked where Salman worked, when the baby was due, where they lived. Her father and mother smiled in his company. She'd felt his eyes follow her. He sleeps in Zarhawar's room. He would be at breakfast. She drifted off, dreamt and stirred when his hand went to her cheek.

***

Shahay fiddled with her sleeves. Too frequently her eyes met Mohammed's over breakfast. Her mother and *Nya* noticed.

Nya's hand stifled a yawn and diverted attention. "I need to walk today. Will you all come with me? Amineh told me the Rose and Jasmine Garden at Shakir Parian Park is very beautiful. There's a new artisan's village nearby."

Mohammed, Zarhawar and her parents readily agreed. She shivered when *Nya* slipped her Walther PPK to Mohammed.

Arriving at the park Shahay was baffled. *Nya led* the walk with *Mor!* Women, elders or not, did not lead mixed genders walking in public. And Nya's eyes swept from one set of park visitors to another. Trouble? It was as if she were on guard. And Mohammed's hidden pistol?

Shahay tightened her grip on Zarhawar's hand. He looked up at her, then quickly around. Her eyes too now took in faces ahead, behind, to each side. So far she saw only couples, some with young children, some older, strolling innocently in the fresh sunlit breeze.

Roses stood unattended, watchful. Nervous birds gurgled, fluttered and chirped in the foliage.

Nya, with Bibi at her side, persisted in the lead as *Baba* and Mohammed followed. *Nya* stopped suddenly. Her eyes fixed ahead. Mohammed's hand went instantly to the pocketed PPK even as his eyes swept fore and aft. In the distance a couple approached. Shazia already bustled toward them... Her words carried.

"Ali, Ayesha! I'm so happy to see you! It's been almost a year. How was your flight? Are the girls with you? Coming behind? Good."

Shahay turned to see Mohammed's mouth open. Her father, face expressionless, exchanged glances with him, slowly shaking his head. *Nya* returned with Mohammed's parents.

"Hi son" his father said. "Surprised?" His hands went to Mohammed's shoulders.

He turned and offered his hand to *Baba.* "I'm pleased to see you again. Please, bear with me. My wife has asked to speak for us..."

Ayesha, chin lowered, spoke through Shazia. "First, we apologize to you, to your wife and your daughter. We were wrong to doubt our son, and even more to doubt the daughter of Mehmoud. *Nya* keeps us informed of her study and progress. Time has allowed us to reflect since our meeting in Baseer's *qila*. We were blind to many things. We respect and honour the courage of Mehmoud's daughter. We'll be forever grateful to her for clearing our son's name. I beg you, your wife and daughter of Mehmoud to forgive our blindness."

Her father's lips traced a smile as Nya translated. He took Ali's hand and nodded. *Mor* gathered Ayesha's arm and walked with her.

Shazia came to wrap Shahay in her arms. "I dreamt Mohammed might find a beautiful and courageous woman. In you, he's found her. *Alhamdullilah!*" A smile traced her lips. "If only he wasn't such a monkey. Poor you."

"He doesn't look – Oh! He learned to tease from you? Perhaps... perhaps he's more like a donkey."

"Yes, a donkey. I like it. Good spotting." Shazia grinned.

***

Shahay had never asked *Baba* for such permission. Her eyes lowered.

"*Baba*, you've spoken of my marriage with Mohammed's parents. He and I haven't spoken. I ask your permission to speak with him."

Baba nodded. "This afternoon we'll walk with his parents and the children. *Nya* will remain. Speak with him then."

***

Shahay sat facing Mohammed. Over his shoulder *Nya* read at the corner windows in the living room's far end, greying hair peeking round the wingback's edge.

She knew that custom had protected but also cocooned her. Freed of its shield she found herself in open space, unguarded and vulnerable. But for his sake, for his honour, she needed to forestall his words and the promise they would bear. Words burst suddenly from her lips like water from a collapsing dam.

"I must speak first so you will understand. You *don't know*. You *won't want* marriage with me. I'm not – I cannot bring dishonour... What they did–"

Mohammed gripped both her hands, insisting on her eyes. "Please, forgive me. Courage makes you reflect on honour. I know what men can do. If speaking of it helps, please do so. But if it brings back horrors, don't. I thank Allah you survived."

She wagged her chin. "But I must tell–"

Mohammed's tone softened. "My honour differs from yours. I'll be honoured if you'll marry me. You bettered and destroyed trained killers who meant to murder you and Zarhawar."

She shuddered. "Yes, but I bring dishonour–"

His head shook. "No. Forgive me. I watched you fight for your life against three attackers. Then, you saved both yourself and your son at the hands of your kidnappers. If that weren't enough, your words at the enquiry protected me, again at the risk of your life. You've filled my thoughts since we met. Now you're a student, studying for a brilliant future. I'd be a fool if I weren't honoured."

Her eyes swam. "But your right..."

He shook his head again. "I don't know *such a right*."

She gulped the words. "But... still, I have shame and night-mares... If we marry, for now I don't know if I'm able... able to be a wife for you."

He moved across to sit beside her. His hand found her streaming cheek. "Cruelty scars both men and women. I promise, your patience will be mine. I have nightmares too, dreams of being unable to save my men. Now, I dream of being by your side. You'll decide when we may be close. We wouldn't skirmish now if we wished to be apart. I beg you, give us both peace. Each of us has much to do and much to say. I can't think of life without you."

Shahay let her gaze meet his. "Nor I without you. Yet, while I study, I must be here with *Nya*. And you must finish in Karachi. And in Batmalai...

"In Batmalai, what?" Mohammed leaned forward.

"When we... when it's time, may we marry there?"

"Of course. It's where I hoped we would marry... So many problems. It's almost impossible for us. I'm surprised you speak of marriage. *Nya* says I'm just a donkey for you."

Shahay looked up, startled. "But I wasn't–" She saw his face and felt her lips begin to answer.

He feigned a frown. "Is it my ears? Do I bray? It's my long nose isn't it?"

She mimicked his furrowed forehead."You once compared me to a horse!"

"Yes. A fine Arabian... But a donkey? A lesser creature? I suppose I'll have to bear such cruelties. Mercy. "

A smile traced her lips.

Mohammed released his breath. "You see. What woman can resist a donkey who makes her smile?"

"We'll live then in my country, in Pakistan?"

"Yes. It's what I'd like. Where better than in Batmalai, near your family?"

Her eyes closed. His arms surrounded her, drawing her in. His fingers lingered on her cheek. She covered them with her hand.

End Notes

A. *Language, Dialect*

Pukhto/Pashto is the language of the Pukhtun/ Pashtun People:

Shahay's people are variously referred to as Pashtun, Pushtun, Pakhtun, Pukhtun, Paxtun, Pathan. Their spoken language has different dialects. She lives in Batmalai, Bajaur, FATA (now Khyber Pukhtunkhwa) northern Pakistan. There she speaks *Pukhto*. Her people are Pukhtun. Were she from Kandahar, Afghanistan she would speak *Pashto*. Her people would be Pashtun. *Pashto* and *Pukhto* are words of the same language, with the same meaning, expressed in different dialects.

Pukhto as a written script descends from both Arabic and Persian precursors. Differences in rendering *Pukhto* and *Pashto* words into Roman script arise from attempting to transliterate the distinct sounds given to the word in, say Batmalai or Kabul (*Pukhto*) on the one hand, and Khandahar (*Pashto*) on the other. An example: Shahay's sister is Farikhta in Asadabad (*Pukhto*) but would be Farishta in Khandahar (*Pashto*).

B. *Pukhtun/Pashtun Customs*

Pukhtunwali – way of the Pukhtun. (Seeks familial *ezzat* (repute) through *nang* (honour)); celebrates *melmastia* (hospitality), *meranah* (manly chivalry), *namous* (purity of women and family honour), *gheyrat* (physical courage), *sabat* (steadfastness), *isteqamat* (persistence, constancy), *imandari* (righteousness); demands *badal* (see above) (redress and reciprocity); insists on *burabu'ree* (intrapersonal equality), *aza'dee* (personal independence); acknowledges *nanawati* (**a**) a procedure in which a protector (*hamsaya*) may, at his discretion, give sanctuary (*nanawati*) to a supplicant pursued by a third party; *nanawati* (**b**) a formalized process of expiation in which a wrongdoer, by presenting, e.g. sheep or goats, to the aggrieved party thereby expresses remorse, accepts shame, and obliges forgiveness and impunity; permits *swara* (a compensation which may take the form of giving a child, almost always a daughter, of a family deemed to have offended to the offended family); abhors *herus* (greed); punishes *tor* (illicit sex) with death; resolves disputes through a *jirga* (consultative council of elders.)

C. *Realities and Fictions*

1. Denver

The University of Colorado located in Denver is real. Its medical school is located at the Anschutz Campus, Aurora, Colorado. The school has a distinguished record of innovation, training and research.

The Craig Hospital, is a renowned Denver institution specializing in neuro-rehabilitation of BI and Spinal Cord injury patients. It's TBI (traumatic brain injury) program is located in Colorado Springs.

2. Bajaur, Pakistan

The Salarzai Leader in Pashat, Bajaur is Faqir Emir Shahab uddin Khan Salarzai. Incidents alluding to the Leader in *The Leopard's Daughter* are created entirely by the author and are fictional.

The November 6, 2008 suicide bombing in Batmalai is real. Since then Shahab uddin Khan Salarzai has directed a masterful cooperative defence of his people, seeking reconciliation where possible, and directing the *lashkar* to fight when necessary. He and his family, his supporters and their families, are under constant threat of death. Over one hundred and forty of the Pashat Khan's friends and allies, the leaders of their people, have been assassinated between

August 2008 and today.

On December 24, 2010 a female suicide bomber blew herself and forty-seven innocent civilians up in Khar as ration seekers lined up at a World Food Program give-away. Over one hundred were wounded. The dead and wounded were predominantly Salarzai displaced by fighting.

Batmalai, Pashat and Khar are real as is the village of Kaga. Khar is Bajaur's administrative centre.

Numbers of US Special Forces, hired private contractors and CIA undercover operatives entered Pakistan in 2005 under the guise of providing help with catastrophic results of Pakistan's earthquake. Pakistani government agencies cooperated to ease normal passport controls thus permitting US 'construction workers' to enter. In the spring and summer of 2010 US SOF were operating more or less openly in FATA, the broader Pukhtun Frontier area in which Bajaur is situated.

3. Karachi

The Aga Khan University Hospital is a leading Asian hospital. It is a private, not-for-profit teaching hospital with a medical school for 500 students, an associated school of nursing, 560 patient beds and 17 main Operating Theaters with 4 additional Operating Theaters for general Surgical Day Care and 2 for Obstetrical/Gynaecology patients.

4. Kunar Province, Afghanistan

Camp Karzai above the Ghakhi Pass in Kunar Province, Afghanistan is/was real. It was under JSOC command and largely staffed by CIA Special Activities Division (SAD) personnel, private contractors, Delta Force and Special Forces for whom, like their *takfiri* adversaries, the Afghan-Pakistan border, (the Durand Line), was a fiction. The base was abandoned in the Fall of 2010. The evacuation may have been connected to the catastrophically bungled rescue operation for kidnapped British aid worker Dr. Linda Norgrove at the village of Dineshgal, Kunar Province nearby Karzai. Dr Norgrove was killed October 8, 2010 by a grenade thrown by one of a rescuing rookery of Navy Seals. The Seals' command chain knew of, but deliberately ignored local elders' negotiations with the kidnappers which, according to the elders' uncontroverted testimony, was to effect her immediate release on receipt of a ransom. Regrettably, if typically, the US military initially lied about the circumstances of her death only later to relent, thus confirming the accuracy of details insisted on by locals.

Marah Warah is a village lying at the base of the inclined Ghakhi Valley in the district of Marawara northeast of Asadabad, the capital of Kunar Province, Afghanistan. US special forces, together with regular Army and Afghan troops acting on intelligence of doubtful provenance, launched a series of ill-conceived and incompetently managed battalion sized operations (Operation Strong Eagle I, II and III) in villages of the Ghakhi Valley on June 29th, July 20th and August 2nd (2010) in a vain attempt to capture the capable hostile commander, Qari Zia ur Rahman, who, according to unverified and suspect American intelligence, allegedly commanded a brigade of Al Qaeda's Shadow Army, the *Lashkar al Zil*. Al Qaeda sources denied that Qari Zia ur Rahman was one of theirs.

The Craig Joint Theatre Hospital (CJTH) in Bagram is real (and bears no relation to the Craig Hospital in Denver, Colorado). CJTH deservedly honours Staff Sergeant Heathe Craig of the 159th Medical Company, 10th Mountain Division. On June 21, 2006 Sergeant Craig, holding on to wounded Pfc 'Brad' Bradbury as the two were hoisted off a ridge line, fell to his death with his patient when the UH60's hoist malfunctioned. Had Sergeant Craig survived, it would be unsurprising were he to acknowledge that he was one amongst many skilled and able medics of ISAF forces regularly risking, and sometimes tragically giving their lives to save comrades, wounded or ailing civilians, and even insurgents in the field.

The village of Mangwel, in Konar District, Afghanistan where Laila and Mohammed learn the U Col visiting speaker is serving, is real. A US Special Operations Alpha (ODA) platoon served there, brilliantly commanded by Major Jim Gant. The Major's remarkable career ended when lesser men, likely envious of his remarkable service, succeeded in finding regulations which he'd breached.

The Mohmand villagers Gant and his platoon assisted, lived with their families. Against regulations, Major Gant lived there with his family, specifically the woman he loved and married, Ann Scott Tyson. Such other regulations as he breached (drugs, booze) were then and are now routinely broken, with less cause, by serving senior officers both stateside and elsewhere. Gant was ousted from the Green Berets, demoted, and accused by Lt General John F Mulholland of bringing 'disrepute' to Army Special Forces and 'disgrace' to himself as an officer and a gentleman. History will instead likely pin those accusations and worse on the bumptious Mulholland and other pettifogging bureaucratic commanders who lacked Gant's grounded insights into war fighting and his courageous success in implementing those insights.

Captain John Grant in *The Leopard's Daughter* is a fiction. None of John Grant's words, actions or opinions should be construed as those of Major Jim Gant (with whom the author has neither met nor spoken.)

D. *Medical*

1. Captain Montoya's Traumatic Brain Injury (TBI)

Montoya's blast TBI is characterised by a percussive shock to the brain, rebound injury (temporal lobe bleed) and (minimal) projectile penetration (cerebellar dura). The dura mater is a two-layer membrane just below the bone of the skull. The TBI initiates global neuroinflammation.

2. Surgical response

Montoya's surgeon performed double decompressive craniotomies at the sites of two focal injuries, removing shrapnel at one, burrholing and dealing with a brain bleed at the second. He leaves drains at both sites. Craniotomies dramatically reduce brain swelling (oedema). That's vital because brain swelling compresses capillaries, (small blood vessels) reducing, sometimes eliminating blood flow, thereby expanding the bruised area and killing brain tissue (tissue necrosis). (*cf.* *http://repub.eur.nl/res/pub/12218/080423_Engel%2C%20 Doortje%20Caroline.pdf*)

Decompressing craniotomies are state of the art but don't completely eliminate expansion of bruising. Bruising induces reparative neurochemical reactions, a direct consequence of which is neuroinflammation. Uncontrolled neuroinflammation (a cytokine storm) results in tissue necrosis (unnatural death of tissue from injury or illness by contrast with apoptosis, natural death of tissue over time). Sufficient brain tissue necrosis may irreversibly degrade balance, speech and coordination, together with emotional and intellectual processes.

3. Neuroinflammation and a Speculative Mitigating Protocol

EG McKeating and PJD Andrews summarise cogently the role of cytokines (tiny proteins that act on cells) in traumatic brain injury (*British Journal of Anathesia* v. *http://bja.oxfordjournals.org/ content/80/1/77.full.pdf*). Their meta-analysis of medical literature cites in particular the work of Sawhami et al. (*Journal of Cerebral Blood Flow and Metabolism 1996; 16:pp.378-384*) showing that inhibition of the cytokine Tumor Necrosis Factor Alpha (TNF-alpha) activity in rat brain is associated with cerebroprotection after closed head injury.

The protocol initiated by Mohammed to mitigate Montoya's brain damage borrows from the controversial work of Dr Edward Tobinick with Alzheimer patients. (*http://www.expert-reviews.com/*

doi/full/10.1586/ern.10.52) Tobinick patented an Enbrel delivery technique for use in neuroinflammatory pathological processes. Enbrel inhibits TNF-alpha cytokines.

Inflammation of neurological tissue, characterized by cytokine elevation, is present in Alzheimers, arthritis and traumatic brain injury. Neuroinflammation in TBI is a consequence of the primary trauma and the flooding of the brain with pro-inflammatory neuro-chemicals meant to protect and heal injured cells and tissues in small-scale trauma. TBI typically couples neuroinflammation with swelling.

In moderate to severe TBIs, oedema compresses capillaries starving brain cells of blood-borne oxygen. Reparative neuro-che-micals then signal for more (pro-inflammatory) helpers because anoxic brain tissue dies. More inflammation incurs more swelling, increasing cell death thus attracting more neuro-chemicals. In a nutshell, neuroinflammation consequent to TBI is characterised by a circular chemical cascade (a cytokine storm) that promotes intra-cranial swelling (oedema) resulting in long term damage to neurons and, in moderate to severe cases, often significant motor, cognitive and emotional impairment. In TBIs microglial cells and astrocytes produce both microphages, meant to play both neuroprotective and reparative roles in injury recovery, and cytokines which, if microglia remain activated, accentuate neuroinflammation leading to neuronal cell death. (cf. *http://www.jneuroinflammation.com/content/5/1/28*)

Would cytokine fusion proteins (e.g Enbrel) help by mopping up excess cytokines? It might seem not because the molecule size of commercially prepared fusion proteins (like Enbrel) seems too large to cross the blood brain barrier (the BBB). But failure to cross the BBB would reduce or eliminate the medication's availability precisely where it's most needed. So the argument goes.

Dr. Tobinick's Alzheimer's protocol targets Batson's plexus (that is, the CVS or cerebral venous system) with Enbrel injections. His therapeutic evidence, so far without conclusive double blind research corroboration, suggests post-injection attenuation of neuroinflammation in Alzheimers and arthritic patients. Why wouldn't it work with TBI neuroinflammation?

4. Objections to the Possible Protocol

Tobinick's claims may seem improbable because of the blood brain barrier difficulty cited above. How could Enbrel molecules reach the brain parenchyma (the working mass of brain tissue where all the damage is) if they're too large to pass through the BBB?

Here wrong assumptions are made.

First, the blood/brain barrier permeability is known to be compromised in neurological trauma. This opens the possibility of enbrel inmigration across the BBB. Secondly, the criticism assumes that TNF-alpha attenuation requires unidirectional transportation of enbrel molecules, that is, it assumes that enbrel molecules (think of them as TNF-alpha-specific sponges) must cross the BBB into parenchymal tissue to sop up excess pro-inflammatories. To put it another way, it assumes the sponges can work only if they go find the TNF-alpha elements. But they don't have to if excess TNF-alpha can cross the BBB (exit the parenchyma) to meet enbrel molecules, that is, if excess TNF-alpha can get to sponges.

If osmosis (the spontaneous spreading of particles from an area where they're concentrated to an area where they're not) works across the BBB, and it does, migration of the enbrel molecules into the parenchyma is unnecessary. It suffices that excess parenchymal TNF-alpha emigrates into the cerebral venous system (Batson's Plexus) where it can be sopped up by Enbrel injected into the CVS.

Recent studies on amyloid plaque formation, central to the pathogenesis of Alzheimer's Disease, seem to confirm the principle that the BBB functions neither as a barrier to migration of plaques formed outside the brain into the parenchyma nor to emigration of plaques found within it (cf. *https://www.nature.com/articles/mp2017204*). The study is consistent with and indeed suggestive of the contention that mitigation of neuroinflammation may be effected by extrathecal injection of TNF-alpha inhibitors into the CVS – Tobinick's idea.

Etanercept (Enbrel) is a master regulator of neuroinflammation through its action on a specific cytokine called TNF-alpha (tumor necrosis factor alpha). TNF-alpha is produced by two types of white blood cells (leukocytes), a major function of which is cell repair. Etanercept (trade name Enbrel) is a commercial (Wyeth, Amgen) long-lived TNF-alpha inhibitor. It works as a chimeric, that is, by mimicking the role of receptors which absorb TNF-alpha, inducing ambient TNF-alpha to bind with it thus reducing its morbid inflammatory consequences. Normal cell repair (gliosis) is unaffected.

Dedication

For The Tarkanri Salarzai and Martyrs of November 6, 2008

Shahay, the Leopard's Daughter, lives in the village of Batmalai in Bajaur. She is a member of the Tarkanri Salarzai. Her people, one of many Pukhtun tribes, are at war. They're defending their freedom, religion, culture and traditions against takfiri zealots.

Three respected Salarzai leaders from Batmalai went to Bajaur's administrative capital of Khar August 26th, 2008. Malik Bakhtawar Khan, Malik Shah Zarin and Maulvi Sher Wali unsuccessfully sought government cooperation in raising a self-defence militia (lashkar) against the zealots. Takfiri operatives assassinated them on their return. A council of headmen (jirga) met November 6, 2008 in Batmalai to form a lashkar. A suicide bomber in their midst blew up himself together with twenty-six of the leaders and elders of the Salarzai and allied Utmankhel tribes. The Prologue to The Leopard's Daughter offers a fictionalized account of this tragedy. Since then, to the date of this writing, scores more Salarzai leaders and elders, brave and honourable men, have been assassinated by the takfiri.

The Salarzai lashkar is made up of farmers, labourers, workers, students, merchants and hunters. Ranged against it are hardened takfiri equipped with modern arms, financed by Gulf money and supported by rogue elements within official government agencies. While their arms are old and light the Salarzai and their allies from the Utmankhel and

*Mamund peoples nonetheless are amongst the most effective anti-tak-
firi fighting forces in the Afghan-Pakistan theatre. In their courageous
and principled resistance they're led by Shahab Uddin Khan, the Pashat
Khan.*

Martyrs of November 6, 2008 Batmalai Bombing

Name	Martyr's Village
Malik Fazal Haq	Rashe Derai
Malik Qaiser	Raghagan
Malik Fazal Karim	Baro
Malik Khan Pachai	Koye
Malik Lal Pur	Koye
Malik Abdus Salim Khan	Koye
Malik Wazir	Thaley
Malik Wazir	Thaley
Abdur Rahman Khan	Thaley
Malik Bahader	Thaley
Malik Sher Bahader	Thaley
Malik Namoos Khan	Thaley
Malik Kabul Khan	Thange
Malik Jabar Khan	Ghakhy
Malik Mian Noor	Ghakhey
Aman ullah	Ghakhey
Shah Sawar Khan	Ghakhey
Malik Sakhi Gul	Pashat
Malik Shamas ur Rahman	Sango
Malik Darwaish	Chanargo
Malik Sarwar	Chanargo
Malik Mirak	Shahgai
Malik Burhan U din	Ghara
Malik Salim	Chalargan
Malik Bach	Batmalai
Zakir Ullah	Batmalai

Acknowledgements

A novice writer of fiction needs guidance lest, like an unschooled swimmer, he perishes with impoverished pen strokes. When a Canadian author and friend, Marlyn Horsdal, offered this unblushing metaphor I sought the assistance of distinguished UK editors. Initial drafts were returned blood- and tear-stained, chunks of hair strewn amidst the pages. I am grateful to Jacob J Ross, to the gifted novelist Emily Mackie, to Bryony Pearce, Sheila McIlwraith, Aisha Rahman, Thalia Suzuma and Edward J. Handyside. Without them *The Leopard's Daughter* would have remained unrelieved fantasy. Each afforded critical direction and careful commentary. 'Grateful' is, of course, inadequate. (I'm particularly sorry for the hair.)

Closer to home, I've benefitted from the critical reading by Teresa Schapansky, author of the exquisitely written *Memoirs of A Pakhtun Immigrant (www.teresaschapansky.com)*, the most quintessentially Canadian memoir of the recent era.

Pashtuns of Afghanistan and Pakistan have been described as lawless, dangerous and primitive, invariably by peace loving, law-abiding and civilized invaders. These would-be conquerors have generously dispensed their wisdom alongside their cultural insights to Pashtuns they deemed benighted. Remarkably, Pashtuns have resisted such dispensations. I'm deeply indebted to a range of polyglot, university educated Pashtuns, to Tayyab Ali Shah, Maryam Tayyab, Alem Zeb, Farhat Taj, Shehnaz Haqqani, Malik Khalil, Balqees Sayyed, Haleema Shah (who will either be a poet or an astrophysicist and may well be both), Muhammad Khurshid, Drs Shazia and Inayat Ali Shah, and Dr. Amineh Ahmed Hoti. All are honest, courageous and deserving of their Pashtun pride.

I am grateful to my wife, Lee, whose patience with a perpetually distracted writer has been his comfort.

Authors of fiction often admit to 'borrowing' from many sources, almost always and conveniently, too many to recall. This masquerade permits an easy, if undue presumption of authorial wisdom and intellect rather as larcenous billionaires may present their fortune as achieved through hard work and – modesty aside (as it must be) – a certain *genius*. One of my thefts is so obvious I am driven, reluctantly of course, to confess. Mehmoud alerts Mohammed (Ch.10) to America's arrogance in imagining its role as 'saving brown women from brown men.' This sardonic gem is stolen from Gayatri Spivak's incisive commentaries on West-centric colonial arrogance.

I would prefer to imagine that any errors, mistakes or infelicities in *The Leopard's Daughter* are entirely the fault of those who've assisted me. Alas, that too would be fiction.